Posing in Paradise

A Harry Reese Mystery

The Harry Reese Mysteries

Always a Cold Deck

Humbug on the Hudson (short story)

Crossings

Kalorama Shakedown

A Charm of Powerful Trouble

Fair Play's a Jewel

Posing in Paradise

Emmie Reese Mystery Short Stories

The Birth of M.E. Meegs

Hidden Booty

Psi no more...

For a glossary of period terms, biographies of the characters, and a complete chronology, please visit:

HarryReeseMysteries.com

Posing in Paradise

Robert Bruce Stewart

Street Car Mysteries

Florence, Mass.

Street Car Mysteries

streetcarmysteries.com

To the denizens of Northampton,
both the fictional and the real

As some of the dialogue includes archaic slang, a glossary has been provided at the end of the book.

You'll find more information on the series at our Web site:

HarryReeseMysteries.com

1

I arrived home after a best-forgotten day at the track to the all too familiar clack of a typewriter.

"Hello, dear." As usual, she spoke without lifting her eyes from the page before her. "Any luck?"

"Luck?" Good God, what did she know? Was it the bracing scent of the turf? I checked my shoes. Nothing.

"You said you hoped to finally get that check today. The Amalgamated Which-Its of Podunk."

"Oh. Bad news there. The Amalgamated Which-Its of Podunk are in receivership."

There was an abrupt halt to the clatter. She looked over at me with concern. Emmie never nags, but she does sometimes look at me with concern. The effect is such that I wish she'd take up nagging. I'd wager if Xanthippe had mastered the technique, she might have shamed Socrates into some occupation more befitting a man with a family, and generations of indifferent students would have been spared having to feign an understanding of whatever it was he was trying to get at.

But it was no use stalling with ruminations on the Western philosophic tradition—Emmie was still looking at me with concern.

While lunching in O'Brien's saloon I had anticipated this precise scenario. That was three shots and a beer chaser after I'd learned the fate of the Amalgamated Which-Its of Podunk and immediately before an acquaintance I knew only as Snide Sam proposed an excursion to the pony races at his expense. Needless to say, I'm not the sort of naïf who falls prey to fellows whose names are preceded by adjectives—not even with three shots and a beer chaser under my belt. Sensing this, Sam bought me a half dozen shots more.

By the time we boarded the train out to Jamaica—the Queens County Jockey Club being that week's host—the scenario of my homecoming had been elaborated. Now when Emmie shot me the concerned look, I merely smiled, then plopped my winnings on the table beside her. In my most ambitious version, they totaled fifteen hundred dollars. But that was before we met the two girls.

"What's for dinner?" I asked.

Her look changed from one of concern to something combining vague amusement with mild derision. This is Emmie's trademark, and I'd grown to find it comforting. Which ought to give you some idea of her repertoire.

"I'll see if I can scrape another round of gristle off last Sunday's ham."

"Sounds delightful. Any mail?"

"A second notice from the grocer, a third from the butcher, and I believe that intriguing mauve envelope is a shut-off notice from the telephone company."

She went into the kitchen and I picked up the daily dunning from the table. I'd had too Protestant an up-bringing to simply toss unpleasantness in the trash, but I *had* taken up Emmie's habit of placing it out of sight. We kept a pile of scrap paper beside the telephone for jotting messages, and I flipped over the missives from the butcher and grocer and added them to the stack. In doing so, I overturned the topmost piece there. It was a short letter from Emmie's mother begging her to come for a visit. There were three more similar letters below that, all dated within the last few weeks and of increasing urgency.

I replaced these and moved on to the vase of flowers Emmie kept on a small table by the door. It occurred to me that the intriguing mauve envelope would look especially intriguing beneath the white porcelain. That space, however, was already occupied by an intriguing blue telegram from her mother dated that very day. It was short, but to the point:

For God's sake, Emmie! Respond!

I replaced it with the mauve envelope and carried it into the kitchen.

"Your mother seems to be hinting at something."

"She's just having trouble with the cousins again."

A widowed uncle of Emmie's had died three years before and his three children—twin boy and girl, now about nineteen, and a younger boy, maybe twelve—had gone to live with Emmie's mother at her home in Northampton.

"What's the little truant up to now?"

"It's not Pluribus this time, or at least not him primarily. It's Hal and Gloria."

Emmie's uncle had been born during the Civil War, and the patriotic euphoria that ensued had made a deep and lasting impression. The girl, Gloria, was first to emerge from the womb and the welcome boy that followed was—in keeping with the theme—dubbed Hallelujah. When seven years later a second boy came along, he naturally was christened Pluribus. Actually, E. Pluribus, with the "E" not standing for anything, so far as anyone knew. In Emmie's family, none of this passes as remarkable.

"I thought they were both working?"

"They are. It's their romantic entanglements. It seems Hal has set his sights on a cook some years his senior."

"What's that to your mother? Ben Franklin swore by it."

"Swore by what?"

"The advisability of taking an older lover."

"Well, Mother is in the opposing camp. She says the cook has given absolutely no encouragement. And what's worse, his folly has made him an object of amusement for the other boys, and that in turn has led to several violent altercations."

"Ben never mentioned violent altercations. What's the trouble with Gloria?"

"With her, it's just the opposite. Mother says she's far *too* friendly with the young men, and fears she may be dispensing her favors indiscriminately."

"Which favors specifically?"

"Mother doesn't itemize. But working in a hotel as Gloria does, she doesn't lack for opportunity. And, of course, Pluribus is still skipping school."

"Sounds as if they have poor Mother surrounded. But you aren't anxious to enter the fray?"

"Harry, you know full well I'm in the middle of *The Circensiad*, which may be my most original work."

I knew little about the work in question, but Emmie described it as a melding of the best elements of Virgil's *Aeneid* and those of the children's book *Toby Tyler, or Ten Weeks with a Circus*. It was due to this stunning disregard for salability that Emmie's earnings as a writer had yet to reach, after four years, double digits.

She now began what promised to be a stinging coda:

"Besides, with money so tight and you..."

In mid-sentence, she stopped, sniffed the air, and proceeded to change the subject. "Harry, are you wearing scent?"

"What?"

"Smells French."

"I don't know what you're talking about, Emmie."

We sat down to our warmed-over gristle and by un-spoken agreement let both matters drop. But Fate had other plans.

Complex plans, as it happens. Though convoluted might be closer to the mark. Or maybe tortuous. In fact, plans so lacking in any kind of organizing principle it's taking a liberty to call them plans at all. I suppose it would be more accurate to call them the whims of a capricious deity. Just the sort of things Aeneas et al. faced on a near-daily basis. But where they were heroes of the Golden Age, I was an out of work insurance inves-tigator living in Brooklyn and decidedly ill-equipped for taking on deities—capricious or otherwise.

I wonder if I've entered into this the right way. I can't help but think I've taken things a bit fast, leaving you unprepared for the ludicrous saga which follows. Let me try another tack.

There are, I think it's fair to say, two sorts of people: those who've attended a literary dinner where the host drowns in his own blancmange, and those not so un-lucky. Now, even if we broaden the distinction, say to those who've attended a literary dinner where the *osten-sible* host *appears* to have drowned in his blancmange, well, there's no disputing that this group must be infini-tesimally small. Speaking as an insurance man, though not an actual actuary, I would guess one's odds of attend-

ROBERT BRUCE STEWART

ing such a fête are less than one in three million—and for a thirty-year-old American male with no known cultural aspirations, one in three hundred million.

Unless, that is, he has gotten himself entangled with someone like Emmie. You see, Emmie is one of Mother Nature's problem children, those unpredictable creatures who make for amusing anecdotes, but problematical spouses. Put simply, within Emmie's radius of influence, laws of probability are flouted with abandon, and actuarial tables pass into nothingness.

It may sound as if I'm complaining, but on this particular evening I felt a nostalgic longing for Emmie's eccentric habits. They'd been in abeyance since two years before, when her literary ambitions had evolved into something of an obsession. From that point on, life had become both duller and financially more precarious.

That's not to say that our current pecuniary predicament was unique in the annals of our marriage. A graph charting the family income over the previous five years would closely resemble the swells and dips of an ocean in turmoil. One moment we're living high, traveling to Europe on a well-appointed steam yacht. A week later we're in a French resort town wondering how we'll pay the hotel bill and make passage home.

Part of the problem is the nature of my business. I investigate insurance fraud cases and am usually paid by commission, say 15% of the recovery. If it's a large case, and all goes well, I can make a tidy sum. If, on the other hand, the case goes poorly, or the client goes into receivership before mailing my check, I come out with nothing to show for my efforts but the experience. And that's not a medium of exchange most tradesmen are willing to accept, having vaults of it themselves.

There had been a time when Emmie brought in a sizable income of her own. Not through her writing, but via her lucky deck of cards. By the time of our marriage, Emmie had developed an affection, but no special talent, for gambling. What she did have a talent for was what the uncharitable call duplicity, and the charitable, the art of deception.

It was Emmie's double-dealing at bridge with the well-heeled matrons of Brooklyn which would have financed our sojourn in France, had she not lost it all to a more skilled cheat on the way over. But she learned from that experience, and, more often than not, Emmie's gifts with a cold deck offered something of a buffer when things were tight. Until, that is, her writing eclipsed all else.

The day following our dinner of gristle began on a promising note: a suspicious conflagration had rendered an idle—but well-insured—factory into ash and a potentially fat fee. By the time I reached the scene, the arsonist had confessed—and, sadly, implicated the owner, rendering both the policy and the fat fee moot. It's an unfortunate facet of my business that my success depends on the competence of amateur crooks. I sometimes wonder if it wouldn't improve my lot if I were to publish a line of helpful pamphlets, such as *How to Torch a Building, How to Fake Your Own Death, How to Poison a Spouse,* and *How to Burgle Your Own Home.*

In fact, I went to my office and spent the remainder of the day doing nothing so productive. I stared out the window and heaped a scorn born of envy on all the passersby who seemed to be in a good mood. It cheered me some, but they were unmoved.

That evening, I arrived home to find the janitor on

the stoop leaning on a broom. As a broom leaner, he was an artiste, but on this occasion he had taken the thing to a whole new level: simultaneous with the broom leaning, he held out a slip of blue paper.

"Come fer yer missus," he told me. "Anutter wire from 'er poor mama. Want me ta read it?"

It was generally taken as a given that anything lacking an official wax seal was fair game for Mr. Bagley.

"Sure—what's it say?"

"'Crisis! Da end is nigh!' That's it."

I took it and turned to go up the steps. But with uncharacteristic energy, the janitor stretched out an arm and stopped me.

"Guess you can't be bothered with a poor ol' widow. You got yer own problems."

"What would you know about my problems?"

"One of 'em come by, jus' a while ago."

"Who came by?"

"Big ugly guy. Widt a cauliflower ear, an' a split lip dat ain't healed right."

"No one I know. Did he give a name?"

"Said Sam sent him, 'bout da five C-notes you owe 'im."

"Five? What'd you tell him?"

"I told 'im, ain't no way you can come up widt five C-notes."

"What would you know about that?"

"Only what I hear."

"And read. What else did he say?"

"He says he guessed ya could if ya try hard enough."

As I proceeded up the steps, he called after me.

"Don' forget, rent's due Monday."

Upstairs, I found Emmie on the phone.

"It's someone named Sam, for you," she said, handing it over. "I'll be starting dinner.... How do you like your ham bone?"

"Naked, and steaming hot. Like my women."

"Why don't I spritz it with something Parisian and leave you two alone for the evening?"

I held the phone and waited for her to go into the kitchen. If you're thinking Emmie had evinced some form of jealousy, let me correct you. I've tried everything short of adultery to rouse the green-eyed monster, but it's never so much as lifted an eyelid.

I put the phone to my ear.

"Say, Sam, good to hear from you. That was quite a day we had, wasn't it?"

"Yeah. An' the night after."

"I missed that. What happened the night after?"

"Them dames you hooked me up with took me for three hundred bucks."

"Did they? Little vixens. Say, while we're on the subject, I don't suppose you know what happened to my watch?"

"What watch?"

"My watch. Gold, with an inscription from the Countess de la Salsiccia. It held some sentimental value...."

"To hell with your damn watch. I'm looking to get compensated for the dough your pals relieved me of."

"Certainly you aren't accusing..."

"No games. You set me up and now you'll pay me back. Three hundred. Plus the hundred I lent you."

"Not that I'm admitting culpability, but that makes only four hundred."

"Another C in interest. And if I don't get it by Monday, it will be a hundred more. You got that?"

The irony was that I had assumed the two French girls were friends of *his*. I considered pointing this out, but fellows called Snide tend to have a low tolerance for irony. I was still mulling my response when the phone went dead. Apparently the telephone company's patience ran shorter than Sam's.

I brought Emmie's telegram into the kitchen and handed it to her.

"It seems the end is nigh," I said.

"Hmm. Mother must be reading the Sunday paper."

"I suspect it's more serious than that. Maybe we should go up there."

"We? You'd be willing to come along?"

"They are family, Emmie."

She looked at me warily. "Why do I get the sense there may be some connection between this sudden tug of familial obligation and the phone call from that ill-mannered Sam? Or is it that French scent you were wearing yesterday? ...Ah, I see now. It's all one."

Among the things I like least about Emmie is how transparent she finds me.

"Well," she went on, "it so happens, I've decided to go myself. I've already bought my ticket for tomorrow."

"What changed your mind?"

"Mother's pleading, of course."

One of the other things I like least about Emmie is how impenetrable I find her. There was some chance she was telling the truth, but I thought it a slim one. No, something else had changed her mind. And since she hadn't divulged what it was, I surmised it must be something of a sinister nature.

That evening, when she went back to her typing, I

pretended to be looking for a book and used this subterfuge to perform a search of the apartment, seeking evidence of some communication which would explain Emmie's sudden change of heart.

Eureka! There, beneath a sheaf of typewritten manuscript, lay hidden an envelope from one Margaret Cable of Northampton, Massachusetts—and postmarked the day before!

"Harry, why in God's name are you rifling my papers?"

"Rifling your papers? Don't be absurd. I was looking for that book...."

"What book? When did you take up reading?"

"I resent that, Emmie. You know what book, George Ade's latest."

"I gave that to you for Christmas. You've been reading that hundred pages of doggerel for four months."

"There's a lot to take in. He presents a very nuanced case. *True Bills* is not a book to be read in a day. And it's at least a hundred and fifty pages."

The look she presented me now was light on the vague amusement—but the derision had quite ably taken up the slack. Forced to retreat, I abandoned the incriminating letter unexamined.

The next day, Sunday, struck me as an auspicious one for travel. Especially since it preceded Monday, which had taken on a troubling, ill-omened sort of cast. I might have preferred another destination, but no doubt the respite would do me good. What sort of reception would await me on our return I left uncontemplated. All I could do was hope for the best. And since hoping for the best probably wouldn't by itself fill my days, I added a second item to the agenda: derailing Emmie's literary career. Of course, since her literary career had never been railed to begin with, it really came down to setting her free of her delusions. I knew there'd be some unpleasantness about it, but, in time, I felt sure she'd thank me.

On the way out of the apartment, an image of the gorilla with the cauliflower ear passed before me. I returned to the bedroom and picked up the lucky deck which Emmie had neglected to pack.

2

For the third time, Emmie's head fell back against her seat. Then it slid to the side. And then, for the third time, her mouth gaped open. I don't think I'm betraying a family secret when I say this was not Emmie's most flattering pose.

We'd spent the afternoon visiting a school chum of hers in Mt. Carmel, Connecticut. Several bottles of wine later, we boarded an evening train for Northampton. Emmie already looked in need of a nap. What's more, it had been a sunny, warm day, and since the only ventilation came via the narrow transom above the windows, the car was hot and airless. And if that wasn't enough, she appeared to have chosen a very dull book for the trip.

The first two times she'd gone under, I'd gently shaken her awake. Then she'd return to her book, and, within a page or two, fall back asleep. I saw no point in repeating the futile exercise. But it so happens we were on one of those locals unable to go ten minutes without stopping in some burg no one's ever heard of. Well, I suppose someone has heard of them. Otherwise there wouldn't have been a constant parade of people sidling up and down the aisle, with nearly every one of them stopping a moment to stare at Emmie's yawning gob.

I thought as a matter of simple chivalry I ought to make some token effort at saving her further embarrassment, so I tried using the pile of belongings on the seat beside her to brace up her head. But no matter how I assembled the amalgamation, her head would soon be flopping over and her mouth gaping anew.

"If I might offer a suggestion...." A middle-aged woman was speaking from across the aisle. "Why not something along the lines of a flying buttress?"

"Flying buttress?"

"Yes, something offering structural opposition to the head. For instance..."

She came over and began rearranging the pile of belongings.

"Oh, I hope I'm not being too forward."

"No, not at all," I assured her.

"I don't claim any expertise in these things, but I've just returned from a tour of French cathedral towns."

"Ah. Say no more."

She rebuilt the pile and then positioned Emmie's left arm so the elbow sat on the pile and the hand offered a brace for the head.

"There!"

Emmie's mouth still fell slightly ajar, but I left this trifle unremarked upon and congratulated the woman on her architectural acumen.

"Some of those cathedrals have stood for a thousand years," she informed me.

Here she proved far too optimistic.

She sat back down, very proud of her construction, and it worked well enough until Farmington, where she left the train. But then a lurch sent Emmie's head in the opposite direction. Now her mouth yawned wider than ever.

"I think what you need, if I may be so bold..." An older gent from behind me injected himself into the project.

"By all means," I told him.

"I think what you need is tension." He came around and pointed to Emmie's jacket. "May I?"

"Certainly."

"What we need to do is create a cantilever. It's the same idea as a suspension bridge. It's all dependent on anchoring the cables at the abutment."

He piled Emmie's personal effects on the tail of her jacket, then stretched the neck of it up and around the top of her head, which he made sure leaned slightly in the opposite direction.

Structurally, it was convincing. But the aesthetics left a great deal to be desired. Emmie looked as if she'd entered holy orders unexpectedly and then had to improvise the costume. Nonetheless, I heaped praise on the fellow's efforts and bade him a fond farewell as he exited the train.

The cantilevered jacket held until we crossed into Massachusetts. But then another untimely lurch as we came into Southwick cast the abutment asunder. Before I could intervene, Emmie's torso had gone lateral and her head had plopped down into the aisle, where a small child found herself suddenly face-to-face with Emmie's open mouth. She (the little girl, not Emmie) gave an ear-piercing cry and ran off after her mother. Emmie, now roused, righted herself.

"Impertinent child," she said.

As she rearranged her pile of belongings, I picked up the library book, which had fallen on the floor. It was *Roderick Hudson,* by that well-regarded soporific, Henry James.

"Care to give it another try?"

"It's a very good book, Harry," she said, taking it.

"Is that why you haven't made it past page three?"

"It's the wine, and the heat."

"Why can't you admit you find James as dull as everyone else?"

"Don't be absurd, Harry. James is one of the preeminent writers of our time."

"I never noticed you showing any interest in him before."

"It's only now that I feel prepared to take on his genius."

"Well, after three rounds, I'd say his genius has you on points."

"Quit needling me. What worthy use have you made of *your* time since we got on the train?"

"Oh, this and that." I felt reasonably sure Emmie wouldn't be amused by the various engineering schemes she'd been made a part of.

"Well, there'll be no allowance for your lackadaisical attitude when we get to Mother's. I bought your ticket, but don't for a minute think this a vacation. There'll be plenty of work for you to do."

"Such as?"

"I'll have my plate full dealing with the twins. So, among other things, you'll need to keep an eye on Pluribus."

"Now, look here, Emmie. You saddled me with that little fiend last time and I won't stand for it again."

I was referring to the winter of '03, a year or so after these cousins had gone to live with Emmie's mother. Pluribus had been missing more days of school than he attended, and as the titular male of the family, I was tasked with instilling some discipline. I tried beating him, but my heart wasn't really in it, and a few days after my feeble paddling he went back to playing hooky. I knew then I'd have to outsmart him, and by the following morning I had what seemed like a foolproof plan. I walked him to school and there confiscated his boots, leaving him in his stocking feet.

It was freezing out, and there was a foot of snow on the ground, so I felt confident I'd solved the problem. But no such luck. When I arrived with his boots at the end of the school day, he was nowhere to be found. He'd won another child's off of him flipping pennies. Now the mother of this other kid was trying to blame me for her own failures—I mean raising a son dim-witted enough to wager his boots in a game of chance—in January, yet. I offered him Pluribus's boots, and they were taken, but then the mother insisted I accompany them to a store and buy replacements for the lost ones.

That evening, I had no trouble putting my whole heart into the paddling I gave the little reprobate. Then, just to be sure, I offered him five dollars to run away from home. During our next visit, we settled on ten, but he'd apparently welched on me.

"I simply won't do it, Emmie. I'll deal with the twins."

"Harry, do you really feel equipped to handle a nine-teen-year-old girl of questionable judgment, and who is, let us say, immodest by nature?"

"This particular girl, or are you speaking generally? And what do you mean exactly by handle?"

She made a noise. Emmie makes quite a number of noises. So many, it can be difficult to distinguish one from another. Not that it matters, since they all seem to mean the same thing: a contemptuous disapproval. Though a few might more accurately be said to convey a disapproving contempt. It all depends on what angle you look at it from. Unfortunately, she didn't leave it at that.

"Harry, what time do you have?"

"Nearing six, I'd imagine." Her change of subject had caught me off guard.

"Why not consult your watch?"

I made a show of feeling my pockets. "Must have left it at home."

"Did you?"

She reached down into her bag and pulled out a gold watch. She dangled it before me. It was mine, all right.

"It arrived by messenger this morning, while you were bathing."

"Must have left it on the car coming home, and some good Samaritan sent it on."

"How would this good Samaritan know where to send it?"

"The inscription is to *Signor Reese*."

You might be wondering why I had a watch inscribed to *Signor Reese* from the Countess de la Salsiccia, especially if your familiarity with Italian is sufficient to recognize *salsiccia* as the word for sausage. Since a complete explanation might tax a work already larded with anecdote, however relevant, I'll give you the abbreviated version: it involves Emmie.

"Don't be obtuse, Harry. The fact is, it was Elizabeth who returned your watch."

"Elizabeth? How'd she get it?"

"I believe I know the answer to that, given that French scent you were wearing. But that's enough for now. *You'll* be looking after Pluribus."

She picked up her book and once more joined battle with the genius James.

Elizabeth was another school chum of Emmie's.

Though in Elizabeth's case, I use the word chum loosely. She and Emmie had been having a running feud since just before Christmas of '01, when Elizabeth was forced to spend a night courtesy of the District of Columbia, in the municipal jail—an occurrence for which she not unjustly blamed Emmie. As far as I knew, they weren't even on speaking terms. So I couldn't imagine how Elizabeth had gotten ahold of my watch. Unless, as Emmie implied, she was acquainted with the French girls....

Barely thirty seconds later, the genius James won round four. The little woman was out cold. The train had grown crowded and I moved over to allow a fellow to sit beside me, just opposite Emmie.

Her mouth again fell agape and I considered recreating the cantilever, but I didn't feel my skills were up to the task. Plus, it would mean denying the fellow sitting beside me the show he was enjoying. He seemed to find Emmie's mouth infinitely fascinating. He leaned one way, and then another, as if he wanted to get just the right angle. Then he took her chin between his thumb and forefinger, and gently shifted her head into a ray of sunlight.

"Ha," he said, leaning back in his seat. "Just as I thought, little Emmie McGinnis."

I wasn't quite sure what to make of this. I'm as open-minded as the next fellow, but there are limits.

"Little Emmie Reese now. And I'd appreciate it if you weren't so familiar with my wife."

"Too late for that. But congratulations! Nice piece of dental work you got there."

I'd heard a good many colloquialisms in my time, but none as novel.

"That gold inlay," he elaborated. "Bottom left, second molar. That's my work. Look at it. Ten years later and still a perfect fit."

I looked over, but the light wasn't right, so he took hold of her head again and turned it until I could see.

"You mean you didn't know about it? Where your treasure is, there will be your heart also. So reads the Good Book. I knew her father, you know. Great fellow. A drunk, sure enough. But never a mean one. Though I do remember something about him cheating his partner out of the business."

Emmie had told me essentially the same tale, if not in those words. Nonetheless, I felt constrained to defend her family's honor, however tenuous, and assured him the story was pure calumny. He nodded, and said he was sure I was right. But the smirk that followed said otherwise.

The conductor came by and Emmie's dentist pointed to her gaping mouth.

"What do you think of that?" he asked.

"Talk to him," he said, looking my way. "It's his wife."

The trainman walked on and my seatmate stared at me, perplexed.

"Philistine," I explained.

As we rounded a bend, Emmie's book slipped from her lap and her dentist picked it up.

"Good God! She's reading this?"

"Trying to. Seems to have a tranquilizing effect."

"Have you looked at this book?"

"Me? No, I prefer to give genius a wide berth."

"Genius? Let me read you a passage from the opening page." He flipped through and then cleared his throat. *"Her misfortunes were three in number...."*

"Whose misfortunes?"

"The who isn't important, just listen to what follows. *Her misfortunes were three in number: first, she had lost her husband; second, she had lost her money; and third, she lived at Northampton, Massachusetts!"*

He slammed the book shut and glared, as if waiting for me to express equal umbrage. Frankly, my views on Emmie's hometown weren't far removed from James's. But I'm always willing to play to the house.

"The scoundrel!"

He liked that, but I regretted having encouraged him when he next stood up and tossed the book out the open transom.

"He's coming to town next week," he said on sitting back down. His nonchalance amazed me. I could only assume he'd never crossed swords with the employees of the Brooklyn Public Library. "The fools actually invited him. Ought to be burning him in effigy. And his damn books."

"James is coming to Northampton?"

"Didn't I just say so? Giving a lecture at the college, next Saturday."

Ah. The fog began to clear. I now had some idea of what had changed Emmie's mind about visiting her mother. The letter from Miss Cable must have informed her that Henry James would be coming to Northampton. You may well ask why she would care about an author she had never read visiting a town two hundred miles from Brooklyn. Like all things involving Emmie, the answer is not a simple one.

About two years before, Emmie began writing a work which centered on a young mother of questionable character. This young mother was, very obviously, a fictionalized version of Elizabeth, the former school chum I mentioned earlier. And the book, actually a trilogy of novellas, was Emmie's latest broadside in their running battle. The portrait it painted of Elizabeth was not a flattering one. Of course, if you knew her as I do, you'd know how impossible it would be to paint a flattering portrait of Elizabeth. Now that I thought about it, it wasn't at all surprising that she would know a pair of light-fingered French girls.

To return to the crux of the matter, Emmie had been trying desperately to get her book into publication for the last year and a half. When the publishers themselves had all rejected it, she began insinuating herself into any literary circle that would have her. Whereupon she would fawn over any writer she thought capable of giving her career a leg up.

Nothing has come of all this ingratiating and I suspect that's due to Emmie's insistence that her oeuvre, like James's, is that of a genius. She tells me an author who lacks faith in her own work will get nowhere. And I suppose she's right. Still, even to those who've fallen into the bad habit of novel writing, her unstinting self-praise must be a bit off-putting.

"'The Lesson of Balzac,' he's calling it," her dentist confided.

"Who?"

"That arrogant ass James. His lecture. It's titled 'The Lesson of Balzac,' as if he knows anything about it."

"I take it you won't be attending?"

"*Attending?* He's the one who should be getting the lesson! I'd attend to that, all right. Whole town's gone senile. Even old Mr. Cable. Says James is his dear friend and his lecture will be most edifying."

He repeated the word edifying in a way that might have given the genius James second thoughts about including Northampton in his itinerary. But his quoting of old Mr. Cable interested me most. Any remaining fog obscuring Emmie's motivations had lifted.

Among the literary figures she had approached was this same George Washington Cable, the well-known writer of old New Orleans who had himself spent some time on the lecture circuit. He was an authentic southern gentleman, but had resided in Northampton for the last twenty-odd years. What's more, Emmie was acquainted with his daughters, particularly with Margaret. Emmie had already made practical use of this friendship, and though the old man hadn't been much help to her in his own right, he had offered to put her work before others.

I concluded from this body of evidence that in her letter Margaret Cable had suggested there might be an introduction to Henry James in the offing. Hence Emmie's change of heart toward visiting her mother *and* her sudden interest in the sodden prose of her fellow genius.

The train slowed and Emmie's dentist got up from his seat.

"I get off here—they're stopping at the State Hospital for me."

Did I mention there was a lunatic asylum in Northampton? Remarkably, as near as I can ascertain, no member of Emmie's family has ever been an inmate.

As he went off, the conductor came by and announced Northampton as the next stop. I shook Emmie awake. She fussed with her hair some and then searched about her seat.

"Where's my book, Harry?"

"Your dentist threw it out the transom. Why haven't you ever mentioned the gold inlay?"

I've never quite understood the craze for taking snapshots. But I'd give an eyetooth for a record of Emmie's expression at that moment—though perhaps not a molar with a gold inlay.

3

Gathering up the mystified Emmie and her impedimenta took some time, and the conductor was already blowing his whistle as we descended from the car. We could see Emmie's mother and the two boys at the far end of the platform. Walking toward them, we passed a young couple perched on the steps of a car. The male lead handed his female counterpart a little bouquet of what looked like forget-me-nots, then they entered into what's known in the theatre as a warm embrace.

"I'll be coming back through three weeks from Tuesday," he told her, with a far weightier delivery than the line could bear. "Will you wait?"

"I'll count the hours...," came her suitably breathless, if unoriginal, reply.

"Gloria?"

Emmie had recognized the voice of her cousin.

"Cousin Emmie! This is Floyd, my darling fiancé."

The whistle blew again and the train started moving. Gloria gave a little stage squeal, and like a providently positioned walk-on, I reached up and swung her down from the steps. Floyd was standing there looking like a confounded puppy, mouthing the word fiancé as if its introduction had come as something of a surprise. Had she said, "This is Floyd, my darling wombat," I doubt his expression would have been appreciably different. No, I've gone too far. There was a dark foreboding about the eyes which the word wombat is unlikely to elicit in any but its bitterest enemies.

"Farewell, my beloved," Gloria called to him. She put a damp handkerchief to her cheek and squeezed out a makeshift tear.

He waved to her meekly, like a dispirited automaton. All he could manage by way of dialogue was a weak "Bye."

"I'm so glad you're here, Emmie," Gloria said, while slipping her arm into her cousin's. She appeared to have mislaid all memory of Floyd, still waving from the slow-moving train.

"I'm glad too, dear—"

She broke off as our attention was drawn to an altercation down along the platform. Fists were flailing.

"Oh, no, Hal's at it again...," his sister told us.

The boxers broke off, but traded taunts as Hal's opponent jumped aboard the last car of the quickening train.

"Hal! What *is* the matter with you!" Emmie's mother admonished.

"Not my fault," he said, picking up his hat. "Sorry about that, Cousin Emmie."

"We can talk about it later," she told him.

With the disagreeable encounter forgotten, we all exchanged the proper little hugs, kisses, and handshakes requisite of a clan reunion. Though I happened to notice Pluribus's bussing of Emmie veered some from the norm. He was still just twelve, but nearly as tall as her, and he gave her an embrace which I thought not in the least way cousinly. It took some effort on her part to peel him off.

We started toward the cab stand and found Gloria already up ahead. She had stolen away from us unseen and was now involved in a second tender embrace, equal in warmth to that of the earlier scene.

"I didn't think you'd come," the chump-of-the-moment told her.

"How could I not come...."

One had to respect her consistency. Her delivery was every bit as breathless as in the scene with Floyd.

"I brought you these, forget-me-nots," she added thoughtfully, while handing him the secondhand bouquet. This time, instead of introducing us, she subtly waved us on from behind her back.

With the others distracted, I took the opportunity to pull Pluribus aside.

"What are you still doing here?"

"Aren't you glad to see me, Cousin Harry?"

"I'm not your cousin. And the deal was for you to leave town. I expect you to return that ten dollars—if you have any sense of honor."

"Sorry, Cousin Harry. Don't got either one. But I do got somethin' worth at least ten dollars."

He pulled a watch out of his pocket. Yes, it was mine. I cuffed him and took the watch. He wandered off, rubbing his head.

"Harry!" Emmie had been nearer than I realized. "If you'd attach the fob properly, you wouldn't keep losing it."

This is a prime example of what passes for sound reasoning with Emmie—and just a dip of the toe into that dark pool of irrationality known as Emmie-land. Little did I know then, before the week was out, I'd be up to my neck in it.

Gloria trotted up to us as we descended to the street. "That was Sol. He's on his way back to New York."

"A Hebrew?" her aunt inquired.

"He never said so, but from the looks of it I'd guess he is."

The girl's words took me by surprise, and I turned to find Emmie in much the same condition.

"I wonder what she means by *it?*" I whispered.

"Harry! They're innocents, for God's sake. You saw where they come from."

Given the rundown of events in the brief time since we'd disembarked from the train, calling these cousins innocents struck me as itself rather naïve.

But Emmie had something of a point. She was referring to an excursion the six of us had made to the old family homestead the previous summer. As the crow flies, the farm couldn't have been much more than ten miles from Northampton. But it turned into a two-day affair. It was first necessary to take a train to a depot conveniently sited along an isolated stretch of river. Next, one waited for an infrequent and excruciatingly slow trolley, one of those rural lines which carry both freight and passengers. The kind that stops at all the farms along the way to dispense empty milk cans and indispensable gossip.

Sometime after noon we arrived in the little hamlet proper, and then trudged three miles up a rocky hill named for one of nature's plagues—Locust Hill, I believe they called it, but it might have been some other arthropod altogether. We passed several farms of increasing dereliction until finally coming to a cellar hole about the size of our dining room back in Brooklyn. This, they informed me, had been the barn, and a smaller hole just beyond it, the house where these cousins were raised—as was their father, Emmie's mother, and their Aunt Nell before them.

When Emmie's uncle died and the children came to live with her mother, the farm was seized for unpaid taxes. That had been just two years before our excursion, but already it had been so thoroughly scavenged by the neighbors, all that was left were the cellar holes and a couple dozen misshapen fruit trees. On coming down the hill, we learned we'd missed the last train and would need to book rooms in the hotel—a fine enough place, provided you aren't wedded to amenities like indoor plumbing. That was my last visit to the country.

Hal had gone ahead to have our luggage placed on a cab, and we found him there on the street exchanging taunts with a rough-looking fellow of about the same age.

"Harry, do something!" Emmie insisted.

"Why me?"

"Oh, please, Harry," her mother couldn't resist adding.

I'm not normally one who allows women to shame me into doing things dangerous to my well-being. But Emmie's mother looked at me so pleadingly I couldn't bring myself to refuse—especially since I planned to hit her up for a loan before we left town.

The two adversaries had moved closer and I slid in between them. "Now, fellows, let's not—"

Next thing I knew, I lay on the ground with the rest of the family looking down at me. To their credit, only one of them was grinning.

"He got you a good one, Cousin Harry," little Pluribus gloated.

Hal helped me up and then Gloria handed Emmie one of the pre-moistened handkerchiefs she'd brought as props for the farewell scenes.

As she dabbed at my eye, Emmie couldn't keep from smiling herself.

"Glad you came, dear?"

Since there wasn't room in the cab, Hal suggested the two of us take a streetcar.

"Let's just walk, if you don't mind. I spent the last two hours in a steamy railcar staring at your cousin's dental work and I could use some fresh air."

The truth is, I was in no hurry to arrive at Emmie's childhood home. The house was a modest one, suitable for a family of three perhaps, but a bit cramped for six. And though I was getting hungry, I wasn't looking forward to one of Mother's meals. Emmie was no virtuosa in the kitchen herself, but her mother held fast to the double-B school of cooking: boiled or burnt.

We were passing near Rahar's Hotel and I suggested we stop in for some refreshment.

"Aunt won't be pleased if we're late for dinner."

"It will give the women time to catch up on things. I doubt they'll even miss us. A tall beer would go down really easily right now."

"Beer? It's Sunday, Cousin Harry. You won't get a beer anywhere here. Isn't that the law in New York?"

"Listen, no one beats the Empire State when it comes to feigning piety. We have the exact same law—but not the bad taste to enforce it. Come on, I'll let you buy me a lemonade."

"All right. I wanted to ask your advice about something anyway."

We went into the dining room and I saw a thick slab of beef being brought to another table.

"How are you fixed, Hal?"

"What do you mean?"

"Can we afford a couple steaks?"

"Oh. Sure, I suppose. But..."

I ordered them before he could finish his sentence.

"What I wanted to talk to you about, Cousin Harry…"

"Let's make it Harry."

"All right. What I wanted to talk to you about, Harry, is your courtship of Cousin Emmie."

"Courtship?"

"Sure. How you led up to the proposal."

"Proposal?"

"Asking her to marry you. Aunt says you courted her for most of a year."

"Did she?" I found that odd, since Emmie's mother had been there at the time and knew full well our courtship, such as it was, lasted something less than a week.

"Sure. And she said she only gave her permission for the wedding when she was certain you truly loved her daughter."

"She said that?"

"Sure."

Emmie's mother seemed to be suffering from some form of dementia. I attributed it to her addiction to the Catholic Mass. Though raised a Congregationalist, she couldn't get enough of the Latin liturgy, and the longer the better. Paradoxically, Emmie's Irish father never set foot in a church of any denomination.

In fact, we were married in rather a hurry, and at the *insistence* of Emmie's mother. It wouldn't be accurate to call it a shotgun wedding, since no actual firearms were displayed either before or during the ceremony, but there was a similar air of urgency.

I'd never quite realized just how callow a youth Hal was. But I suppose that might be expected of a boy raised on a subsistence farm perched atop a rock-strewn hill named for an insect.

"I think your aunt is misremembering some details

of the affair," I told him. "But why's that important?"

"Well, let me ask you this. Suppose there were people who stood in the way of your marrying Cousin Emmie. You wouldn't have let them stop you, would you?"

"How many of these hypothetical people are there? And just how big are they?"

"You're teasing me, I know. I suppose they told you about my attachment."

"Is it an attachment?"

"Is for me. She's not keen on it yet."

"Well, you can't *make* her feel the same way about you. Maybe she just prefers another type."

"It's not that. She won't see anyone. Says she can't. Says she couldn't leave the people she works for."

"As a cook?"

"Yes. But she looks after the younger kids quite a bit—their mother died last year."

"Well, there *are* married cooks."

"That's what I say. She sees it different. Then there's Aunt. Says I shouldn't be seeing a girl that much older. Does twenty-seven sound so old to you?"

"Not since I hit thirty. Listen, Hal, things will work out. If not with this girl, then someone else."

"But it's her I love."

"Look, if the girl consents to marry you, no one can stand in your way. You're old enough to make your own mistakes."

"You mean decisions."

"When you look back, you'll find the distinction a murky one."

"Will you at least talk to Aunt?"

"Sure. But it's you who will have to talk to her in the end."

"Yes, I know you're right."

"Sure I am. But what's with the fighting? Does that have something to do with this girl?"

"Oh, just people riding me. Think I'm making a fool of myself over Lottie. That's her name—Lottie Flagg."

"That sort of thing usually doesn't come to blows."

"Maybe I'm being a little thin-skinned."

"How'd you meet her?"

"We've been doing a lot of work over at the house. Me and Mr. Grundy, the plumber I work for."

"How's that going?"

"Sure beats working in a mill, or on the farm. And there's always work. Once people get used to flush toilets, there ain't no going back."

While he absented himself inspecting those of the hotel, I took the opportunity to fortify the lemonade with a few shots of rye from my flask. I wanted to take the kid's mind off his love life. Of course, one can never be sure how drink will affect a person.

After Hal generously paid the tab—and then greedily drained both glasses—we made our way to the house. Emmie's mother was annoyed, but not so much as Emmie. I found her in Gloria's bedroom unpacking.

"Where were you, Harry?"

"Hal had some things he wished to consult me about. How to court and propose to a woman. I thought it best explained privately."

"He'd have been better off consulting the barkeep. You were in a bar, weren't you?"

"You're forgetting the Sabbath, Emmie. Not a drop to be had. What'd you have for dinner?"

"Boiled cabbage and something resembling sausage. And you?"

"Oh, about the same."

"By the way, I'll be in here with Gloria. You'll be in with the boys."

"Three to a bed?"

"Take a room at a hotel if you like—provided you can afford it."

"I'll take the couch."

Gloria entered the room and closed the door behind her.

"I'm so glad I have you together," she whispered. "One can't have a serious conversation out there. I need some advice. About things...."

"I think maybe I should excuse myself."

"No, please, Cousin Harry. I'd like to hear about it from your side too."

"My side?"

"Hear what exactly?" Emmie asked.

"Well, Cousin Charlie was there when you picked out... I mean, when you met Harry. He said you told him how much you wanted to leave Buffalo and go to New York, and then, not two weeks later, you married Harry and moved to New York."

"Gloria, you don't honestly think I married Harry just to get to New York?"

"Oh, no, Emmie. Of course not. Only you did find him awfully quick. Were you sure he was the one when you let him seduce you?"

"Gloria! I did not let Harry seduce me."

"That's right," I agreed. "She seduced me."

"Oh! That's better still! And once she had, you were so in love you proposed immediately, then took her to live with you in New York?"

"Brooklyn, to be precise," I told her. "I'd hoped to

use her dowry to pay my past-due rent."

"Dowry? Did you have a dowry, Emmie?"

"Harry's attempting to be amusing. I did have some modest savings."

"I have sixty-eight dollars."

"That's more than Emmie had, but a good deal less than the five hundred she promised."

"Promised?"

"Don't listen to anything he says, Gloria. You and I will have a long talk later."

The girl nodded and obediently left the room.

"Harry, quit teasing her. Can you imagine what sort of man she might wind up with?"

"Reminds me a little of me, poor sap."

Suddenly, we heard Hal shouting. I followed Emmie out to the dining room, where he had mounted a chair.

"I want you all to know, I've made my decision. I will be marrying Lottie and there will be no more talk about it."

"Hal, I can't let you—" Emmie's mother tried to interject, but he cut her off.

"No, Aunt! I love you like a mother, but there is a time when a man must make his own life! And that time is now!"

He just stood there beaming for a few moments, daring anyone to contradict him. Then he stuck the knife in my back.

"How was that, Cousin Harry?"

"Swell, Hal. How about getting down now and going to bed?"

I reached out to help him, but he waved me off. Then the chair collapsed and Emmie's mother looked at me reprovingly.

"Oh, Harry. What did you tell the boy?"

"Can't remember precisely...."

I escorted Hal to his room, and there found his vile brother going through my bag. He was eyeing my favorite tie. I thought long and hard about choking him with it, but settled for another cuffing.

Then, feeling a sudden nostalgia for Brooklyn, I went off looking for Gloria. She was in the kitchen, putting dishes in the cupboard.

"Say, that sixty-eight dollars you mentioned. I don't suppose a little loan..."

"Sorry, Cousin Harry. It's in the bank."

The speed with which she replied led me to think she'd been prompted. I turned to find Emmie in the doorway with her arms folded, grinning a self-satisfied grin.

"Nice try. Don't forget, tomorrow you need to escort Pluribus to school. And then see he stays there."

"Any leg irons about the house?"

4

There were, alas, no leg irons about the house. But I did manage to come up with something nearly as good during a long, sleepless night. The couch was in desperate need of restuffing, and about a foot too short. What's more, I'd swear I heard someone leave and then reenter the house, twice. And they were pretty clumsy about it both times.

The next morning I forced Pluribus into some pants of his brother's, a couple sizes too large. Then I strung a length of rope through the belt loops, cinching it good and tight. At the back, I tied a knot modeled on Gordius's, leaving about six feet of rope free. It was, for all intents and purposes, a leash.

I expected Emmie and her mother to object. But it tells you something about the kid's character that the only comment from his aunt was to remind me to make sure he wasn't carrying his jackknife, while Emmie merely smiled, then wished us a pleasant day.

We arrived at the school with an entourage of jeering children. I took it as a given that Pluribus had annoyed each and every one of them, and now they were paying him back in kind. But the little scalawag was immune to humiliation and found the whole scene thoroughly amusing. His teacher at first smiled, a little wickedly I thought, and I took that as encouraging. But then she insisted I remove the leash.

"What would happen if Miss Fuller saw him like that?"

"Miss Fuller?"

"The principal. Or someone from the school board. Oh, no, you must untie him."

I saw through her feeble objection. There may have been those determined to keep the little truant in school, but I sincerely doubted his teacher could be counted among them. In fact, I'd wager she abetted his escapes in any way possible. I mean, who in her position wouldn't?

Luckily, I had anticipated she might take this attitude and had prepared accordingly. I cut through the rope and yanked it away. Much to the amusement of the other children, the too-large pants fell to his knees before he could pull them up. It wasn't as sure-fire as tying him to a cast-iron radiator, but even a practiced malingerer like him would find it difficult to make an escape while holding up his pants.

I went outside and camped myself under an elm. It was an agreeable spring day and I had a perfect vantage from which to watch the entrance. I must have dozed for a spell because I was suddenly jarred awake by a prolonged squeak. That cunning teacher had opened a window. As I say, it was an agreeable day—but certainly not so warm she needed to open a window. I was onto her game. There was Pluribus, seated just beside the window. The one window Miss Slyboots thought fit to open.

About ten seconds later, he made his leap out over the sill—just enough time for me to get up and put on my hat. He charged off and I followed. The little beast must have found something to use as a belt, because his hands were free. I wouldn't have been the least surprised if his teacher had provided him the replacement.

We went a few blocks, first to the south and then to

the west, and eventually met up with a railroad line, the same one Emmie and I'd come into town on. He was, of course, in much better shape, and I never could have kept up if he hadn't stopped every hundred yards or so to taunt me. He was doing just that when a guy wearing a white smock stopped me.

"Say, you seen anyone wandering around out here?"

"Just that damn kid up ahead. You don't happen to have a rifle, do you?"

"Rifle?"

It was then I connected the white smock with the nearby State Hospital and decided that maybe I should be more guarded in my language.

"Sorry. I meant, you don't happen to have the time?"

"Oh. Just after eleven. This fellow I'm looking for, he might be disoriented."

"Misplaced a patient?"

"Yeah, that's right."

"I'll let you know if I see him. What's he look like?"

"Oh, kind of ordinary. But probably acting a little odd."

He continued on into a copse and I resumed my pursuit. Pluribus had waited for me to finish my conversation, but now took off along the tracks. Soon after, a train coming from the other direction forced him off the rail bed and I saw him slide down the embankment. Once the train passed, I proceeded to where I'd last seen the little hellion.

While still some distance away, I came upon an older fellow climbing up the embankment.

"You need have no anxiety," the old man told me as we met. He had to be at least sixty, with a big white beard and a rather pompous way of speaking. "There will be no more trouble. And I shall issue a full and unconditional pardon."

"Pardon?"

"Yes, full and unconditional. You have nothing to fear. Now, if you'll excuse me, I have affairs of state to attend to."

With that, he descended the embankment on the other side of the tracks and wandered off. Meanwhile, I went on to where I'd seen Pluribus disappear a little while before.

As I got nearer, I could see what looked like a wide ditch, or small elongated pond, at the base of the slope. While climbing down to follow him, I slipped on a muddy patch and fell forward, toward the water. I put my hands out to catch myself and they landed in some reeds—the right one holding a man's shoe. His foot was still in it. But he wasn't going anywhere.

When I'd picked myself up, I could see he was lying face down and half submerged. The reeds concealed him unless you were right above him. I crouched down and inspected the body. There was a gash at the back of his head, but the blood was mostly dry. Then I rolled him over. It wasn't easy, because rigor mortis had begun to set in and his suit had sponged up several gallons of the brown water. He looked vaguely familiar, but more likely just one of those fellows that look like a thousand others. He was thirty-something, clean-shaven, with brown hair, and nothing else about him seemed the least bit distinctive.

I checked each of his pockets and found them empty. Not even any spare change. I turned him back over and started up the embankment. Then I saw it: Emmie's library book.

It seemed improbable that a book tossed from a moving train, even one thrown by an enraged dentist, could actually kill a man. On the other hand, what if it had merely knocked him senseless, and he'd then stumbled into the ditch and drowned? I checked it for blood. Nothing. Besides, I wondered, how could a book so deathly dull cause so acute a wound?

A more likely possibility was that he had been walking the tracks as a train came by and something protruding from it caught him in the head, a not-infrequent occurrence.

I climbed up to the tracks and began walking toward town.

"Where you going?" It was Pluribus, calling from behind me.

"Where do you think? To call the police."

"I didn't do it, you know."

"Maybe not. But a couple hours under the lights, and they'll squeeze a confession out of you, all right. Those boys can work wonders with a rubber hose."

He ran up beside me.

"You know, Cousin Harry, you got a real peculiar way of bein' funny."

"Wait 'til the cops start asking who cleaned out the corpse's pockets—you'll find that plenty funny."

"What makes you think I did?"

I stopped walking and looked at him.

"Well, anyways, I didn't."

He emptied his pockets as if to prove it. All he had was fifty cents, which didn't seem excessive for a little thief like him. Just the same, I confiscated it.

"What's this place called? I mean, whose property is that with the ditch?"

"That ain't a ditch. Part of the old canal. Why do we need to tell the cops?"

"If we don't, that old man will. Then we'll have to explain why we kept quiet."

"Him? He's one of the nuts, from the hospital."

I stopped again.

"Did you say canal?"

"Yeah. Long time ago, before the railroad. There was a canal that ran 'long the same route."

Unless you happen to have been privy to my earliest cases involving Emmie, you might well be asking yourself why it was significant that this corpse was lying in a canal, even an abandoned canal. Well, I will endeavor to explain—at least as far as anything involving Emmie can be explained.

The first case was back in Buffalo, where we met. Emmie's uncle by marriage had disappeared and was presumed drowned in a boating accident. In truth, he was alive and well and living under an assumed name in Toronto. That is, until he was shot dead.

Sometime after we became suspicious of the boating accident story, but before we'd visited Toronto, Emmie developed a theory that her uncle had been murdered the previous winter and his body kept refrigerated in the Erie Canal. It was an absurd theory, with no substantiation in fact. But Emmie liked it, and some months later when writing short articles for English newspapers, she made use of it. I should note, these "articles" were, for the most part, pure fancy. But since she was paid just thirty-seven cents per placement, and the newspapers had names like *The Leek Times and Cheadle News,* there wasn't much room for complaint.

Later, when her article featuring the refrigerated

body was found in the pocket of a corpse floating in a canal in Lincolnshire, the local constabulary contacted her, and she, with some help from yours truly, solved the case via the mail.

Then there was a murder-for-insurance scheme we became involved with the next spring, which included a woman who was redundantly poisoned and tossed into one of the industrial canals off of Newton Creek in the north end of Brooklyn.

I've left off mention of another corpse found in the feeder canal at Glens Falls for brevity, but that case occurred immediately after the episode in Buffalo and just previous to Emmie's journalism career.

Finally, there was the time in Washington, which, strictly speaking, didn't involve a corpse, but a dead-drunk Irishman. Hoping to have found another body, Emmie was offended at his still having a pulse and attempted to finish him off with a length of lumber.

I think that about concludes the chapter on corpses in canals.

"How about we make a deal?" I asked the kid.

"What deal?"

"Well, how would you like to impress your Cousin Emmie?"

"Impress her how?"

"Show her that corpse."

"Instead of the cops?"

"We'll let her show the cops. You run home and find Emmie. Tell her you got away from me and came across the body in the canal. Make sure you mention the canal."

"What if she won't come?"

"She'll come, all right. Just remember the part about the canal."

"OK."

"And give her this." I handed him the book.

"What's that?"

"What's it look like? Just tell her you found it near the body. And one more part of the deal. I keep that four bits."

"It's all I got."

"Had. It's either that or the rubber hose. Take your pick."

He consented and then started off in the direction of home. But a moment later, he stopped and turned back.

"What if she wants to just go and tell the cops?"

"Well, think up some reason you can't."

"Like what?"

"I don't know, use your imagination."

He stood thinking for a moment, then looked up. "Won't have to, I guess."

On that cryptic note, he ran off.

Only then did I notice what he was using to hold up his pants: my favorite tie.

"I see you caught up with the boy." It was the fellow in the white smock I'd encountered earlier. He'd come up the embankment just as Pluribus had gone.

"Yes, and I think I saw the fellow you're looking for."

"Yeah? Where?"

"Back that way," I said, waving a thumb vaguely behind me. "But he seemed to be wandering back to the hospital."

"Oh, yeah? How'd he look?"

"Dapper. Offered me a full and unconditional pardon."

"Oh.... Yeah, Mr. Anthorn's always doing that. Thinks he's William McKinley."

"Doesn't look much like McKinley."

"Try tellin' him that."

"Doesn't he know about the assassination?"

"We thought about lettin' him know, but what if he took up being William Jennings Bryan? All that speech-making. Who's got the stomach for that?"

"Better the lunatic you know...."

"That's the thinkin'. Well, I better head after him."

I wished him good luck and continued toward town.

There may not be much to be said for a town like Northampton, but I will say this: it's one of the few places a man with fifty cents in his pocket can spend an entire afternoon in a saloon—lunch included—and still have enough for a modest tip.

I figured I needed to stay out of sight, to give Pluribus time to coax Emmie into accompanying him back to the body. My plan was a simple one, and seemingly flawless. Once she had seen the sodden corpse, Emmie's passion for waterway murders would be rekindled. And soon, all thoughts of a literary career would slip from her mind.

When I got to the house, only Emmie's mother was there, incinerating a chicken.

Someone rang the bell and I answered the door.

"Hello—you must be Harry. I'm Margaret Cable. Is Emmie about?"

"I'm afraid she's out on a case."

"A case?"

"I mean, she's out. Shopping or something."

"Oh. Well, I just came by to tell her the arrangements have been made."

"Arrangements?"

"Yes. She's been invited to the dinner my father is hosting this Sunday. For Mr. James."

Before I could respond, Emmie arrived and greeted her friend. Then she led her out on the walk, where they chatted beyond my hearing.

So it was just as I had deduced: Emmie had come to Northampton not in aid of her mother, but to gain an introduction to the genius James. I felt sure there was little chance her prose would so impress the great author that he would take her on as a protégée—Emmie's writing runs unswervingly to the lurid. Just the same, I considered it in my best interests to put the kibosh on the meeting. That gave me just six days to distract her so absolutely she would forget all about her authorial ambitions.

A few minutes later, Miss Cable left and Emmie entered the house.

"So, how'd you spend your afternoon?" I asked.

"Care to guess?"

"Can't imagine. Shopping?"

"Harry, of all your idiotic gags, this was the most pathetic. Did you honestly believe I'd fall for that yarn about a body in the canal?"

"I don't know what you're talking about, Emmie."

She made one of her more elastic noises—it starts out as a sort of hum but slowly evolves into a disbelieving "yessss." The general implication is that she's skeptical.

"What did that little heathen tell you?"

"Just what you instructed him to, I imagine. I had no idea you two would start working together. From now on, I'll take care of Pluribus and you can watch over the twins. You can begin tonight with Gloria. Now, if you'll excuse me, I should go help Mother." She started toward the kitchen, but then stopped and turned. "By the way, Harry. It's you who will be explaining the condition of that book to the librarian."

"Me? He's not my dentist...."

She left before I could finish my sentence.

I know what you're probably thinking. You're thinking that Emmie's reaction to being told by her prevaricating cousin that he'd seen a body lying in an unused canal bed was the natural one. And, I admit, you may be right. But with Emmie, one must always consider the deeper, darker possibilities. Which in this case included the possibility that she *did* accompany Pluribus to the body and was now merely trying to mislead me.

It wasn't until after dinner that I was able to interview the little trickster himself. I opened the session by cuffing him and taking my tie.

"You broke our deal," I told him. "Emmie says you never took her to the corpse. I guess now I'll have to turn you over to the cops and their rubber hose."

"What was I supposed to do? Drag her out there? An' besides, you go to the cops, an' you'll have some explaining to do yourself. Especially now."

"What do you mean, especially now?"

"The body. It ain't there."

"What do you mean, it ain't there?"

"Gone. When Cousin Emmie wouldn't come with me, I went myself. It ain't there."

"Then someone else must have called the cops and they took it away."

"Don't think so. No one was around."

"Maybe you were just looking in the wrong ditch?"

"No, I wasn't looking in the wrong ditch. Come on and see if you don't believe me."

"All right. But if you're lying, *I'll* be taking a rubber hose to you."

When we reached the tracks, I posed a question.

"Remember this morning, you asked what to do if Emmie wanted to call in the cops? I told you to use your imagination, and you said you wouldn't have to. What was that about?"

"The dead guy. He's the one Hal was fightin' with yesterday."

"The fellow who punched me?"

"No, the one before."

"But we saw him get on the train."

The kid shrugged.

I couldn't be positive he brought me to the right spot—the sun was setting by then and things have a way of looking different that time of day. There were no signs of a body having been dragged off. But there did seem to be an area where the reeds had been flattened. Then I saw a shoeprint in the mud. It was mine.

5

"What do you think happened to it?" the little pestilence asked.

"Your guess is as good as mine. Probably better."

I climbed back up to the tracks, with him on my heels.

"What do you mean by that? You think *I* moved it?"

There wasn't much point in interrogating him. He was an inveterate liar, worse even than Emmie, who I had no doubt began her dissembling in the cradle.

"You going to investigate this murder?" he asked. "Like those others?"

I stopped and eyed him warily. "What makes you so sure he was murdered?"

"The bash on the head."

"Could have been hit by something thrown from a train."

"Like what?"

"A dull book."

"That book you found? You couldn't knock someone out with that. An' if it wasn't murder, why else would someone move the body? Musta been to cover it up."

"Did you leave the house last night?"

"No. Why?"

"Did Hal?"

"Not that I noticed."

When we got back to the house, Emmie greeted me in one of her less-than-genial moods.

"Where have you been, Harry?"

"Went for a stroll."

"Don't forget, you're to keep an eye on Gloria this evening. I dropped her off at a friend's house for a whist party. She'll be leaving there sometime after 10:30." She handed me a little slip of paper with directions. "Just make sure she doesn't stop anywhere along the way."

"You're worried she has some rendezvous planned?"

"Yes. I interrupted one last night."

"When was that?"

"Half past twelve, maybe one. She left the house and I followed her. She headed toward the Plymouth, the hotel where she works. I confronted her and she made up some nonsense about meeting another girl for a late-night walk. She returned to the house with me, but today I did some snooping. Apparently she's been seen with a man staying at the hotel. His name is Mortimer Vincent."

"*The* Mortimer Vincent?"

"You know him?"

"I'm astonished you don't recognize the name, Emmie. He's a noted author."

"*You* know a noted author? Author of what, pray tell—burlesque skits?"

"You wound me, Emmie. Mr. Vincent has written some very popular travelogues. He's been all over the world—China, India, Africa... Kalamazoo."

"Well, then, you can introduce yourself as a fan when you see him."

"When I see him?"

"Yes. You have plenty of time to stop by the hotel and make clear to him his advances toward Gloria are not welcomed by the family. And if he persists, you will take action."

"Will I? What sort of action?"

"Don't threaten him physically, but do convey the seriousness of the matter. When you finish with him, you can go and escort Gloria home."

I saw no point in arguing and left the house resigned to perform my familial duty—provided it could be done without risk of bodily harm.

The Plymouth Inn was an incongruity. In New York, it would have compared well against the smaller second-class hotels. But for a town like Northampton, it felt ostentatiously ornate. Great slabs of marble, palm trees, and giant urns graced the lobby. It may have passed for elegant in the daytime, but in the dim light of evening, the overarching effect was inescapably funereal.

"I'm here to see Mr. Vincent," I told the clerk.

"Is he expecting you?"

"No. The name's Reese. Harry Reese."

He went to a switchboard and phoned the room. While still on the line, he called over to me. "Does Mr. Vincent know you?"

"Ah, no. Not really."

He spoke some more on the phone and hung up.

"Room 412. To the right off the elevator."

I may as well confess that Emmie's doubts were well-founded. I'd never read a single one of Mortimer Vincent's books. We had met briefly six years before, when I was investigating a large claim on his fire insurance. There were certain features of the case which raised suspicions, but, regrettably, nothing rising to the fraudulent.

I wasn't at all surprised that the fellow opening the door and introducing himself as Mortimer Vincent didn't recognize me, and for two very good reasons. In the first place, we had only met that once, several years before.

And in the second, he wasn't Mortimer Vincent. I don't profess to powers of perfect recognition, but the man standing before me was about fifteen years too young and six inches too tall. What's more, he seemed to be a genuine Englishman, as opposed to a supercilious American affecting a patrician accent.

Once we'd dispensed with introductions, he offered me a drink, and this cordiality went a long way toward making up for his inauthenticity.

He handed me a short glass and we sat down in two huge wing chairs.

"Now, what can I do for you, Mr. Reese? A question about my travels?"

"Actually, it's a purely domestic matter."

"Oh, I've been all over the States."

"No, I mean *very* domestic. It involves one of the hotel's chambermaids. A blonde girl, named Gloria..."

"Oh. Is she your—"

"My cousin, by marriage."

"Well, I can assure you, I've never given her the least bit of encouragement."

"No?"

He sounded sincere, but I noticed some beads of sweat taking shape about the brow. Then his upper lip quivered, ever so slightly. Frankly, it would have been difficult to blame the fellow if he *had* given her just a little encouragement. Gloria was a girl with very definite attractions. She had naturally wavy hair, and affable blue-gray eyes. She was just the right height—not threateningly tall, yet well above squat—and what showed of her figure held out great promise. Most winning of all, she had the smile and manner of a true peasant girl— approachable to a point just short of wanton. If she *was* still in her virginal state, as Emmie had implied, it was something of a miracle.

"Friendly, of course," he said. "But nothing more." Then he took out a handkerchief and undercut his credibility while wiping his brow. "Has she complained?"

"No, no. The family's just worried."

"I give you my word, you have nothing to fear from me."

"Fine. But, ah... just whose word is that?"

"I beg your pardon?"

"I told the clerk I didn't know Mr. Vincent because we'd only met briefly and I doubted he'd remember me."

"Oh, I see. Well, it's nothing nefarious, I assure you. I'm Mr. Vincent's valet. Joe Griep's the name."

"Pleased to meet you."

"Likewise, I'm sure." He reached over and shook my hand. "Well, perhaps I should explain. You see, Mr. Vincent has embarked on a tome with the unfortunate title *The Shire Towns of Old New England*. And there are quite a few of them, you know. So he sent me here to gather material. He's particularly interested in Shays' Rebellion."

"Ruthlessly crushed, wasn't it?"

"Yes. You're something of an historian?"

"No, not at all. But one of the more enduring legacies of the Spirit of '76 is an intolerance for any sort of revolutionary spirit. Shays' Rebellion, the Whiskey Rebellion, Southern secession, Haymarket, Homestead— all crushed ruthlessly. But let's get back to your masquerading as Mr. Vincent."

"Well, originally he was to come here, but then learned he needed to stay in New York. There was some trouble with proofs of a prior book, so he sent me in his stead. When I arrived, I of course intended to use my own name. But the clerk naturally assumed I was Mr. Vincent, and I thought, why not? No harm in it, and I'd most assuredly be treated better than I would be as Joe Griep."

"And no one suspects?"

"No, just the opposite. I've been invited by Mr. George Washington Cable himself to attend a dinner he's giving on Sunday for another author."

"Henry James..."

"Yes, that's right. Are you familiar with his work?"

"Never read a word, but I can attest to its efficacy, provided you're battling insomnia. Don't expect a scintillating evening...."

"No? Oh, well, I don't get many chances to attend these sorts of things. I certainly don't want to snub the man."

"That's very white of you. Of course, there is some hope the dinner will rise above the literary doldrums: my wife's attending as well. And if her dentist shows up, all bets are off."

"Oh, your wife... You won't give me away, will you?"

"No, no. Mum's the word."

"Thank you. How about another drink?"

"Thanks, I will."

"I wonder, since you're a native... I wonder if you would mind answering a question for me."

"I'm just visiting—it's my wife who's from here."

"Well, maybe you'll know just the same. It's about this referring to the town as Paradise. I can't quite make out what's meant by it. I mean, is it safe to assume they're being ironic?"

"No, sadly, they're not. It's just an extraordinarily

pure strain of mawkish chauvinism, born of one of P.T. Barnum's stunts."

"P.T. Barnum?"

"Yes, the impresario of hokum. Do you remember Jenny Lind, the opera singer?"

"Before my time."

"Before mine, too. I believe it was in the 1850s. Barnum got the idea to bring her over from Europe and promote a tour of the U.S. The Swedish Nightingale, he called her. Worked the press in the usual Barnum way, so before she'd even set foot in the country, people were clamoring to buy tickets. Given this puffery, any town granted a performance would have an irrevocable imprimatur of cultural sophistication. Naturally, the citizens Northampton couldn't pass up the opportunity."

"Yes, I suppose, but..."

"There's more to it. When she arrived here, and before she'd even sung a note, they treated her like royalty. Later she returned the compliment by referring to the place as the Paradise of America. No doubt they'd poured her full of hard cider, but I imagine the perpetual adulation contributed equally to her delirium."

"Only in America," he said, then raised his glass. "Well, here's to Paradise."

"Here's to delirium."

We drank and he refilled our glasses, then made a suggestion.

"If I might be so forward..."

"Be as forward as you like."

"It's concerning your cousin. Far be it from me to give advice on a matter such as this, but given her... predilections, don't you think perhaps some other form of employment might be more suitable?"

"Maybe. But given her predilections, I'd be surprised if she hasn't snared some poor sucker before the summer's out, regardless."

"Yes, I don't envy you. Ceaseless vigilance is called for."

"Or resignation to the inevitable."

"But wouldn't that be disastrous for the girl?"

"Not if it were the right mark... I mean, the right fellow. Say someone like you. Steady income. Seem straight enough. Though I suppose your employer might not be too keen on the idea."

"On the contrary, he's suggested, not too subtly, he feels a feminine sensibility might round out the household, and taking a wife should be given serious consideration."

"Meaning him, or you?"

"Me, most definitely. Mr. Vincent abhors the idea of a wife for himself."

"Well, here you have a girl willing and able. Trained as a chambermaid, used to hard work. And you'd be doing all right for yourself. She's willing and able in that department, too."

"All true, I suppose. But there is the matter of deportment. Mr. Vincent is an exceedingly proper man. There is a casualness to Gloria which he might find off-putting."

"Oh, we can polish her up."

"That's possible," he acquiesced. "But then there's also the matter of her education. Ours is a literary household. Mr. Vincent and I often discuss what we're reading at any given moment."

"Oh, she can read. Made it through three years of high school, more or less. Just a matter of you setting her onto the right books." He didn't seem convinced. "Look, when do you leave town?"

"Early next week."

"Doesn't give us much time, but we'll see what we can do."

"I suppose there's no harm in that. But there is something else to consider."

"What?"

"Would she be happy? Traveling incessantly. Living in hotel rooms..."

"Are you kidding? A nineteen-year-old girl who grew up in a farmhouse the size of this sitting room?"

"And what would your wife's family say?"

"Yes. There'd be some squawking there.... But not if they thought she was eloping with the famous author Mortimer Vincent!"

"But surely, once they learn the truth..."

"By then you'll be back in New York."

"Actually, we go next to Argentina."

"That should be safe enough."

"It is an interesting proposition, Mr. Reese. But I would like some time.... The matter of her bearing still gives me concern."

"Yes, of course. But don't worry, we'll take care of that. Well, I need to be going. You think it over."

I left the hotel and found my way to the house of the whist party, then waited outside. They emerged as a raucous mob. Seven or eight girls, all chattering and laughing at once. Rather than announcing myself, I decided to follow at a safe distance until they separated. But they were so wedded to one another's company that instead of simply going their separate ways, they collectively walked each girl home in her turn. There then followed a tedious series of good-byes on her porch. I was eyeing one of these sessions from behind a large rhododendron when someone tapped me on the shoulder.

"Just what do you think you're doing, friend?"

He was a stout, middle-aged burgher with gray hair.

"Ah, I was just following those girls. See that one there...."

I wish I'd been more succinct with my answer. As it was, he hit me with a force I thought unfairly inconsistent with his physique.

"Daddy! What is it?" one of the girls called from the porch.

"On my way home from the lodge and I find this miscreant watching from the bushes. He was following you."

"Me?"

"Who else, missy? Another of your assignators?"

The gaggle moved off the porch and stood over me.

"Is that you, Cousin Harry?" Gloria asked.

"Yes. Just wanted to make sure you got home OK."

"From behind the bushes?"

"Didn't want to intrude."

She helped me up. As we started for home, the others watched, commenting in hushed tones. It's mere conjecture on my part, but I'd wager none of it was flattering to yours truly.

"Did Cousin Emmie send you to spy on me?"

"Not to spy, just to make sure you made it home without any detours. I stayed back because I didn't want to interrupt you and your friends. By the way, I stopped by and saw Mortimer Vincent earlier."

"Why?"

"I met him in New York a few years ago and saw he

was staying here. When I mentioned you worked at the Plymouth, he told me you had met."

"What did he say about me?"

"Very complimentary."

"Really?"

"Yes, he had great things to say about... the way you make the bed."

"Oh. Nothing about me personally."

"Sure, but I don't want to give you a swelled head."

She smiled, sincerely pleased.

"What do you think of him?" I asked.

"He seems so... so debonair. And I love the way he speaks, don't you?"

"Yes, he's the real thing, all right. It's amazing he's still single. But I imagine there aren't many women who'd enjoy all that travel. One week you're in Timbuktu, the next week on the French Riviera. Must take some getting used to."

"It sounds terribly romantic."

"I suppose. But having traveled a fair amount myself, I can vouch that there are some real drawbacks. Tiny, noisy hotel rooms, harboring not-so-tiny, noisy vermin, who run about all night long. And often the food is barely edible. I can't speak with any authority on the fare in Timbuktu, but the natives of Passaic, New Jersey, have some very strange ideas regarding cuisine."

"Couldn't be much worse than Aunt's cooking."

"Point well taken."

"But it's the other part of his world I could never fit in with. You know, rubbing shoulders with the swells. Knowing all the proper things to say. Which fork should you use for your salad, which spoon for the fruit cup."

"Which knife to plant in a rival's back...."

"What do you mean?"

"Well, with a fellow like Mortimer Vincent, you're bound to have competition. Carpe diem must be your watchword. Or watchwords."

"Carpe diem?"

"Seize the man."

When we arrived at the house, Gloria went to her room and I joined Emmie in the kitchen.

"What happened to your eye? Did you have a confrontation with this Mr. Vincent?"

"No, you have him all wrong, Emmie. Never met a straighter fellow. The girl's just naturally infatuated."

"Well, I'm glad to hear it."

"In fact, he'd be quite a catch for Gloria. Well-to-do, respectable."

"Isn't he a good deal older than her?"

"About my age—I doubt he's much over thirty. And I'd think a more mature fellow would be what's needed in Gloria's case. A fellow like Floyd wouldn't stand a chance."

"Floyd?"

"The first fiancé we met at the depot."

"Oh. Yes, I imagine there's something to what you're saying. But what sort of man would arrange a late-night rendezvous with a chambermaid?"

"Emmie, I think you leapt to a conclusion there. If you met the fellow, you'd realize the idea is absurd."

"I suppose that will have to do. But that still leaves your eye."

"Oh. The father of one of Gloria's pals seemed suspicious of my intentions toward his daughter."

"What were you doing to his daughter?"

"I wasn't doing anything. I was just standing behind a rhododendron, watching."

"Watching?"

"It's not what you think...."

"Never mind, Harry. Her father appears to have the situation well in hand. I'll see you at breakfast."

By morning, the corpse in the canal had more or less slipped from my mind. But as I prepared to leave the house, Emmie reminded me of it.

"Don't forget, you're to visit Hal at work this afternoon. See what you can learn from Mr. Grundy in regard to this cook. I'm hoping we can enlist his help in putting an end to the affair. Oh, and do keep a lookout for any more stray bodies."

Her quip seemed practiced. As if she wanted to mislead me. I left the house, but then circled around and planted myself where I could watch Emmie. She was helping her mother with the dishes. As I watched, I developed a theory. It seemed highly unlikely that Emmie, even with Pluribus's help, could have carried the corpse up the embankment. But what if she decided to sink it in the canal? Just as she had imagined the culprits in Buffalo did, five years before.

Why would she sink it, you may ask, not being yourself sufficiently acquainted with Emmie's warped school of logic? To keep others from finding it while she investigated, of course.

Once the breakfast dishes were disposed of, I expected she'd leave the house and initiate inquiries. Instead, she sat down at the table and began going over one of her manuscripts. But I wasn't fooled. If I knew Emmie, she was still plenty preoccupied with that dead man submerged in the canal, and her apparent nonchalance merely an act for my benefit.

My only fear was that this might prove too simple a

case, and the distraction from things literary too ephem-
eral. So I thought I'd muddy the waters. I made my way
to the *Northampton Daily Herald* and arranged for the
placement of a classified ad in that evening's edition.

6

Meeting Mr. Grundy, Hal's boss, turned out not nearly so awkward as it might have—given that he was the aggrieved father who found me lurking behind his rhododendron the previous evening.

"Sorry about the eye, Mr. Reese. But when you got a daughter that age, you get a might combunctious."

"Ah, well, say no more, Mr. Grundy. I perfectly understand."

"Yes, I figured you would. You having Gloria to look after. That girl's to the worse-ward of my Jane. But they're all brassy nowadays. Not like their mothers."

Apparently Mr. Grundy was ignorant of the fact that Gloria's mother had run off with an organ salesman soon after the birth of her younger brother.

"Say, Hal. I think we must have left that convincin' wrench back at Mr. O'Donnell's house. Why don't you run back and get it?"

"All right."

Hal left and Mr. Grundy offered me a seat.

"I expect you're here to talk about Hal's fatuation with Lottie, Mr. Cable's cook."

"Yes. Only I wasn't aware she worked for Mr. Cable. Is that George Washington Cable, the author?"

"The venterated man himself. I was the one that warned Mrs. McGinnis about the affair."

"Affair?"

"I use the word as presagement of the potentialities."

"Ah, I understand. So you see them as ill-matched as well?"

"Not just ill-matched—ill-omened, I'd call it. I haven't got nothing against the girl, mind you. Not that she could get away with calling herself a girl. Thirty, if she's a day."

"Twenty-seven, Hal tells me. Still, if they care for each other..."

"She don't want nothing to do with him! That's the complexing thing. Why go after an old maid that hasn't the time of day for you, when there's plenty of ripe young ones just begging to get their finger ringed?"

"Love is rarely logical."

"You never said a truerism, Mr. Reese. Take my Jane. I know she's been seeing one of these fellows from over at the hospital. That's who I thought you were. See, he hasn't got the manners to come by the house, proper. Just meets her on the sly."

"Maybe she's worried you wouldn't approve of him."

"Why would I? With a better man right under her nose."

"You have someone else in mind for her?"

"Well, I guess you seen right through me. Sure, I'd like nothing better but for her to take up with Hal. I haven't never met a boy as primticular as that kid. Don't drink. Don't gamble. And no sneaking around in bushes. There was a time they saw quite a lot of each other. Before this other fellow showed up. It's just a matter a getting them back together."

"I suppose that would have advantages for Hal, too."

"Why sure, ain't no better business than plumbing. And when I'm ready to retire, it'd all be his!"

"And at the same time, you'd be keeping it in the family."

"And what's wrong with providing for my little girl?"

"Nothing, nothing at all."

"When the boy gets back, we'll all head over to Mr. Cable's and you can meet this Lottie. You'll see what I mean."

Shortly after, Hal returned with what looked like an inarguably convincing wrench and the three of us boarded Mr. Grundy's van. It was a large wagon pulled by a small horse, so whenever we came to a hill, Hal and I were obliged to get out and push. Making the task all the more tedious, the rear wheel on my side was oddly eccentric. It took us half an hour to travel the one mile to Tarryawhile, the manse of the venerated Mr. Cable. Venerated, I suppose, by the same type who find it charming to burden a home with a quaint name as he had.

It was a well-appointed suburban house, not as grand as I might have expected, but congenially situated on a street with the equally quaint name of Dryad's Green. I feel some friend should have alerted the old man to the second law of real estate: two quaints make for insipid.

The door was answered by Margaret Cable, Emmie's friend I'd met the day before.

"I thought you had finished, Mr. Grundy."

"Oh, yes, Miss Cable. Finished with the preliminary work. But without emancipating the trap subsequent to the one we attended to priorly, well, you'll end up just where you started in a week or two."

"I don't remember a stuck drain ever presenting such a problem before."

"Oh, it was more than just stuck, Miss Cable. If you forgive me saying so, you had a clog of monumental audacity. By the way, this is Mr. Reese, Hal's cousin."

"Yes, we've met."

"Hal, you take the tools down to the cellar—I'll be with you in a jiff."

Once his assistant had gone, Mr. Grundy continued. "You see, Miss Cable, Hal's family is of the same mind as you and me. I mean, regarding Hal and Lottie. I thought maybe you could take Mr. Reese to the kitchen for some coffee."

"Oh, I see. Yes, all right."

Mr. Grundy followed Hal down to the basement and Margaret led me into a hall. There I was surprised to see President McKinley descending the stairs.

"Hello," I said. "How stands the Republic?"

He gave me a bewildered look, which was explained when Margaret introduced the old gent as her father. On closer inspection, I realized he was somewhat older than the fellow who'd very obligingly given me a full and unconditional pardon, but otherwise the spitting image.

"This is Mr. Reese, Father. He's married to Emily McGinnis. You remember Emmie?"

"Oh, yes. I see." Apparently my relationship with Emmie was sufficient to explain my greeting. "Good afternoon, Mr. Reese. But I'm afraid I must be off. What time is Mrs. Tibbitts arriving, Margaret?"

"Not until this evening, after dinner. I'll be meeting her at the depot."

"Then I'll see you at dinner. Good-bye, Mr. Reese."

He shook my hand and then put on his hat and left us.

"Mrs. Tibbitts?" I asked. "That wouldn't be the former Elizabeth Strout, would it?"

"Yes, it would." She spoke with a certain resignation,

then bit her lower lip. "But please, Harry, don't mention it to Emmie. Elizabeth swore me to secrecy. And she can get *very* sarcastic."

"Yes, I've been targeted myself. And carry the scars to prove it. But don't worry, I won't say a word. Is her visit also related to Henry James coming to town?"

"So she tells me, but I think she has something more in mind. On the day I received Emmie's letter asking about Mr. James's visit, I also received a letter from Elizabeth. When my father said he thought he might be able to arrange a meeting with Mr. James for Emmie, I happened to mention that fact in my reply to Elizabeth. It was in her next letter that she asked about coming to town the same weekend, ostensibly to hear Mr. James's lecture."

"So it's no mere coincidence."

"No, I fear not. And given the current state of relations between the two of them, I can't help but suspect she has something up her sleeve. Especially since the first part of Emmie's novel was published in the alumnae magazine. As I'm sure you know, it's a very thinly veiled satire of poor Elizabeth."

"Not that poor Elizabeth doesn't deserve it."

"True enough. But now *I'm* caught in the middle. And they're both such formidable personalities."

"Does Elizabeth know Emmie's been invited to dinner Sunday?"

"No, not yet. But there's no way I'll be able to avoid telling her."

"My guess is she'll try to find some way of scuttling it."

"I don't see how she'd be in a position to do that. Of course, she is Elizabeth...."

"Yes, she is that."

"Well, why don't we go in and you can meet Lottie. She really is a wonderful woman, you know. We all adore her. And now she's really become part of the family. You see, our mother died last year. But I don't want you to think any of us would want to stand between her and her happiness. It's just that…"

"She doesn't return Hal's feelings?"

"Honestly, I'm not sure she doesn't. I think perhaps she's just worried about appearances, for his sake, as much as her own. But she won't confide in us about it."

We went into the kitchen and I met Lottie. She was certainly senior to Hal, but there wasn't anything old-maidish about her. In fact, she was remarkably well-preserved for a woman who'd probably been in service for ten years or more. She smiled when told Hal and his boss were in the basement, but too inscrutably for me to derive any meaning from it.

She sat down and had coffee with us, but the conversation never went beyond the casual. She didn't mention Hal, and I didn't feel comfortable broaching the subject myself.

By the time the trap subsequent to the one attended to priorly had been emancipated, it was nearly six. We helped Mr. Grundy load his van for the downhill ride into town and then Hal and I left for home.

"Do you know that fellow you had the altercation with at the depot?" I asked. "The one who boarded the train?"

"Yeah, sure, I know him. Why?"

"Was he one of those riding you about Lottie?"

"With him there's something more to it."

"Like what?"

"Well... for one, he's been sugaring up Jane, Mr. Grundy's daughter."

"Why would that bother you?"

"I just don't like him. I don't mind her seeing fellows. Just not him. I had to warn him off from bothering Gloria a while back."

"What's his name?"

"Bill McCrea. He works at the hospital. Why?"

"Just curious. Do you know where he was off to?"

"No, but must be somewhere north of here."

The evening newspaper was waiting on the porch. I picked it up and, as Hal went inside, I found my ad:

To whom it may concern,
Your activities at the old canal have been observed. If you would like to resolve the matter amicably, meet at said location at midnight. Must come alone.

I folded the newspaper in such a way that the ad appeared at the top of the single column showing. Then I went inside, where I found Emmie in Gloria's room. I nonchalantly placed the paper on the dressing table before her. She glanced briefly at the page, but then went back to brushing her hair.

"Did you meet Mr. Grundy?"

"Yes. As a matter of fact, for the second time."

"For the second time?"

"It turns out he was the fellow who caught me off guard last night."

"I hope you apologized."

"For getting in the way of his fist?"

"For ogling his daughter. What did he say about Hal?"

"Well, he'd like nothing better than to get him ogling his daughter."

"What are you talking about?"

"It's Mr. Grundy's wish to have Hal hitched to his daughter Jane."

"Because he thinks so highly of Hal?"

"Yes, that. But also to keep the business in the family. I met Lottie as well."

"The cook?"

"Yes. She happens to work for the Cables."

"Oh?"

"Yes, Mr. Grundy needed to emancipate a trap there and I came along and had coffee with Margaret and Lottie in the kitchen."

"Emancipate a trap?"

"Argot of the guild."

"What was she like? As old as Mother makes out?"

"About your age. And very pleasant. I think your mother's negative opinion is based mainly on Mr. Grundy's biased intelligence."

"But is it true she isn't keen on Hal?"

"It's not clear if it's him so much as circumstances. The age difference. And apparently she's pretty devoted to the Cables. By the way, how'd you get on with Pluribus?"

"Oh, that problem's solved."

"You chained him to his desk?"

"Nothing so primitive. I came to an arrangement with him."

"What sort of arrangement?"

"You'll find out when the time comes."

Her words had an ominous quality, and the smile she sent via the mirror did nothing toward reassuring me.

When she went off to the kitchen, I retrieved the newspaper. I couldn't be sure she had actually read my ad, so another attempt was in order. I thought about circling the ad in pencil, but decided that was a little too obvious, so I circled the one immediately below. Unfortunately, without having read it.

I placed the newspaper beside Emmie's usual seat at the table. When she sat down, she again glanced at it, but then pushed it aside, toward Hal. He picked it up and exhibited a definite interest.

"Who circled this ad?" he asked.

"Which ad?" Emmie asked in turn.

"This one from a man selling 700 board feet of ash flooring."

"I must have done it, unconsciously," I told them.

Emmie displayed a smile not terribly unlike the one she'd sent my way in the bedroom earlier, its precise meaning equally obscure.

After dinner, Emmie and her mother played Hal and myself at whist until about ten. Then I was once again sent off to escort Gloria home. She and her pals had gone out that evening to the small vaudeville house. By the time I arrived, the show had ended and Gloria stood among a scattering of people out in front of the theatre. She was in a close huddle with a fast-talker wearing a plaid jacket. What's more, his hands were in his pockets, his hat was pushed halfway back on his head, and he had a cheek full of chewing gum. Yes, there was no doubt about it, he was a sheet music salesman.

"Say, you look like *you* oughtta be on the stage," he told her in the oily drawl of a practiced drummer.

"You think so?"

"Sure! Just lookin' at you, I can see you got talent."

"You can?"

It was a pretty tired routine. One that would garner nothing more than a bottle to the head in New York. Even in a town like Northampton, I couldn't imagine it had much play. But when dealing with girls who grew up on hills named for insects, all bets are off.

"Say, friend." I tapped him on the shoulder.

"Hey, there. Something I can do for you?"

"Well, it's none of my business. But I thought you should know the girl you're working on is the police chief's daughter."

"That right?" he said, seemingly unimpressed. "Well, got to hit the road early tomorrow. See you folks."

"That wasn't very nice, Cousin Harry."

"Look, Gloria, you hook up with a fellow like that and you're going to find yourself abandoned in some two-bit mill town, unwed and... how-come-ye-so."

"How-come-ye-so?"

"I thought that was a New England expression. Well, you'll find yourself carrying a come-by-chance."

"Come-by-chance?"

"In the pudding club?"

"Pudding club?"

"All right, knocked up."

"Oh. You don't think I'd hop into bed with a man like that, do you, Cousin Harry?"

"No, but one can't be too sure." We walked on a little, but then something struck me. "Say, you didn't mean to imply you might hop into bed with a man not like that, did you?"

"Well, when the time comes. I mean, it worked for Cousin Emmie."

I wasn't prepared to enter into a discussion of the

mechanics involved in come-by-chance prevention, so I asked her about her day at work.

"All right. Same as any other day."

"Did you see Mr. Vincent?"

"Mortimer? Only for a minute or two."

Mortimer? When we arrived home, Hal informed me that Emmie had gone out for a walk.

"Kind of late for a walk. Did she say where to?"

"No. It was right after Aunt went to bed. She said she needed some air."

I pretended to read the paper, then when Hal went to bed, I slipped out of the house and made my way toward my midnight rendezvous. By the time I reached the tracks, Pluribus was beside me, carrying a lantern.

"Thought we'd need this, there bein' no moon."

"Thanks. Now you can get back home."

"Fat chance. See, I know why you circled that ad, Cousin Harry."

"Why?"

"'Cause you wanted Cousin Emmie to see the one above it! The one the killer put in."

"Killer?"

"Sure! It had to be him. He knows you saw the body, before he had a chance to hide it. Now he's willing to pay you to keep quiet. An' you wanted Cousin Emmie to see it, so she'd believe us about finding the body."

"You read a lot of dime novels?"

"What makes you say that?"

"Never mind. Yes, that's exactly right."

I checked my watch—almost midnight. We weren't more than a couple hundred yards from the ditch he called a canal.

"Look!" he whispered. "A lantern. An' there, on the

other side! Another one. Now they're both gone out!"

I'd only seen one dim light. Now he doused his.

"Why'd you do that?"

"Ta give us the element of surprise, a course. I'll tell you what, you head to where that first lantern was, and I'll sneak over to the other side. Just to make sure they don't get the jump on you."

"Get the jump on me?"

"Sure!"

He slunk off and I continued down the tracks. It was nearly pitch black, but in the shadows below, I thought I could see the reeds that edged the old canal bed. Then I didn't see much of anything. I'd been sapped on the back of the head.

7

I awoke to a vision of Emmie, illuminated in the soft glow of a lantern. She was once again hovering above me and dabbing at my skull with a wet handkerchief.

"You let him get away, Cousin Harry," Pluribus chided.

"How thoughtless of me. So, which of you hit me?"

"Don't be absurd, Harry. It had to be the murderer. I don't suppose you caught sight of him first?" Emmie asked.

"I couldn't see a thing."

"You must have anticipated the possibility that the killer would read your ad. Why else put it in the newspaper?"

"Until now, I doubted there was a killer. I'm still not convinced. I put the ad in purely for your benefit. Are you sure that little brat didn't sap me?"

"Why would I do a thing like that, Cousin Harry?"

He held up his lamp and the long shadows across his face gave him an even more malevolent look than normal.

"He was with me, on the other side of the canal."

"So there really were two lanterns?"

"Oh, yes. But the murderer had his set so dim I couldn't really make him out. I can't even say it was a him."

"Do you think he saw you?"

"He definitely saw my lantern, but it was also set low. I would think at most he could identify my sex."

"So I take it you did come out with the truant yesterday?"

"Of course. But when I didn't see any evidence of a corpse, I assumed you two were playing horse with me, so I swore Pluribus to secrecy. Then when I learned that you came back out here with him after he told you the body had been moved, I began having second thoughts. Given your propensity for indolence, it seemed unlikely you'd go to that much trouble simply to mislead me."

That's the strange thing about Emmie-land: on entering it, even the most contorted reasoning seems somehow to make sense. Which explains why I wasn't the least bit surprised by what followed.

"Now we should get on with the dragging," she announced.

"Ah. Because, naturally...?"

"Because, *naturally* the murderer must have weighted the body and sunk it in the canal."

"Just like those fictional fiends in Buffalo."

"Or the very real murderess in Lincolnshire."

"Well, why don't we leave the dragging to the police?" I suggested.

"The police? How long will that take? No, Harry, we must strike while the iron is hot."

She then bent down and picked up a length of rope. Something glittered at the end of it.

"Is that a grappling hook, Emmie?"

"Of course. What did you think we'd use, a hat pin?"

"You came out here at midnight equipped with a grappling hook?"

"I certainly couldn't count on you to. Let's get on with it, shall we?"

I don't know if you've ever tried dragging the bed of

a muddy-bottomed canal by the light of a couple kerosene lanterns, but it's exhausting work. It wasn't five minutes before I willingly turned the job over to the little annoyance standing beside me.

Twenty minutes on, we had a pair of old boots, one broken pot, and the skull of a very large dog. Then the hook caught on something meatier.

"Wait!" Emmie shouted. "We can't risk the hook tearing up the corpse. You'll both need to wade out there and pull it to the bank."

"How can we be sure it isn't the carcass of a horse?"

"That's a risk you'll have to take, Harry. This is the least you can do. So far you've left everything to Pluribus and me."

I let the runt take the lead. He took off his shoes and rolled up his trousers, then trudged through the mud to where the hook had stuck. He felt about in the dark water, then shouted, "Look!"

He held an arm up out of the water. He tried pulling it, but the corpse didn't budge.

"There'll be stones in his pockets," Emmie told him. She knew all about sinking bodies in canals.

Per her instructions, he emptied the pockets, but still couldn't move the body.

"Go on, Harry!" Emmie egged. "It must be stuck in the mud."

So I had to take off *my* shoes, roll up *my* trousers, and wade out into the mire. I didn't enjoy the ooze rising up between my toes, but the tin cans and odd bits of discarded metal I encountered worried me more. All in all, it seemed a wonderful opportunity to contract lockjaw.

The corpse was indeed stuck in the mud, and it was

all we could do to break the bond created by the suction. But once we had, the body became semi-buoyant and we could fairly easily work it to shore. It was just a matter of not minding the smell. Which was no small matter. We pulled it up the bank some and then went back to the water to wash off the mud.

"I guess now we can call in the police," I said, while putting on my socks and shoes.

"And tell them what?"

"Tell them the truth."

"Yes, the truth. I can just hear you now, Harry. 'Well, officer, Monday afternoon I came across a corpse. Then, rather than reporting it, I had my wife's young cousin tell *her* about it. Sometime later that day, the corpse disappeared. But instead of reporting *that,* I put a cryptic ad in the newspaper. Later, after being knocked unconscious by someone I presume to be the murderer, I dragged the old canal, with the help of said young cousin.' Yes, Harry, an excellent idea. By all means, go to the police."

"I don't think *I* should be saddled with the notion of dragging the canal."

"*Saddled with the notion?* If it wasn't for me, we'd still be missing a corpse!"

This is another telling aspect of Emmie-land. Within its precincts, even the most rational of men—i.e., me— appears to be acting like a lunatic. Before I met Emmie, I'd never even considered acting as a metronome while co-authoring a treatise on lascivious pirates, or collaring a substitute escaped convict while impersonating a Washington policeman. But in Emmie-land, even the commandeering of a canal boat full of contraband Chinese girls seems hardly worthy of mention.

"What do you suggest we do?" I asked.

"Put the corpse back where you found it in the first place. Then tell the police that we only now happened upon it."

"At two o'clock in the morning?"

"Well, we'll have to place it now, then later come out for an early morning stroll."

So we positioned the corpse as I remembered it, then made some effort at hiding all the tracks we'd made on the muddy bank.

It must have been past four when we got to bed and not yet seven when Emmie woke me by dripping ice water on my face, a favorite technique of hers.

"Come on, Harry. Breakfast is ready. And that corpse isn't getting any fresher."

Emmie led me stumbling out of the house a short while later and then stumbling along the railroad tracks. By now, we both knew that length of canal intimately and had no trouble finding it. The body was another matter. It had, for the second time, disappeared.

"I don't believe it," I said, and I didn't. In spite of her denials of having seen the body that first day, I suspected that Emmie had been behind the submerging of it. Even if there *was* a murderer and it was he who had sapped me. Emmie does these sorts of things just to keep the rest of the world off balance.

"Do you think the murderer sank it again?" she asked, too innocently I thought.

I gave her my best soul-piercing glare, confident it would impel her to truthfulness. But all for naught. She was looking down at her feet.

"No, apparently not. Look, Harry."

She pointed at a pair of trails in the mud, which

seemed to indicate the body had been dragged away from the canal. But they only reached as far as the soft ground extended, and the grass beyond was too short to tell.

"I wonder where they could have taken it?" she said.

"They?"

"Surely it would take two men to move it any distance."

"I guess. But maybe the murderer had a wagon."

"But the road's on the other side."

"He could have driven it up along the tracks."

"What if a train came while he was doing it?" she asked.

"They don't seem to run too often on this line. Maybe he knows the timetable."

"Now we have some real food for thought."

"A little too much. I was sated last night."

"There seem only two suspects," Emmie announced as we made our way toward home. "There's the hospital patient that both you and Pluribus encountered that first day...."

"And?"

"And Hal."

"Pluribus told you about recognizing the corpse then?"

"Yes. But where Hal might have had a motive, he doesn't seem to have had opportunity. And while the patient had opportunity, we know of no motive. Of course, if he's unbalanced..."

"I think we can scratch President McKinley off the list."

"President McKinley? He suffers from delusions?"

"Didn't seem to be suffering—enjoys them, from what I could tell. But the victim had already been dead for hours when I saw him roaming about. Rigor mortis had set in, so death must have occurred sometime during the previous night. Besides, he doesn't seem the type. He's more the benign lunatic. And too fastidious a dresser to be mucking about in the mud, weighing down corpses or dragging them up embankments."

"That's too bad. It just leaves Hal. But if he'd gone out that night, you would have heard him."

"Well, I've been thinking about that. I heard someone go out and return, twice. When you told me you followed Gloria out, I assumed it was the two of you. But if that were the case, I would have heard her go, then you go, then you both return together. When you and she left, I must have thought it was one person. Then you returned together."

"So someone else went out?"

"It would seem so. But I'm not sure of who, or when."

"Could it have been Hal?"

"The runt insists he didn't hear Hal go out."

"Of course, any number of others might have wanted this Bill McCrea dead."

"How'd you learn his name?" I asked.

"Same as you, I imagine. By asking Hal."

"Well, Mr. Grundy suspects he was chasing after his daughter, and he was none too happy about it. He thought I was McCrea when he slugged me. Come to think of it, Hal mentioned McCrea had been bothering Gloria, though it sounded like that was sometime in the past."

"Let's work on finding some suspects further from home. Maybe someone he worked with. The spot where the body was found isn't far from the hospital."

81

"I did encounter someone from the hospital that morning, just about where we are now."

"But that would also have been hours after the killing. Why was he here?"

"Looking for President McKinley."

"And you spoke with President McKinley as well?"

"Briefly. He told me I need have no anxiety, and gave me a full and unconditional pardon."

"Then he must have at least seen the body."

"Maybe. But when I mentioned the pardon to the hospital attendant, he told me the President is pretty free in handing them out."

"But you didn't tell the attendant about the corpse?"

"No, I was saving the corpse for you, Emmie."

"That was very thoughtful of you, Harry. But what *did* you tell the attendant?"

"Only that I'd seen the President wandering back toward the hospital, which was true."

"Well, we need to get in and talk to His Excellency. Find out if he did see anything. Maybe the murderer coming back to sink the body."

"Why don't I go? He already knows me. I think the attendant called him Anthorn. And maybe you could go by the depot and find out where McCrea was going Sunday evening, and when he returned. Be more efficient that way."

"Yes, good idea, Harry."

I have to confess, my real concern wasn't efficiency but that once the hospital staff met Emmie, there'd be no getting her out again.

While she continued on toward town, I started up what they call Hospital Hill. Just inside the entrance of the large and imposing building, a woman in white sat at a reception desk.

"I've come to visit my uncle, Mr. Anthorn, currently in the role of William McKinley."

"Oh. John Anthorn?"

"Yes, that's right. Uncle John."

"And your name?"

"Harry Reese. Uncle on my mother's side, you see."

"Hmm. Well, Mr. Anthorn should be reading to the laundresses."

"Reading to the laundresses?"

"Yes, all the patients are given occupations. Or, most."

A fellow also in white passed nearby and she called to him.

"Joel, could you take Mr. Reese here to the laundry? He's come to see his uncle, Mr. Anthorn."

"Sure. Come with me."

We went out into the sun and he led me toward a little brick building.

"What's reading to the laundresses entail?" I asked.

"Well, everyone has his little job. And since he's not much use on the farm, the doctors came up with this. He reads the women romance novels while they work. Supposed to be reading them sermons, and Bible verses, but they're not too fond of that and it was hard getting them to work. With the romances, none of them want to miss an installment."

We walked into the steamy room and there on a short dais stood Anthorn, covered in perspiration and looking as if he were delivering a stump speech at some Amazonian outpost. He read in a rich, sonorous voice, and with well-placed dramatic touches:

"The gallant Frenchman arose with alacrity from his velvet chair, and came forward with a bow such as only a Frenchman knows how to make."

Here the orator bowed as only a man imagining himself a dead Ohio Republican imagines a Frenchman to bow.

"'How can I serve mademoiselle?' he asked politely.

"'Monsieur has need of help in his lace factory—I seek employment,' was the response, in clear, sweet tones, while the tint deepened upon the maiden's cheek, as she pointed to the advertisement in the paper which she carried in her hand."

Anthorn pointed likewise, then contorted his face in the way of a blushing maiden. I can't say I would have mistaken it for that of a blushing maiden, but the laundresses seemed to buy it. When the sighs subsided, he continued:

"'Mon Dieu! I was sure she was an aristocrat come to give an order,' monsieur mentally ejaculated, while his suave bearing underwent a sudden change."

I don't know what the author had in mind here, but I feel certain it wasn't the look of utter horror evinced by President McKinley. Even the washerwomen looked taken aback.

"Excuse me, Mr. President," the attendant interrupted. "But your nephew here has come for an audience."

Anthorn stopped reading and looked at me—then a spark of recognition.

"Yes, of course."

A sopping wet blouse hit the attendant in the face.

"You're on your own," he said, ducking out of the room.

"Maybe we could speak a moment outside, Uncle John?" I suggested.

"Certainly. Ladies, I will return as soon as I've dealt with this petitioner."

We exited to a chorus of hissing.

"How is your mother?" he asked, as we strolled.

"Couldn't be better."

"And the campaign in the Philippines?"

"Ah. The rebellion has been quelled."

"Excellent. Now we can teach our brown brothers to govern themselves."

"I believe that's Cuba you're thinking of, Mr. President. In the Philippines we executed the democrats *because* they wanted to govern themselves."

"You're sure it isn't the other way around?"

"Reasonably sure."

"It's all so damn confusing. That's why I left the matter to Teddy."

"I wonder, sir, if you remember our meeting yesterday. Out by the old canal."

"That was you, was it?"

"Indeed it was, sir. Do you remember seeing another fellow? He was, if I remember correctly, lying face down in the reeds beside the water."

"Ah, yes. No doubt the work of an assassin."

"Assassin?"

"If it isn't the damn anarchists, it's disgruntled office-seekers. Far more dangerous than people think. Look what happened to Garfield in Washington."

"Or yourself in Buffalo."

"Buffalo? I've never set foot in Buffalo."

"Ah, that explains it. Tell me, did you recognize the victim of that assassin?"

"Certainly! The Secretary of the Treasury."

"Secretary of the Treasury? Then that would be Mr...."

"Mr. McCrea, of course."

"Yes, of course. And no doubt killed because...?"

"Yes, no doubt."

He raised his eyebrows briefly, but if he was signaling something, its meaning was opaque.

"Well, leaving that for the moment, did you see anyone else about?" I asked.

"Are you mad, sir? Of course I did. You!"

"I was thinking besides me."

"Not that I recall. Are you an anarchist?"

"Anarchist? No, certainly not. Though I do get a little annoyed by functionaries from time to time."

"Say, Mr. President..." We were interrupted by Joel, the attendant who'd escorted me out to the laundry. "You better get back to your sermonizing. The girls are starting to walk off the job."

"Duty calls, sir!" the old man proclaimed, then went back to his dais.

"Poor Uncle John," I said.

"Poor? I thought he had money."

"I was speaking of his condition."

"He don't seem to mind. Likes it here. Other day was the first time he'd wandered off."

"Monday morning?"

"Yeah. He told you?"

"Mentioned something. When was it exactly?"

"Wasn't here when we took roll in the morning, but he was back before lunch."

"So by noon?"

"Earlier, maybe half past eleven. Why?"

"Just curious. He mentioned a fellow named McCrea."

"McCrea? He wasn't here Monday. Got a few days leave to see his mother. She's ill, apparently. He left late Sunday."

"Uncle John confuses things."

"Oh, he's not so bad. You should see some of the cases we get. You ever try getting Napoleon to change his underwear?"

"Ah, no, not that I recall. Well, thanks for the help."

8

I went back to the house hoping to catch up on my sleep, but Emmie's mother stopped me at the door and sent me to procure victuals for the midday torment. At the grocer's, I ran into Margaret Cable.

"She's here, Harry. And it's just as I suspected."

"Elizabeth, you mean?"

"Yes. She has a plan. A diabolical plan."

Then she held a finger to her lips, as if she feared we might be overheard by one of Elizabeth's agents. It was completely irrational, but gives you some idea of the trepidation the woman provokes in her friends. And if they should consider ending the friendship, they need look no further than Emmie for an example of what would lie in store. Over the last several years, she'd been subjected to a long series of persecutions, ranging from petty embarrassments to outright slanders—and all at the hands of this most cunning of rivals. So it came as no surprise that the plan was a diabolical one.

In fact, Elizabeth's plans came in only two varieties, the purely venal and the diabolical. The diabolical usually included a strong element of venality, but in cases involving Emmie, it need not. Emmie, it's true, could give as good as she got, and with the latest round—her loosely fictional biography of Elizabeth—might even be said to have come out on top. But for ordinary humans, i.e., those constrained by the laws of science and logic, acquiescence to Elizabeth's will is the only safe course.

Our transactions completed, we left the shop. Margaret took my arm and led me down a side street. Then checked to be sure we hadn't been followed.

"You won't believe it, Harry. Elizabeth wants to stage a sham dinner!"

"A sham dinner?"

"Yes! She's even brought a false Henry James. He's staying at one of the hotels."

"So she plans to have Emmie attend this sham dinner...."

"Yes! And then give her manuscript to Elizabeth's Henry James."

"Sounds overly elaborate, doesn't it? Why not simply steal the manuscript?"

"Do you really need to ask that? Can you imagine Emmie's mortification when she discovers she's been fooled by an English confidence trickster pretending to be Henry James?"

"English confidence trickster?"

"Well, Elizabeth said he's an Englishman, and a friend of her father's. Have you ever met her father?"

"Only indirectly, via Emmie's book."

"Well, I have met him and Emmie's portrait does him no injustice. Years ago, he tried to interest my father in some South American oil fields, and when that got him nowhere, he suggested a game of poker. It was only when my father explained to him how card cheats are handled in his part of the country that he left us in peace."

"It's nice to know Elizabeth comes by her talents naturally. Where is this dinner to take place?"

"Our house. You see, Father is giving his dinner at the Plymouth Inn, where Mr. James is staying. And Elizabeth has already charmed Father into allowing us to entertain some friends the same evening. The whole thing's laughable. I mean, how could anyone who's read even one of Mr. James's books not see through it? All it will take is one question about some passage, some use of language, to reveal the man as an impostor."

"Well, you're probably safe on that score. Emmie hasn't made it through five pages, let alone an entire book. Had you really arranged a place for Emmie at the real dinner?"

"Yes, and I've said nothing to Father about her not going. I haven't decided which course I shall follow. It looks to be a choice between Scylla and Charybdis. I was hoping you might have some suggestion."

"Which one's the whirlpool?"

"Charybdis, I think. But forget the metaphor. I assume, as Emmie's husband, you want me to foil Elizabeth's plan. Which I have no qualms about doing—as long as it doesn't look as if I'm responsible."

"Yes, very wise. Well, to be honest, and this is strictly on the q.t., I have, for my own reasons, set about a plan to scuttle Emmie's literary ambitions."

"Are you saying you are in *favor* of going forward with this deception?"

"Not on the record. Suppose you keep all options open for now, and we see if we can't come up with a scheme which shields us both from their respective wraths."

"All right. I don't really see how that's possible, but we do have some time to think about it. Good-bye, Harry."

"Good-bye, Margaret."

She went off toward home and I made my way to the butcher's. When I emerged, I saw Emmie waving at me from across the street. As I got nearer, I assayed her mood as less than cheery.

"Well, Harry, I've just wasted three hours confirming the obvious."

"What's that?"

"The evening we saw Bill McCrea board the train, he had purchased a ticket to South Deerfield, *and* another for the return. The ticket-seller remembered McCrea because of the fight he had with Hal."

"It was obvious he was going to South Deerfield?"

"No, don't be such a gink. Let me finish my account without any of your simple-minded interruptions. McCrea took the train to South Deerfield, arriving at around seven. He went immediately to a hotel and checked in, making a point of telling the clerk he had to leave the next morning. He went up to his room and wasn't seen again by the clerk. But he must have left the hotel by the rear stairs and gone back to the depot, where he boarded the southbound 7:25. So as not to be seen, he boarded from the side facing away from the platform, but a porter helping an elderly woman on the train heard the conductor admonishing McCrea for not boarding properly. That train arrived in Northampton at about a quarter to eight. I found no one who remembered seeing him disembark, but no doubt that's because he again used the side facing away from the platform."

"So McCrea merely wanted it to *appear* that he was going out of town."

"Yes, of course! The fight with Hal was just to make his exit more worthy of note. From that, we may deduce he had some ulterior motive. And, ironically, that is confirmed by his boarding of the train in South Deerfield, where he would probably not have been remembered if he hadn't taken pains to go unobserved. Clearly, this was a bungled attempt at establishing an alibi."

"There's only one problem with that."

"What?"

"Well, if he were the killer, he'd naturally want an alibi. But he was the victim."

"Oh, but that's just my point. What difference does it make? Surely, you concede that McCrea must have been up to no good, or why else would he need an alibi?"

"A not unreasonable conclusion. So?"

"Well, then who really cares? Do you realize how much effort we've put into solving murders of people so unscrupulous, so vile, that the world is better off without them? All that nonsense up in Maine about rhyming slang and promiscuous eels, for what?"

"To bring to justice the murderer of a young woman?"

"She was an unprincipled blackmailer! A human bloodsucker!"

"True. But she had a brother who was fond of her."

"Brother... pfft."

"I never thought I'd hear you talk this way, Emmie. Why, when we met in Buffalo..."

"Buffalo! Yes, let's remember Buffalo. Where we fingered the father of my cousin Charlie's poor fiancée."

She did have a point there. Things had never been quite right between ourselves and Charlie's now-wife. And it probably wasn't going too far to think it had something to do with our having her father sent to the state penitentiary for a life term. But I thought it only fair to present the other side.

"He *had* killed Charlie's father, Emmie."

"Oh, that bigamous beast! Good riddance to him! No, Harry. I won't be dragged into solving another un-senseless murder."

"Unsenseless murder?"

"Well, you admit McCrea was up to no good. Perhaps murder himself. So now the world has one less killer, thief, blackmailer, etc. Who really cares? I've had enough, Harry. I simply won't charge off hither and yon, gathering little crumbs of evidence, being misled by doddering witnesses, and wasting untold precious moments of time. I live now only for my art. Murder be damned!"

"That's a dangerous attitude to take in this genre, Emmie. I hope you'll reconsider."

"I will not reconsider. You may do as you like, Harry. But leave me out of it!"

We'd been conducting this little tête-à-tête on Northampton's principal thoroughfare, and just at midday, so it isn't terribly surprising we'd attracted a small audience. They seemed to have interpreted our colloquy as some sort of impromptu performance. At Emmie's concluding line, they applauded. She pretended to be nonplussed, but I could tell she was flattered.

I must say, her change of attitude alarmed me. Evidently, I'd underestimated how difficult it is to derail literary delusions once they've taken root.

All three cousins returned home for lunch that day. We had sausage. I never would have guessed you could ruin sausage simply by boiling, but apparently you can.

I've told you some about the early life of Emmie's cousins, but have yet to really capture the details. I will take as an example table manners. Pluribus was, of course, a lost cause. But let us look at his siblings. Imagine two children, born on a hill named for an insect, whose mother abandons them at seven, and whose father, by all accounts, is himself no slave to propriety.

Whether they availed themselves of utensils at the farm, I can't say. But even after three years with Emmie's mother, they still harbored suspicions toward forks.

In fairness, they were impressively deft with a knife. Gloria could detach a bit of sausage and toss it into her mouth with a precision which would stir envy among the habitués of a waterfront saloon. Nonetheless, I couldn't help but wonder if such a talent might not narrow her options matrimonially. True, she had no shortage of suitors—but how many of them had seen her dismember a bratwurst?

Since I had more or less settled on this so-called Mortimer Vincent as her future mate, I needed to find some way of convincing him that Gloria would pass muster with his employer. And to achieve that goal, some sort of training would be essential.

It's odd, isn't it, how sometimes what seems like an unsolvable conundrum can suddenly seem solvable? Odder still is how one solution can sometimes resolve two conundrums at once. This was one of those happy occasions.

That afternoon, I again visited the home of the Cables. Lottie answered my knock and informed me that I would find Margaret in the garden entertaining her guest.

"Hello, Harry." Elizabeth greeted me with a warm embrace, in itself highly suspicious. "I understand you're going to help us play our little joke on Emmie."

"I never said that exactly."

"No. Nor did I tell you he had, Elizabeth," Margaret clarified.

"Details. Tell me, Harry, can you think of a surer way to destroy her literary ambitions?"

"I'd hoped murder would do the trick."

"Murder?" Margaret seemed incredulous. "It sounds rather harsh, doesn't it?"

"No, not murder *her...*"

"Too bad," Elizabeth chimed in. "I think what Harry is referring to is Emmie's avocation as a sleuth. A pursuit far more fitting for her talents than is her writing. Yes, Harry, by all means let's get Emmie back to her ratiocinations. And what better means than bringing about her utter humiliation before the great Henry James?"

"Utter humiliation?" Margaret asked.

"Just a turn of phrase," Elizabeth told her. "We, her friends, are simply endeavoring to bring her to her senses. Or as near to that as Emmie is capable."

"I think she may have trouble viewing it quite so benignly," Margaret pointed out.

"Perhaps. But surely it's me with whom she'll be most upset. And I, frankly, relish the thought."

"But I'm the one who shares a bed with her."

"Yes, however do you bear it?"

"Well enough. How goes your marriage, Elizabeth? Last time I saw Tibbitts he was sleeping on our couch."

"Touché. We have our rapprochements. Now and again. But I don't think you're in a position to object, Harry. You see, I know all about your outing to the Jamaica racecourse."

"So it *was* you who returned my watch?"

"Oh, yes. I found it in the possession of my protégée, Mélisande."

"Protégée?"

"Perhaps not a precise portrayal, but near enough. She gave me a complete account of the excursion."

"Did she? I don't suppose you also convinced her to

return the three hundred dollars she and her friend took from the fellow accompanying me? Snide Sam's his name."

"Snide Sam?" Margaret asked.

"Money wasn't mentioned," Elizabeth said. "But she had quite a lot to say about you. It sounds as if you became very friendly in the course of the afternoon. *Very* friendly."

"Friendly, but nothing more."

"Nothing?"

"Well… a warm friendship. But you can't use that to blackmail me. Emmie seems to already have a good idea of what happened."

"How?"

"Can't say. She works in mysterious ways."

"Yes, she certainly does."

"But we might still be able to make a deal," I said.

"What sort of deal?"

"I'm afraid it will necessitate Margaret's collusion as well."

"Oh, no. Now, really…"

"Margaret is only too glad to help," Elizabeth explained. "Aren't you, dear?"

"What is it you have in mind, Harry?"

"Well, your father invited another author to the dinner with Henry James."

"You mean Emmie?"

"In addition to Emmie. Mortimer Vincent, the travel writer."

"Oh, yes. Of course. What does he have to do with any of this?"

"Nothing, directly. But you may be familiar with Hal's sister, Emmie's cousin Gloria."

"I know her by sight. What about her?"

"Well, she's become something of a problem...."

"What sort of problem?" Margaret asked.

"Men, no doubt," Elizabeth told her.

"Precisely. And the sooner we marry her off, the better. Right now, she has her sights set on Mortimer Vincent."

"What? A distinguished author?" Margaret was again incredulous. She was quite convincing at it.

"Well, not so distinguished as you might think. But that's neither here nor there."

"I don't mean to sound cruel. But don't you think she might be a bit too... rustic?"

"That's just it. He's actually somewhat keen on her. But he has some misgivings about her fitting in."

"I still don't see what you're driving at."

"You said earlier your father is expecting Emmie at the dinner."

"Yes, but..."

"Harry," Elizabeth asked, "are you proposing to send Emmie's cousin to the real dinner, posing as her, so she can impress this Mortimer Vincent with her comportment?"

"That's it in a nutshell."

"Don't you see the obvious flaw in that?"

"Which obvious flaw?"

"Won't he wonder why she is there under a false name?"

"Oh, we can be fairly certain there won't be any trouble on that score. But there is another obvious problem."

"Which is?"

"Gloria's comportment isn't likely to impress."

"How primitive is she?"

"Well, let me put it this way: she was raised on a hill named for an insect by a 'widowed' father who spent his days watching his farm go fallow and making sure his neighbors' wives didn't. At least, that's the rumor as his family relates it. Keep in mind, I'm using the word widowed in its euphemistic sense, and the word raised in the broadest sense possible. She has an acquaintance with basic tableware, but anything beyond that might prove a trial for her."

"So what exactly are you proposing?" Elizabeth asked.

"That you take it upon yourself to prepare her for this dinner. Dress, manners, the whole kit and caboodle."

"In just four days? It sounds like something of a challenge.... But even if I were successful, what assurance do you have this Mortimer Vincent will take her to his bed?"

"That, I think, we can safely leave to Gloria."

"All right, Harry. I was facing several days of boredom, and this might offer an amusing diversion. No offense intended, Margaret."

"No, I'm sure not, Elizabeth, *dear*."

"But won't someone at this other dinner be acquainted with Emmie? Margaret's father?"

"Oh, I don't think he'd remember Emmie by sight," her friend told her. "It's been years. And he meets so many people."

"All right, then. I'll do it, for the sport if nothing else."

"There is one other thing," I told her. "I'm afraid I'm currently in the poorhouse."

"So I'm to dress the child?"

"She has some money. But she's pretty tight-fisted."

"Well, you're in luck. As it happens, I won a sizable wager while waiting to change trains."

"What sort of wager?" Margaret asked.

"I don't really think you want to know, dear."

"I certainly do now. Don't you want to know, Harry?"

"I admit to being curious."

"Very well, since you insist. I saw a well-dressed gentleman spit into a cuspidor from five feet away. He looked very pleased with himself and I surmised he was hoping I would respond with some expression of repulsion. Instead, I told him I could achieve the same results from twice the distance. He bet me one hundred dollars I couldn't."

In Emmie's book, Elizabeth's fictionalized self exhibits that talent, but I had assumed it merely another libel abetting her vilification. It was exceedingly difficult to imagine Elizabeth doing anything of the sort. She's a tall, statuesque blonde, highly intelligent, cultured, learned, always impeccably dressed, and nothing short of imperious in manner. Seeing her hit a spittoon from ten feet away would be worth a hundred dollars.

"That is thoroughly disgusting, Elizabeth," Margaret told her. "I suppose you should be congratulated for putting the childish ass in his place. But that might not be the sort of lesson Gloria is in need of."

"No, I've seen her spit almost as far," I confided.

"Might I suggest she refrain from any displays of her marksmanship until after the wedding?"

"Fear not, Margaret. When I finish with her, she'll have every man in the room eating out of her hand. And you, Harry, in turn, will help us pull the wool over little Emmie's eyes."

"I didn't say I'd help. Simply promise not to interfere."

"But we need you, Harry," Margaret said. "To help with dinner. And, frankly, I'd like someone else there to share Emmie's wrath should she catch on. I still don't see how we can possibly pull it off. Do you really think your friend can play a creditable Henry James, Elizabeth?"

"Well enough to fool Emmie."

"But who will play my father? Emmie has seen him often in the past."

"Ah, I might have an entrant for the part of your father."

"Who?"

"Someone who bears a stunning resemblance. As a matter of fact, I mistook your father for him when we first met."

"I know no one in town like that. Is this someone from New York?"

"Yes. Yes, that's right. A fellow in New York. I'll wire him. He owes me a favor."

"The most important goal of the scheme has been left unmentioned."

"I thought Emmie's utter humiliation was the goal?" Margaret queried.

"Yes, but to achieve that, she must hand Mr. James her manuscript."

"Well, I don't think that should be difficult," I said. "Provided she's convinced he's the real McCoy."

"Let me worry about that. Tell Gloria to meet me here at six this evening."

9

Given the formidable task I'd assigned the girl, I thought it only fair I should let Gloria in on the plan. After making inquiries at the desk, I found her changing sheets on the third floor of the hotel.

"I have some good news."

"What sort of good news?"

"It concerns your snaring of Mortimer Vincent."

"Oh!" She closed the door of the room. "Bunch of busybodies working here. Go on, Cousin Harry."

"Suppose you were invited to a formal dinner, one which he's also attending, full of prestigious people? Then he could see for himself that you know how to conduct yourself."

"Well, that might be OK. But do I know how to conduct myself?"

"Frankly, no. But that problem's solved."

"Solved how?"

"I've arranged for a mentor, a Mrs. Tibbitts. You're to meet her at the Cables' house this evening at six. You'll be dining with her."

"I thought maybe Cousin Emmie..."

"Ah. There's the rub. Cousin Emmie is not to know anything about your attending this dinner, or about your meeting with Mrs. Tibbitts."

"Why not?"

"Why not? Well, it's rather complicated. But the crux of it is that you will be impersonating Emmie at this dinner of the literati Sunday evening."

"Literati?"

"Bookish types. Like our friend Mr. Vincent."

"Oh, I see.... But... but Mr. Vincent knows I'm not Cousin Emmie."

"Well, him you need merely impress with your impeccable manners, and your gracious, yet witty, conversation."

"At the same time?"

"Same time?"

"Do I have to be gracious and witty at the same time?"

"No, there's some leeway there. I'd lean more toward the gracious."

"So say, 'Please pass the peas'?"

"Yes, that sort of thing."

"And then tell a joke if things get quiet. I heard a good one from the man in 217. You'll love it, Cousin Harry. You see, this farmer had a daughter...."

"Maybe better stick to gracious your first time in the ring. And I might leave out farms altogether. Remember, six o'clock, at the Cables'. And not a word to Emmie, or anyone else, for that matter."

"Not even Mr. Vincent?"

"No—better leave it to me to tell him."

"All right, Cousin Harry. It sounds like fun!"

I had my doubts about the fun. But if anyone could prepare the girl for the trial ahead, it was Elizabeth. She was as artful as the day is long, and knew all there was to know about leading men by the nose—a talent she'd perfected while working as a professional co-respondent in a divorce ring. I only hoped, for her future husband's sake, Gloria didn't acquire any of her mentor's ruthlessness. Elizabeth had married a New York police detective of the hard-boiled school, but even he had trouble coming to terms with her. Their marriage always seemed about as stable as the last Balkan armistice.

It was now time to arrange for my reproduction George Washington Cable. I wasn't entirely sure what the procedure was for borrowing inmates, but given I had no trouble convincing both him and the staff I was his nephew, there seemed a reasonable chance of success—provided he wouldn't mind taking a few hours off from piloting the ship of state to try his hand at authorship.

I went again to the reception desk and then was sent to the office of a doctor, who explained I could check out my supposed uncle via a procedure much like that used at libraries.

"Generally speaking, we feel this sort of thing is very healthy for the patient. Being around familiar people, sharing memories. Who knows when he might suddenly recapture his identity?"

"Is there really much chance of that?"

"Honestly, no. Still, as I told your sister..."

"Sister?"

"His niece. I just assumed she was your sister. Took him out several times when he first arrived."

"Oh, yes. Of course. Cousin, actually. Cousin Mary. She'll be there, of course."

"I thought her name was something else... Lottie...."

"Ah, Cousin Lottie. She'll be there as well."

"Sounds like just the sort of affair that would do the old boy some good. The important thing is not to excite him. You might remind him of events in the past, old friends, etc. But never deny his authenticity as President McKinley. If he is to be cured of his psychosis, it must come from within himself."

"I see. Tell me, has he ever imagined himself someone else? Say, a well-known writer?"

"He had a brief spell as Edgar Allan Poe. Brought on by a fever, I suspect. But I think he found the poetry too depressing. Your uncle is, if nothing else, eternally optimistic. President McKinley is much more in keeping with that spirit."

"Or was. Until he was shot."

"For God's sake, whatever you do, don't mention the shooting. Who knows what effect that would have on the man."

"Consider it forgotten. Never cared for Roosevelt myself."

"I see. Well, I suppose now you'd like to tell your uncle about your arrangements? It's always best to acquaint a patient with any sort of change as far in advance as possible."

He called to an attendant walking by his open door.

"Pat! Come here, would you?"

It was the fellow I'd met that first morning. The one who'd been looking for Anthorn.

"This is Mr. Reese. He's here to see his uncle, our Mr. Anthorn." The doctor turned back to me. "Mr. Moran will show you the way."

Moran smiled at me vaguely. He didn't seem to recognize me, which came as a relief. At our first meeting, I had betrayed an ignorance of Anthorn and I couldn't imagine how I might reconcile that with being the fellow's nephew.

But if there's one thing I've learned, it's that getting away with impersonations is far easier than you would suspect. People, even people possessing a normal skepticism, have a predilection for believing what you tell them. Just look at how easily his valet can play the part of Mortimer Vincent. A man calls at a hotel and says he's Mortimer Vincent—who's going to doubt him? Provided, of course, they never met the original. This attendant probably remembered meeting someone that morning. And might, if he thought about it, see a resemblance. But there's little reason for him to think I'm other than who I presented myself as. I'm wearing a different suit, we met in different circumstances, and he must see a great many people—patients, staff, visitors, etc.

I probably wouldn't have recognized him either, but he was an odd-looking character, with a small, round head sitting atop a short, thick body. And, since I had just encountered a corpse, the events of that morning were more firmly etched on my mind than had I been out for a morning stroll. It was then, as I went over it in my head, that I remembered something had struck me as not quite right that morning. But what exactly, I couldn't recall.

We found Uncle John outside, reciting to the laundresses as they hung the wash to dry.

"'Monsieur,' Tina answered, more sadly than she had yet spoken, 'you ask of me an impossibility. I cannot marry you.'

"'Ah, mademoiselle!' he exclaimed, 'you know not what you reject—you shall have the finest and loveliest laces; horses, carriages, and jewels; there is nothing that la Belle shall lack, if she will give herself to me.'

"Tina's lips curled."

...And the President's did likewise.

"'I have said no, monsieur. I should scorn to sell myself to any man for gold or the luxuries of which you speak.'

"Her tones were intensely sarcastic, and as she

105

concluded, she drew herself away from the supplicant at her feet with the air of a queen."

The tones of Moran were equally sarcastic when he proposed that the heroine was simply negotiating for a higher price.

"Listen, *monsewer*," he suggested, "give the chippie a couple furs and a warm place to do her business. She'll come around."

He received the customary wet shirt to the face, and I took advantage of the interruption to address dear Uncle John. Luckily, he did remember me.

"Ah! My boy!"

"I've wonderful news, Uncle John," I told him, as we went off along a path. "We'll be attending a dinner Sunday evening."

"What sort of dinner?"

"Well, sort of a masquerade."

"Hmm. Never cared much for masquerades."

"Yes, I know. But you won't need to wear a costume. And it means a great deal to Lottie."

He perked up at the name, and it occurred to me I might be able to convince him that the Cables' cook Lottie and his Lottie were one and the same.

"Lottie hoped you could play the part of George Washington Cable."

"The writer?"

"Yes."

"A southerner?"

I'd forgotten that Cable and McKinley had fought on opposite sides in the war. The intricacies involved in organizing a literary dinner party can't be overestimated.

"Isn't it time to let bygones be bygones? Besides, I believe he's repented on the issue of emancipation."

"Has he?"

"Oh, yes. And it is, after all, for Lottie."

"Well, for Lottie. Yes. All right, I'll do it."

He shook my hand and I took him back where he could resume his reading. Then I proceeded toward the gate.

"So long!" It was Moran, calling from across the lawn. I waved back. It seemed an odd demonstration on his part and that got me to wondering if he did remember me after all. Then I recalled what had struck me as odd that first morning. When I originally encountered him, he asked if I'd seen a fellow who might be disoriented. When I saw him again a little later and told him I thought I might have seen the fellow he was looking for, he seemed a little surprised by my description of Anthorn.

"Back to see your uncle?"

It was the other attendant, the one who had taken me to the laundry the day before.

"Yes, arranging a little family get-together, with the help of one of your colleagues, Pat Moran."

"He's the one who brought your uncle back Monday morning."

"Must have been out all night looking for him."

"Pat? No, he was out of town. Back in Boston. Didn't get in until early that morning. And like I told you, we didn't even notice your uncle was gone until morning roll. Just after seven. But don't worry. It won't happen again. We've been locking the room now."

"Good. Wouldn't want to lose the old fellow."

"No, I'm sure you wouldn't."

He gave me a wink. Apparently he *did* suspect my claim of kinship.

When I arrived home for dinner, I explained to Emmie that Gloria would be going to a friend's house immediately after work and that I would be picking her up later.

"Are you acting as her social secretary?" she asked.

"Merely doing as you instructed, keeping tabs on her. I ran into her this afternoon and she told me about it."

"Ran into her at the hotel?"

"I happened to be passing by. On my way to the hospital."

"The asylum?"

"Yes. Checking up on the movements of my various suspects."

"What suspects? The patient who thinks he's McKinley?"

"Uncle John. Yes, for one."

"Uncle John?"

"I needed a ruse to get in to speak with him. Then there's the attendant I saw that first day, Pat Moran. He wasn't half a mile from the corpse."

"But wasn't he out looking for Anthorn?"

"So I assumed. But I remember now in my first conversation with him, a few minutes before I'd met either the corpse or Anthorn, he told me he was looking for a man. He didn't use the word patient, just suggested the man would be disoriented. When I saw him again just half an hour later, and told him I thought I might have seen the fellow he was looking for, he seemed surprised to recognize my description as that of Anthorn."

"But the timing—McCrea was killed the night before."

"Yes. That's a problem. Supposedly Moran had been

out of town and didn't arrive back until morning. Still, an intriguing clue, don't you think?"

"No, not really. At least, not intriguing enough to abandon my other plans."

"Your dinner with Henry James?"

"That's right. Margaret mentioned it?"

"Yes. You're planning to present him with your manuscript?"

"To solicit his opinion."

"And then his help in getting it published?"

"That's my hope. And what's wrong with that?"

"Nothing. But why couldn't you have admitted that was your reason for coming up here in the first place?"

"In case it fell through. I didn't want to give you another opportunity to gloat."

"Me? Gloat?"

"Admit it, Harry. You take some perverse satisfaction in my literary frustrations."

"That's not true, Emmie. It's just your literary pretensions I'd like to squelch. I mean, all this time spent toadying up to writers whose work you find sleep-inducing."

"In life, Harry, one must frequently be accommodating of others. If, that is, one has ambitions. Something you would know nothing about."

Her barb stung me. I had every intention of enumerating my countless ambitions right then and there, and would have done so gladly if she hadn't left the room while I was still assembling the list.

At eight, I walked over to the Cables' to see when Elizabeth would be finishing her tutorial. Margaret greeted me at the door and we went out to the garden, where Elizabeth had Gloria literally going through her paces.

"Shoulders a little higher. Not too fast.... Go away, Harry. We need another hour at least."

"Shall we go for a walk?" Margaret suggested.

We strolled down to the Mill River, which lies not far behind her house. From there, it flows past the college, ultimately emptying into the Connecticut.

"I don't mind telling you, Harry, I'm having apprehensions about this phony dinner. The whole idea seems ludicrous."

"Well, pretty much anything involving Emmie has an inalterable attraction toward the ludicrous. What gravity is to the rest of us, the ludicrous is to Emmie."

"I don't know if that even makes sense. But even if it does, it isn't Emmie who's responsible. It's us! I mean, having a confidence man play Henry James? And then getting some actor to play my father...."

"Oh, that's all arranged. He's willing and able."

"You've arranged it so soon? Well, even still, I've told Emmie there will be at least one other author at the dinner—a travel writer—and a professor from the college and his wife!"

"Hmm. Well, we'll just need to round out the cast. Nothing insurmountable."

By then we'd come to where the river widens into a large pond, just below the college. The man known as Mortimer Vincent approached us from the opposite direction, smoking a cigar. I introduced the two of them and we made small talk.

"Lovely spot, isn't it?" Margaret asked.

"Yes, lovely," he agreed.

"It's called Paradise Pond."

"Not really?"

"Oh, yes. Really."

"Did Mr. Reese put you up to this?"

"Put me up to what?"

I signaled the valet with a slight shake of the head.

"Oh. Pardon me." He wisely changed the subject by asking Margaret if she would be attending the dinner with James.

"No, my older sister Lucy will be hosting with Father." Then her tone turned mildly facetious. "But, of course, Harry's wife, Emily Reese, will be there."

"Yes. So he's informed me. I look forward to meeting her."

"You haven't told him, have you, Harry?" she asked me.

"Not just yet."

"Told me what?"

"Well, there's been a slight emendation of those plans. You see, my wife won't actually be attending the dinner with James."

"Oh, I'm sorry to hear that. But Miss Cable just said..."

"When I say she won't be attending, I mean *she* won't be attending. She has another affair the same evening. But Gloria will be going in her stead."

"Gloria?" he asked.

"Yes, she enjoys nothing so much as a swish soirée."

"Gloria the chambermaid?"

"One and the same. She's a different girl entirely when she togs up and tucks in the bib with the smart set."

"Are you teasing me?"

"Certainly not. You'll see for yourself, of course."

"I can't wait."

"There is just one thing."

"What's that?"

"Gloria will be appearing as my wife."

"You mean, under a false name?"

"Yes. It's scandalous, isn't it, Mr. Vincent?" Margaret added unhelpfully.

"Oh, I wouldn't call it that. Given the circumstances, quite understandable. Mrs. Reese has another engagement, so someone ought to get a meal out of it."

I could see by her expression that Margaret found his conclusion difficult to credit. But we parted with him cordially, and soon afterwards I was escorting Gloria back to the house.

"How did the lessons go?" I asked.

"OK, I think. How's my walk look to you?"

"Not so very different."

"Really? Because it's just hell keeping it all straight. 'Shoulders higher! But casual! Sway the hips, but ever so slightly. Step lightly, as if you're walking on thin ice.' That's exactly how I felt the whole time."

"Sounds trying."

"It was. But she did take me to the Plymouth for a private dinner. Boy, did I get some looks from the waiters. You know, she made me drink from four different glasses. Why is it considered polite to use so many glasses, Cousin Harry?"

"Well, it keeps the dishwashers employed."

"What was silly was she'd only give me these thimblefuls of wine. She seemed sure I'd get drunk and make a fool of myself. But there is one thing I don't understand. Why is she doing this for me? Are you paying her?"

"Not exactly. But we have an arrangement."

"She's very beautiful, Cousin Harry. I hope you

aren't, you know, behind Cousin Emmie's back."

"Oh, not that sort of arrangement. There's never been any you-knowing between Elizabeth and me."

"Good. I mean, I did think it *unlikely*."

10

As if I didn't have enough on my plate, the next morning at breakfast my nemesis lobbed a bombshell among the soggy eggs and carbonized bacon.

"Is it true you go to Coney Island every day in the summer, Cousin Harry?"

"Only when the horses aren't running," Emmie told him. "Now hurry up, or you'll be late for school. And remember what I told you, Pluribus."

"OK. Sorry."

Until that moment, I'd been lost in thought. Trying to keep track of who'd be masquerading as whom, while simultaneously managing Gloria's love life and, when time allowed, solving McCrea's murder, had gotten to be something of a chore. But the little reprobate's query cut through my reverie like a hot knife through butter.

Emmie as much as told me she'd struck a bargain with him. Now I had a very good idea of the terms: if he went willingly to school, she'd let him come stay with us in New York. And, apparently, she threw in my services as tour guide. You wouldn't think it to look at her, but Emmie has a vicious streak. It lies hidden most of the time, and when not having seen it for a month or so, I can fool myself into thinking it's gone into a semi-permanent torpor. But then it shows its ugly head, and sinks its fangs deep into my softest flesh. I don't know if vicious streaks come fanged as a rule, but that's how I felt.

Making some excuse, I followed my affliction out of

the house. Half a block on, I whistled to him. He stopped and waited for me to catch up.

"Walking me to school, Cousin Harry?"

"Don't Cousin Harry me, you little skeezicks. What sort of deal did you make with Emmie?"

"She said if I told, it would nix it."

"Well, consider it nixed."

"That ain't fair! I'm holdin' up my end. She promised you'd take me to Coney Island."

"Listen, kid, if I take you to Coney Island, it will only be to drown you off the pier."

"You're a cruel man, Cousin Harry."

The little brat actually started crying. I'd no doubt it was an act, but I sensed that I may have overplayed my hand by threatening to drown him. Neither Emmie nor her mother were likely to see the justice in it.

"Look, you don't want to come to the city in the summer. There's no air. Just the dust of sunbaked manure, and the smell of four million perspiring bodies. Hell, everyone there is looking for a way to get out! And a trip to Coney Island ain't no day at the beach. It's just a slight improvement over a stifling tenement. Before you even get off the packed train, three fellows have tried to pick your pocket. After that it's just one small-time graft after another."

"What about the amusement parks?"

"A pretty sad idea of amusement. The lines stretch six blocks. And the whole time you're penned up with a few hundred malodorous bodies that've just spent the night in a stifling tenement."

"What about the freaks?"

"All fakes."

"Well, there's still the ocean."

"Sure. But there's also some lug who entertains his friends by dunking strangers. And if you want to lie down on the sand, be prepared to have your head stomped on by a team of morons playing some primitive form of football. Trust me, the local swimming hole has it all over Coney Island. No, if you're smart, you'll stay right here for the summer."

"Maybe. But I still want to see it."

"Suit yourself. Just don't say I didn't warn you."

We continued along, me trying desperately to think of a strategy. Then it came to me. All I needed to do was lead him into breaking his deal with Emmie.

"It's too bad, really."

"What's too bad?"

"Well, you becoming a little Goody Two-shoes. Spending all day in school. Looks to be a beautiful day, too. I was hoping you'd help me out, solving that murder."

"Cousin Emmie told me to forget all about it. She said the dead man probably deserved what he got anyway. And besides, how can you solve a murder without a body?"

"Shows what little you know. That missing body is our best clue."

"How do you mean?"

"Well, it was moved twice. So not only do we know when the murder occurred, we know the murderer returned the next day, and then came back again Tuesday night. Now it's just a matter of going through the list of suspects and figuring out who had the opportunity to do all three."

"What list of suspects?"

"That's privileged information, I'm afraid. I couldn't

share it with anyone not involved in the investigation."

"You have Hal on your list?"

"He went out that first night, didn't he?"

"Yeah."

"Why didn't you say so before?"

He shrugged.

"Did he tell you where he went?"

"When I asked him, he said he just wanted to get some air. But I think he meant he went out to heave. He ain't used to drinkin'."

"How long was he gone?"

He shrugged again. "I fell asleep before he got back. But Hal wouldn't kill no one."

"Well, then wouldn't it be best if someone clears his name?"

"But no one suspects him. 'Cept you."

"If that body shows up, and you can bet it will, Hal will be top of the list. Must have been two dozen people there at the depot when he lit into the fellow."

"That don't mean he'd kill him."

"I know that, and you know that, but do the cops know it? The only sure way of saving Hal is to find the real killer."

He wavered. Frankly, I was shocked to see he had a selfless bone in his body—no doubt an awfully small bone. He continued on until we were within sight of the school.

"Sure is a beautiful day. Bet it gets awfully stuffy in there."

"Do I get to come back to New York with you?"

"Well... sure, all right." It was nonsense, of course. But I'd managed to mask my insincerity—at least well enough to fool a twelve-year-old who grew up on a hill named for an insect.

"OK, then. Come on!"

He shot up a side street and then stopped and waited for me to catch up. From there we followed a path down a hill, and about a quarter-mile on we came to a copse beside the Mill River, downstream a mile or so from the college. This is where he had his hideout. There was a crude bench fashioned from planks and stumps, and a fire pit lined with rocks. Up above, in a big oak tree, he'd built a crow's nest. He climbed up the tree and then dropped down again with a corncob pipe in his mouth. Next, he pulled a little pouch of tobacco out of a knothole in another tree, then packed the pipe and lit it.

"What's with the Huck Finn routine?" I asked.

"What's wrong with it?"

"Kind of dated, isn't it?"

He shrugged. "So what do we do now?"

"Well, let's see. I suppose you better leave the checking up on suspects to me, otherwise the truant officer is liable to catch sight of you and lock you up in the hoosegow."

"Then what do I do?"

"Why, track down that body, of course. Five will get you ten they took it away along the railway tracks in a wagon, or some sort of cart. Maybe you can see which direction it went, and where it left the tracks."

"What do I look like, the last of the Mohicans?"

"You want to help Hal, don't you?"

"All right. I'll see what I can find. When do we meet back here?"

"Just go home for lunch like any other day."

He took off and I went back up the path and on toward town. I was feeling pretty sure of myself. The next day I'd inform Emmie he'd skipped school and then have the teacher confirm it.

At the depot, I quizzed the porters about the arrivals on the early trains Monday morning. Memories were vague, but luckily Moran's ovate shape was distinctive enough that one fellow recalled seeing him get off a train. So unless he had played an elaborate game like McCrea had, he couldn't be counted as a suspect.

Next I stopped by Grundy's shop. I surprised him as he sat marking a small promptbook with a pencil. He was threading a pipe, he told me.

"I'm speaking metaphortical."

"Ah."

"Redactin' the Bard can only be done with a similarial steady hand."

"Oh, I see."

"Just like a woman."

"Redacting?"

"Threadin'. If you've come to see your cousin, I'm afraid I'll have to disaplease you, Mr. Reese. He's over at Mr. O'Donnell's, subjugating a flange on a turnout."

"Sorry to hear that. You seem to do a lot of work at Mr. O'Donnell's."

"Oh, it's an unjust world, Mr. Reese. Mr. O'Donnell is a highly respected, and very successful, lawyer, but in spite of that, the poor fellow is plagued by bad pipes. It's on account of him building his house on an escapulation, you see. It has a tendency to totter."

"Ah, yes. Always a mistake. Would it be all right if I stopped by there with a message for Hal?"

"Don't see why not. Here, you can take him this persuadin' wrench—that way it won't look like he's malanguishing."

He gave me directions and I started for the door, but then inspiration struck for the second time that still-young morning.

"Tell me, Mr. Grundy. Might I assume from your redacting that you've done some acting yourself?"

"As a matter of fact, I have. Me and the wife organize the annual Elks' dramatical production. A benefit for the lodge's welfare committee. Why is it you ask?"

"Well, there's to be a dinner on Sunday, over at Mr. Cable's house. A literary dinner. But it seems we're short a professor. Do you think you could..."

"Play a college professor? In my sleep, Mr. Reese! Don't I live in a town full of 'em?"

"And do you think Mrs. Grundy could be prevailed upon to attend as well?"

"Oh, without heaveration. She'd be pleased as punch. But she'll insist on having the same appecalation."

"How's that?"

"Well, if I'm to be a professor, it wouldn't do for her not to be one herself. See, we always take the leading roles."

"I see. Well, no problem with that. The only thing is, it's all to be a surprise for one of the guests. My wife, in fact. So you need to keep it under your hat."

"Absolutely, Mr. Reese. I gave a surprise party for my Gladys last year, so I know all about that."

"Wonderful. I'll stop by with the details later."

"Just a minute, Mr. Reese. It might help me to prepare if knew what sort of professor."

"Astronomy? Or maybe geography? Emmie's thoroughly unacquainted with both."

"Shakespeare *is* my forte. And the missus." He

smiled. "I mean, her forte as well. As to the other..."

"Very well, two Shakespearean scholars. By the way, Mr. Cable won't be able to attend, due to a prior engagement. I'll be bringing along an actor to play his part."

Interestingly, Mr. Grundy saw nothing odd in this arrangement. We said our good-byes and I made my way to the O'Donnell home.

A middle-aged maid in a sullen mood greeted me at the door.

"What?"

"I've come with a wrench. For young Hal."

"Oh. Down in the basement.... Banging away. Don't see what he needs a wrench for. All he does is *bang, bang, bang.*"

"Well, this wrench is alleged to have powers of persuasion which may render the banging unnecessary."

"That little thing? Not likely. Just bang in a different key."

"Have they been coming here frequently?"

"Have they been coming here frequently? All spring they've been coming!"

"Even last Monday?"

"Last Monday? Why not last Monday? Oh, lord, now I remember. That was the worst. From just after breakfast 'til I took dinner off the stove. *Bang, bang, bang!*"

She showed me to the basement and there I found Hal, seated in an old chair with his feet propped up. He lifted a large monkey wrench with one arm and then let it fall on a large iron pipe. Then repeated the exercise twice more to round out the measure. When he saw me approach, he hopped up.

"Oh, it's you, Cousin Harry."

"Keeping busy?"

"Oh, I needed to rest.... Some of these pipes just won't give."

"Well, you're in luck. Mr. Grundy sent me with the persuading wrench."

"I suppose it can't do worse than the convincin' wrench."

"The maid tells me you've been working here quite a bit. Says you were here all day on Monday."

"Monday? Oh, yeah. We put on a new elbow. Took all morning. Then we figured, if we found something else, they'd be sure to give us lunch. Have a wonderful cook here. Then, after we ate, Mr. Grundy said it would look bad if we just up and left, so we found something else to bang on until afternoon coffee. Then..."

"Yes, I get the picture. Tell me, ever see anything more of that McCrea character?"

"McCrea? No. Might still be out of town. Why?"

"Oh, I thought I might have seen him once or twice."

"Nothing weird about that. Just means he came back."

"Sure. Well, happy plumbing."

As the maid showed me out, we heard a *ping, ping, ping* from the basement.

"What'd I tell you? *Bang, bang, bang,* an' now it's *ping, ping, ping!* God save us all."

I didn't envy the poor woman, and as I headed off, she lingered briefly in my thoughts. But only briefly. I'd problems of my own. What I needed was a long, contemplative walk.

The way I saw it, I'd just eliminated my final suspect. Suspect number one, Anthorn, aka President McKinley, might have encountered McCrea on the night of his death. But he'd returned to the hospital before the body had been sunk in the canal. And on the night it was carted off, he was locked up tight. Suspect number two, the attendant Pat Moran, didn't arrive back in town until after McCrea had been dead several hours. Suspect number three, Hal, could have left the house and committed the murder. But he apparently had been at the O'Donnell house all the next day, when the body was sunk.

If I wanted to solve the murder of McCrea, I needed to cast a wider net. Though I can't say I felt particularly motivated. As a means of diverting Emmie, it had failed miserably. And her point about McCrea not being worth the time and effort wasn't without merit. All it took were some incipient pangs of hunger to push the crime out of my mind completely.

I'd wandered down to the path along the Mill River and was presently wending my way toward lunch when I encountered Elizabeth, reading as she walked.

"Gripping book?"

"Harry, what are you up to?"

"Just out for a stroll. Lovely morning, isn't it?"

"Don't be a dolt. I'm referring to this idiotic subterfuge. That man Gloria is wooing, he's quite obviously not Mortimer Vincent."

"What makes you think so?"

"Last evening we saw him at the hotel and she introduced me."

"You've met him before?"

"No, but this morning I had Margaret check out one of his books from the library, to help Gloria prepare herself for conversation at the table. Look."

She held the book open to a photograph at the front. Mortimer Vincent looked even less like his valet than I remembered.

"It's all innocent enough."

"So you admit you knew?"

"Yes, I *have* met Mortimer Vincent."

"And so you want me to help you arrange your cousin's marriage to a man you know to be a fraud?"

"Well, not a complete fraud. See, he's Vincent's valet, Joe somebody. Vincent planned to come here to do some research but then couldn't make the trip. So he sent his valet. When he arrived, the people at the hotel mistook him for Vincent and he just neglected to correct them. So, all completely aboveboard."

"How absurd. And how can you claim it's all completely aboveboard when you haven't told Gloria?"

"Well, she'll find out soon enough. And look at the photo—do you think she'd be any happier with that old buzzard?"

"This is like talking to Emmie. Have you considered what sort of place there will be for a girl married to a valet?"

"Vincent—I mean Joe, the faux Vincent—he seems pretty certain the real Vincent will welcome the addition to the household. Apparently he feels the need for a feminine touch."

"Good lord, Harry! Are you pimping your cousin?"

"Not that intimate of a touch. At least not with the real Vincent. She'll just be a sort of maid to him."

"So you've led Gloria into thinking she will be marrying a well-to-do author, while in fact, she'll be nothing more than his maid?"

"Well, of course I plan to tell her all that before the actual wedding. Provided there's time...."

"*Provided there's time!* And you assume I will go along with this?"

Here she forgot with whom she was speaking. I knew Elizabeth far too well to think she ever allowed herself to be inhibited by matters of probity. No doubt she was just fishing for some further inducement. But I would have none of it.

"A deal's a deal, Elizabeth. You may, of course, back out of your end. But in that case, you can be sure Emmie will be apprised of your machinations posthaste."

"All right, Harry. Have it your way. But don't ask me to explain to the girl the logic of your plan."

"Wouldn't dream of it. By the way, don't mention any of this to Margaret—just make things more awkward. But you might tell her that I've found a couple to play the professor and his wife."

"I thought I'd take care of that. What literary types would you know?"

"Dramaturges, the both of them."

"Are you serious?"

"Perfectly."

"I'm surprised you even know the word."

"You should be more careful about underestimating me."

Before departing, she made a noise identical to one of Emmie's favorites. Though I'm sure you wouldn't find it listed in the curriculum, I'd always suspected the talent had been acquired during their time at Smith.

As I made my way up the last block to the house, Pluribus jumped out from behind a hedge.

"I found it."

"Found what?"

"Where they buried the body."

"You're kidding me."

"Why do you say that? Just like you said, they had a

wagon. Couldn't make it out along the tracks, but when they turned off, about a half-mile on, got plain as day. Ground's soft there. They followed an old road for a ways, and then they dragged the body into the woods. There were four different shoeprints, so must have been two of them. They stuck some branches over where they buried it, but didn't do a good job of hidin' it."

His narrative had all the hallmarks of Emmie's literary efforts and I had little doubt she was its author. On parting from me at his hideaway, the brat had probably gone on to school after all. When he came home for lunch, he told Emmie how I had tried to scupper his arrangement with her. Then she concocted this tale and sent him back out to meet me.

"After lunch we can get some shovels and go back," he said.

"Yeah, sure."

We walked up to the house and found Emmie on the porch, her arms folded.

"What are you two conspiring about?"

"Nothin'. I was just showing Cousin Harry my slingshot." He pulled the device out of a back pocket as proof.

Emmie echoed her former friend's noise of a few minutes earlier, then preceded us into the house. But I was on to her.

11

I don't think it would surprise Mr. O'Donnell's maid to learn that on entering the house, we discovered Hal's aunt massaging balm into his muscle-fatigued arm.

"You must say something to Mr. Grundy," she told him. "He can't keep working you this way."

"Plumbing just takes a lot out of a man's arm. That convincin' wrench must weigh twenty pounds. Don't worry—I'll get used to it. You wouldn't want me to lose my job by complaining?"

"No, of course not," she said. "Sit down everyone. Lunch is ready."

The midday meal proved even more of a challenge than usual. Gloria, her lesson of the evening before having taken a firm hold, set the table giving us all a second fork, and then insisted the fork used for the entrée hash not be used for the dessert hash—the challenge being that the two forks, and the two hashes, were indistinguishable one from the other.

When we finished, Emmie beckoned me into the kitchen.

"You can start on the dishes, Harry. I'll be escorting Pluribus back to school. And I intend to speak with his teacher about this morning."

"Do that, Emmie. Let me know what she reports."

"You had better not be encouraging him to miss school."

"Me? Don't be absurd, Emmie. He certainly doesn't need any encouragement from me to skip school."

She tried giving me the dubious eye, but I'd gotten to it first. We stood there for a minute or so, just eyeing each other dubiously until she finally left the room.

By the time she returned, I'd washed the dishes—and then played spectator while her mother rewashed them. Though a horrible cook, Emmie's mother was otherwise an obsessive housekeeper. Her own house was always immaculate. Even now, with three young rustics of questionable hygiene living with her. I remember the first time she visited us in Brooklyn. She disassembled our stove, and then tried to instruct our maid on how to clean between the floor boards. That girl left our service soon after. From then on, we sent the maid on vacation whenever Mother was expected. That is, when we could still afford a maid.

"I apologize for disbelieving you, Harry," Emmie said, once we were alone.

"Disbelieving what in particular?"

"Suspecting that you had incited Pluribus to skip school. I spoke with his teacher, and she confirmed he'd been there all morning."

"Why am I not surprised?" I took on a knowing air.

"Why are you looking at me that way?"

"You invented that story of his."

"What story?"

"His story of finding the trail of a wagon that went from the railway tracks to conveniently soft ground. And then the signs of a body being dragged... and a fresh grave. All a little too gothic—and all very like you, Emmie."

"What are you talking about, Harry?"

"You really know nothing about it?"

"Nothing."

"Then he must have come up with it on his own."

"Are you saying he tracked down the body?"

"No, I'm saying he *said* he did. But since he was in school all morning, he must have made it up. He *is* your cousin, Emmie."

"But you admit you were encouraging him to miss school?"

"I might have mentioned how pleasant a day it is."

"I take it then that you've deduced my arrangement with him."

"Which arrangement, Emmie?"

"You know perfectly well—if he attends school faithfully, he may come to visit us this summer in Brooklyn."

"If he comes to Brooklyn, Emmie, I'll be summering elsewhere."

"Don't be so peevish, Harry. It isn't becoming in a man your age."

"Strangling a child isn't becoming in a man my age either. But that's just what's likely to happen if he and I share the same apartment."

"You know, Harry, there is still the matter of your trip out to the track with the French girls to be resolved."

"French girls?"

"Don't play coy, Harry. I know all about it. I've read Mélisande's account."

"Read her account?"

"Shall I show it to you?"

She went into Gloria's room and came out with a small sheaf of paper and handed it to me. It seemed to be a sort of letter, much thumbed, and written in a barely legible script. What's more, the text seemed to fluctuate between English and French. It was tough going, as the French was all but impenetrable to me. But I could

ROBERT BRUCE STEWART

understand enough of it to confirm it as an account of the
excursion in question. All the significant details were
there, including the trip back on the train when Mélisande had distracted me and taken my watch. It was the
methodology she used to distract which was most damn-
ing....

"I can explain everything, Emmie."

"I seriously doubt it. But there won't be need for
that, regardless. Now that you've agreed to entertain
Pluribus during his visit with us."

"You really can be cruel, Emmie."

"Oh, yes, I can, Harry. And you had better not forget
it."

"Did she send you that? Or did Elizabeth send it
along with the watch?"

"Neither of them sent it. Don't you recognize it? I've
had this for two years now. Surely you haven't forgotten
the visitation?"

Much as I would have preferred to, I had not forgotten the visitation—for the simple reason that Emmie
wouldn't allow me to forget it. I had hoped, however, to
avoid having to explain it to a third party. But now she'd
forced my hand.

Up until this moment, you may have regarded my
depictions of Emmie's eccentricities as playful exaggera-
tions. Sure, she's an odd bird, you're thinking, but they're
not so rare as this Reese fellow seems to believe. Well,
think again.

Back in February 1903, I spent several days in
Cleveland, investigating a life insurance claim. When I
returned, I found Emmie up to her elbows in manuscripts—an enormous assemblage of diaries, letters,
autobiographies, scrapbooks, etc. She told me she had

bought them at some auction house, and was using them to inform her literary work. Randomness being the most salient feature of Emmie's literary work, there seemed nothing remarkable in this.

Then, some months later, she told me a different story. This was just after we'd been up in Maine, where we met a couple of women who were acquainted with Elizabeth. Elizabeth had had a dispute with Tibbitts and gone off to France without him. We knew about that. We now learned that Elizabeth had recently returned to New York with a baby. Presumably, Tibbitts's.

Emmie began by telling me she needed to make a confession. She swore now that the collection of manuscripts I'd seen back in February had not come to her via an auction, but rather via a crate dropped from a mysterious airship flying over Prospect Park. Thinking it a joke, I laughed, and she became angry. Almost livid. She insisted I hear her story out, and so I indulged her.

She told me that she had happened to be out late that night and had observed the airship when she disembarked from a streetcar just outside the park. She followed it, and then witnessed the descent of a crate via parachute. With not another soul in sight, she retrieved the cache and brought it home to the apartment. Later, she learned the crate had been addressed to her, and that the assemblage was all of a piece, a sort of extended family history—the family being that of Elizabeth and her husband.

All quite ridiculous, of course, but I've not yet gotten to the most ridiculous part. You see, among the manuscripts was one dated 1959—fifty-six years *after* the arrival of the crate. What's more, it was written by someone claiming to be the daughter of Elizabeth and Tibbitts.

I assumed it was all an invention of Emmie's, something she'd been working on for years, whenever I was away from home. But there were certain facts that confused the issue. I had only seen the collection fleetingly that previous winter. But Emmie had spoken of various characters—chief among them, a woman named Eugenia, the central character of the collective work. Three weeks after our return from Maine, and six months after Emmie had first mentioned the name, we learned that Elizabeth had named her baby, born that May, Eugenia.

For that, however, I could conceive a rational explanation. Perhaps, in some moment of romantic dreaminess, Emmie and Elizabeth had exchanged their favored names for children, and Emmie had thereby anticipated Elizabeth would name her daughter Eugenia. Militating against this explanation is the fact that neither woman is prone to romantic dreaminess. An alternative explanation was that there had been some more-recent correspondence I'd been unaware of. Unlikely, given the state of their relationship, but still possible.

Curious now, I did some research and learned that there *had* been a smattering of reports about an airship over New York that very night in February. Emmie, of course, might have simply remembered these herself when concocting her story several months later. But it did give me pause.

Adding to that pause, there was another name Emmie mentioned repeatedly: Mélisande. An unusual name which I'd never heard before. Not only that—she shared with me several of the episodes Mélisande had recorded in her unique patois. They bore some telling similarities to the affair at the track, not to mention the trip back on the train.

Well, now you know as much about it as I do. And, I trust, are as confused by it as I am. You can see why I wanted to keep the whole thing hushed up, *and* why I wanted to keep Emmie as far away from that state hospital as possible. Ten years back, reports of airship visitations were common, and I wouldn't be at all surprised if there was an entire wing of the hospital devoted to the humans who hosted them.

Emmie hadn't waited for a response. She sat down at the table with her manuscript and looked it over for the hundred-and-ninth time.

"I'm going out, Emmie."

I said it with all the haughtiness I could muster. But while nothing went on during that trip to the track worthy of a divorce court, it did have its compromising moments. And unless I wanted Emmie to remind me of them until my dying day, I was going to have to go along with her noxious little cousin paying us an extended visit.

"Make sure you close the door," she said, without looking up.

I had no real destination in mind, I just felt any demonstration of indignation worth its salt required a haughty exit. But thoughts of the noxious one brought my mind back to the corpse and its current disposition. His story may have been hogwash, but that didn't mean there might not be a clue out there waiting to be found. And having run out of suspects, I could think of no better use of my time.

I set out on the all-too-familiar route, and once again came upon a hospital attendant walking toward me—one Pat Moran.

"Searching for lost sheep?" I asked.

"Oh. Ah, something like that. Don't worry about

your uncle, though. What did you say your name was?"

"Reese. Harry Reese."

"Say, didn't I see you out here Monday morning?"

"Did you? Oh, yes. I remember."

"Sure you do. And I remember you didn't seem to know who your uncle was at the time. Just told me about receiving the pardon."

"You sure?"

"Yeah, I'm sure." His expression took on a somewhat less jovial aspect. "What's your game, buddy?"

"The truth?"

"Well, you can give it a try."

"Oh, I can do better than that." Almost anything would be better than the truth. "Well, I'm a newspaperman. Visiting from New York. I'm in town to meet Henry James. The author."

"Who's he?"

"Writes rather dull stuff about rather dull people. Very big with the college crowd."

"Oh. No Chinese highbinders, or detectives disguised as opera singers?"

"Not a one."

"That does sound dull.... But what's that have to do with you pretending to be Anthorn's nephew?"

"Well, there's to be a dinner for Mr. James. At the Cable residence. But a... But old Mr. Cable himself can't attend, and I happened to notice that Mr. Anthorn bears a striking resemblance to the fellow."

"I suppose he does, sorta. And you're thinkin' you can use him to fool this James character?"

"Why not? Mr. Anthorn seems game."

"When is this soirée?"

"Sunday evening."

"At the Cables' house?"

"That's right."

"Well, if you want, I could tag along. Help keep an eye on the old fellow."

"But not dressed in white?"

"No, wouldn't wear white. I can look respectable."

"Say, maybe you could play a part?"

"A part?"

"Yes, we're short a travel writer. Ever been to Africa? Or India?"

"No. Went out to Missouri once, to visit my brother. But never Africa. Or India—least, that I remember."

"Well, it doesn't matter. Neither will anyone else. You just might need to come up with some colorful anecdotes."

"What sort?"

"Doesn't matter really, just so they're exotic."

"Oh, I get it. Something like 'Did you hear the one about the drummer of shrunken heads and the witch doctor's daughter?'"

"Yes. Exactly. Do you know where the Cable place is?"

"Yeah, sure."

"Well, would you mind bringing Mr. Anthorn around at about 6:30? I told the hospital I'd be checking him out, but the timing may be tight."

"Wouldn't mind a bit. Well, I'm sure glad I run into you, Mr. Reese."

"Likewise. Oh, one other thing. You'll be playing a man named Mortimer Vincent."

"Mortimer Vincent. Sounds classy, don't it?"

"Very."

"So only you'll know I'm not this Vincent fellow?"

"Yes, and Mr. Anthorn."

"Oh, he'll believe it, all right. Well, so long."

"So long."

As he walked off, his shoes emitted a little squish with each step. Apparently Mr. Moran had been doing some wading. I suppose I should have been a little suspicious about how easily he went along with the outlandish conceit, but at the time I was simply relieved to have extricated myself from a difficult situation—not to mention filling out the dinner party.

I continued on my way and soon reached the little patch of canal where all the various goings-on had gone on. There wasn't enough room for a wagon to run beside the railway tracks, so if one had been out here it would have needed to travel across the ties, and in that case it wouldn't leave any trail.

After about a couple hundred yards, the surrounding ground rose and was now level with the tracks. Then, a few hundred yards beyond that—just where Pluribus had told me—there were clear signs that a wagon had turned off the tracks and onto an old road. They'd needed to make little ramps to get the far wheels over the tracks, and had left some bits of scrap lumber behind.

"Where the hell you been, Cousin Harry?"

It was the little brute himself, emerging from the woods beside the road.

"I thought Emmie took you back to school?"

"She did."

"She told me the teacher said you were there all morning."

"Sure she did. Me an' the teacher have a deal. I stay away, and she reports me present. Says teaching me is a waste of time anyway. And even if I did manage to learn something, I'd as likely use it to no good anyhow."

"Sounds like a good judge of character."

"Did you bring a shovel?"

"Well, believe it or not, I found your story a little difficult to swallow."

"You just come and look for yourself."

We followed the wagon tracks in the road until they came to a halt. Then he showed me the two sets of shoeprints and the marks left by the heels of the dragged body. They led into the woods. Then, at a little clearing, he pointed to a pile of twigs and branches. He pushed them aside with his foot.

"You see?" he asked. "Someone was digging here. An' it weren't for worms."

"No, it weren't for worms."

"Maybe it would be better if we come back, after dark, an' dig it up then?"

"Dig it up? And then what? You remember its condition last time we saw it—we'd need blotting paper. Better if you just tell the police and leave it to them."

"Me? Sure be a lot to tell 'em now."

"Well, we could tell them about the grave anonymously, and let them figure out the rest on their own."

"What if what they figure out is Hal did it? What then?"

"What would you propose we do with the body once we dig it up?"

"Bury it, only better. Further out."

"What difference would that make? Are you assuming Hal had something to do with burying the body?"

"Come on."

We went back out to the road where the wagon tracks were visible in the dried mud.

"Look here." He was on his knees, pointing. I got down beside him. "You see that notch? Goin' across the track of the wagon wheel?"

"So?"

He hopped up and went a half dozen paces back toward the rail tracks.

"There it is again." He went another half dozen paces. "An' again. Every fifteen feet or so. It's a repair, on a five-foot wheel. Only, someone didn't do it right, so it sticks out."

"You figured that out on your own?"

"Sure. Nothing hard about that."

I'd always assumed the kid a near imbecile. This little demonstration kindled in me something resembling respect. Though trepidation comes nearer to it. Somehow he seemed not so dangerous as an imbecile.

"Mr. Grundy's van. It's got a fix just like that, where the rim came loose on the wheel. He did it himself."

"Yes, I've ridden in it. You think Mr. Grundy helped Hal bury the body?"

"Or Hal helped Mr. Grundy."

"Are you suggesting Mr. Grundy killed McCrea?"

He shrugged. "More likely than Hal."

"The body got moved that same night we moved it back to shore. How would either Hal or Mr. Grundy know we had moved it?"

"Promise you won't tell Cousin Emmie?"

"Sure."

"She told me not to tell no one. But when I got home that night, I woke Hal up gettin' into bed. He started asking all sorts of questions. Well, I just told him. I guess I was aching to tell someone. Not every day you get hold of a story like this. I told him how you and me saw the dead man that first day. And then how we had found him sunk that night."

"And then he went out?"

"Not that I saw. I went to sleep and when I woke up, he was coming in the window. Said he'd just been out peeing. He likes doing it outside, so if the neighbors aren't out, he just hops out the window. I'm the same way."

"You might want to break that habit if you come to Brooklyn."

"You mean you'll let me come?"

"I said if."

He broke off two branches from a downed tree and handed me one.

"What's this for?"

"To cover up their tracks."

"Well, what's one more felony?"

12

During the walk back, Pluribus set aside thoughts of the peripatetic corpse and grilled me about New York. I painted it as ugly as I could imagine—and having lived there for ten years, I didn't need to waste much time imagining.

"Ever hop off a streetcar and find your foot's caught in the rotting carcass of a nag?"

"Course not. Neither have you."

"Shows what you know. Summer of '96. Long Island City."

"Thought we were talking about New York?"

"Long Island City is one of the posher neighborhoods of New York—people go there just to soak up the atmosphere. Now you better run along home. You should have gotten out of school by now."

"All right. Where're you going?"

"I thought I'd see where Mr. Grundy keeps his van."

"Grayson's Stable. Back behind the shop. But we already know..."

"We think we know. But I want to be sure before I say anything to Hal."

"You're going to tell him what we saw?"

"I'm going to ask him if he was out that night. But let me talk to him."

"OK by me."

He went off toward the house and I continued on into town. I surveyed the alleys behind the shop, but the only stable bore a large sign reading Clyburn & Sons. In the little yard in front, a fellow was sitting at a bench, mending a bridle.

"I'm looking for Grayson's Stable."

"This is it."

"Mr. Grayson?"

"Clyburn. Grayson's dead. People just ain't used to the new name."

My curiosity was piqued by the fact the sign reading Clyburn & Sons was so old and faded as to be barely legible. "How long's it been?"

"Twenty, twenty-five years."

Like me, you're probably wondering if Henry James wasn't too easy on Emmie's hometown.

"Well, I may be in need of a place to board a horse and buggy. I was wondering about terms?"

"Two dollars a week. Three with feed. You want feed?"

"I can take it or leave it, but the horse might see it differently. What if I needed to take it out at night? Is someone here?"

"No, but you can hitch it up yourself. What do you need to go out at night for?"

"Oh, one never knows when an unexpected exigency might arise."

"Just seems odd, your anticipatin' this thing you don't expect. You aren't up to nothin' untoward, are you?"

"No, no. I can give you references if you're worried. I believe Mr. Grundy keeps his van here."

"That miser? If that's your reference, might be better taking your trade somewhere else."

"Doesn't pay his bills?"

"He pays what he has to, but not a dime more. Look."

He led me inside the building, where Grundy's van was parked.

"Covered in mud. Told him day 'fore yesterday I'd wash it down for two bits. 'Two bits!' he says. 'Nickle, an' not a penny more!' Well, it will be a cold day you-know-where. An' look at that wheel there. Rim came loose. 'I can fix that for you, Grundy,' I told him. 'Won't be more than a dollar.' He laughs. 'I can fix it myself,' he says. Now runs all over town, thumping up and down, covered in mud, looking a real fool."

He had a point. And I noticed something else as I got near the van. An unpleasant odor.

"Wonder where he went, to get all that mud?"

"Told me next day he had work out at a farm late on Tuesday, after I left. Must have been a ways. Ain't rained here in more than a week. But he's an odd fish, him. Daughter, too."

"Jane? What about her?"

"Goes out at night herself. Her and some others. Call themselves the Neigh-itties."

"How's that?"

"Neigh-itties. Neigh, like a horse does, and itties, like... well, itties," he explained. Then he sunk into a whisper, "Short for... you know." He raised his hands up to his chest, palm up, then fondled the air for a good deal longer than necessary.

"Ah. Some sort of secret society?"

"Somethin' like that. Only not too secret. But I wouldn't know anything about that." He nodded toward a big-bosomed woman approaching us. His wife, he said. From her expression, I inferred she'd witnessed his pantomime and was eager to offer a critique. It seemed a good time to make my exit.

That evening, as I prepared to go by the Cables' to pick up Gloria, I asked Hal to come out with me. He tried begging off, a little awkwardly. When I told him it might be important, he acceded, but was now even more nervous.

As we came to the end of the block, he asked what it was about.

"What would you say if I told you McCrea is dead?"

"I... I can't say I'm surprised."

"Look, Hal, did you see him again Sunday night?"

"Why do you ask that? What's Pluribus been saying?"

"Only that you went out that night. Just a few hours after fighting with McCrea at the depot. And the next morning, McCrea was found dead. Pluribus told you that, didn't he?"

"Yeah, he told me. Not then. Not 'til Tuesday night...." He took a deep breath. "Well, here's what happened. That night, Sunday, you remember how drunk I got. I know you put something in the lemonade. Well, as soon as my head hit the pillow I was asleep. Then a couple hours later I wake up, and I'm still feeling pretty fearless. I decided I'd go fetch Lottie and elope with her. Then no one could stand in our way."

"Didn't it occur to you she might feel differently?"

"Well, I wasn't thinking too clearly. I figured if she was at all reluctant, I'd just carry her off. I guess I thought she'd see it as kind of romantic."

"More likely, she'd see it as kidnapping. Did you talk with her?"

"When I get over to the Cable place, and start circling round the house, trying to remember which room's hers, I nearly walked into them."

"Them?"

"She, Lottie, is out there in the garden, talking to a fellow. All whispers. She says, 'I got to go in, but you're barking up the wrong tree.' And then the fellow, he says, 'Then *he* has it.' She doesn't say nothing to that, just kind of waves a hand at him and shakes her head, then goes into the house."

"Was the fellow McCrea?"

"I couldn't make him out yet, but I knew his voice."

"Did you confront him?"

"Not then. Not so near the house. I followed him, down to the river. He was walking toward the college. I called him from behind. He turned, scared. Must not a heard me 'til then. He starts running off, and I pick up a rock and throw it, hard as I can. He falls. I run towards him, but then he's back on his feet and running again. That's when I tripped on a root. By the time I picked myself up, he was long gone."

"What time do you think that was?"

"No idea. Late. But I wasn't paying too much attention to the time."

"Did you know he had some connection to Lottie?"

"Well, I'd seen him talking to her before."

"Is that what the fight at the depot was about?"

"As soon as he saw me there, he starts egging me on. 'How's your girl? Better be careful with her,' he says."

"As if he wanted a fight?"

"Seemed that way."

"So when Pluribus told you about finding McCrea with a cracked skull, you assumed it was caused by the rock you threw?"

"Didn't seem like he was hurt that bad, the way he ran off. But I hit him, all right."

"I think it's pretty unlikely he went another two or three miles and died in the canal from whatever wound you gave him. If it'd hurt him that badly, why not go back to the hospital? It wouldn't have been any further. And he must have had friends there who could have dressed it. Are you even sure your rock hit him in the head?"

"No, just that he fell after I threw it."

"And the same night Pluribus told you about finding the body, he told you the rest? How he'd just come from helping me pull it out of the water?"

"Yeah, he told me all of it. But to tell the truth, I still don't think I got it all straight. I mean, why didn't you and him call the police that first day?"

"Ah. Well, there was something approaching a reason. But you know, the best-laid plans of mice and men.... Let's get back to that night. What did you do after Pluribus told you all this?"

"I... Well..."

"You went and told Mr. Grundy?"

"You know?"

"I have a good idea, but it would be better coming from you."

"Well, I waited for Pluribus to fall back asleep. Then I went off to Mr. Grundy's. I had to tap pretty hard on the window. Woke up his missus, too. He came outside and I told him how I must've killed McCrea. And I asked him to come with me to the police. He knows all of them, so I figured it would go easier on me if he was there. By then I just wanted to get it over with. But he said he didn't think that was a good idea, given it'd been three days by then. He said since no one seemed to be looking for McCrea, better just to get rid of the body and forget all about it."

"Very accommodating. So you went and hitched up

the van. How'd you know where to find the body?"

"Pluribus described it. Only a few places where the old canal hasn't been filled in. Mr. Grundy guessed right where it was."

"So then you took the body into the woods and buried it."

"Yeah."

"But if there were two of you, why'd you drag it? Why not just carry it?"

"Oh, Mr. Grundy's got a bad back. So I had to do the digging, too."

"Ah. So is it true McCrea was seeing Jane, Grundy's daughter?"

"Seeing's just it."

"What do you mean by that?"

"Well, it's nothing I want to talk about. You ask Gloria."

"About what? It wouldn't involve the Neigh-itties, would it?"

"You know about them?"

"Just the name. What's it mean?"

"Oh... You better..."

"Ask Gloria?"

"Yeah. I suppose you'll want to go to the police now. Have me show where the body's buried?"

"No, let's leave that alone for now. It might be better to find out who actually killed him before getting the police involved."

"All right. Well, I'll be off now. If that's OK."

"Sure."

Once again, I found Elizabeth and her pupil in the Cables' garden. Gloria had a short stack of books on her head. When I greeted them, it startled her and they fell to the ground. One lay splayed at my feet. I picked it up and dusted it off. It was one of Henry James's.

"Go away, Harry. I think Margaret's inside making coffee."

I tapped on the screen door of the kitchen and Margaret let me in. Lottie stood at the sink, washing pans. We exchanged greetings, then Margaret and I sat down.

"I've some good news," I told her. "I've filled out the table."

"Elizabeth mentioned you'd found a couple to play the professor and his wife. Are these friends from New York as well?"

"Ah, no. Not exactly. In fact, you know the man: Mr. Grundy."

"Mr. Grundy, the plumber?"

I heard Lottie stifle a titter.

"Yes, it seems he and the missus direct the annual theatrical show at the Elks lodge. He feels sure he can play a convincing professor of Shakespearean studies, and the missus likewise."

"Harry, how in the world do you expect to fool Emmie with a confidence man playing Henry James and a plumber playing a Shakespearean scholar?"

"Well, several rounds of cocktails before dinner, then a liberal use of your father's cellar."

"Elizabeth is handling the libations, so you may be certain there will be plenty to go around."

"Good. I also found someone to play the part of Mortimer Vincent."

"Who? The rag collector?"

"Fellow who works at the State Hospital. Name's Pat Moran."

Lottie dropped a large pan into the sink.

"Sorry," she said.

Margaret shook her head, but at least she was smiling. "A world traveler, is he?"

"Been out to Missouri, he assures me. Plus, he promises an anecdote about a drummer of shrunken heads and a witch doctor's daughter."

"Somehow it seems appropriate," she said. "Having an attendant from the State Hospital."

We heard Mr. Cable call for Margaret from the front of the house and she left the room.

"Did you recognize the name Pat Moran, Lottie?"

"I... No. The pan just slipped is all." She answered without turning toward me.

I can't explain why it hadn't occurred to me before then that this Lottie and Anthorn's niece Lottie could truly be one and the same. I suppose it just seemed too much of a coincidence. But coincidences are, after all, the bread and butter of the detective novel, and this one was far too good to pass up. I probed further.

"You wouldn't happen to be related to a fellow named John Anthorn, would you, Lottie?"

She came over to the table and sat down. "What do you know?"

"Only that Mr. Anthorn has a niece named Lottie who visited him occasionally."

"Not for over a year now. Last time... He just got unreasonable."

"That's how you know Pat Moran? From visiting the hospital?"

"Yes. Don't mention it to Margaret, or the others, will you?"

"All right. But don't they already know about him?"

"No. We come from North Adams. About seven or

eight years ago it started—Uncle John thinking he was President McKinley. No one cared much. He had a business in real estate. Didn't seem to matter, people went along with it. Even greeted him as Mr. President. But then President McKinley, the *real* President McKinley, was said to be coming to town. Uncle John, he started getting angry. People thinking he *wasn't* the real President. Well, that got them worried. And that's when the doctor sent him to the hospital here."

"And that's when you moved here?"

"I'm his only family. And I'd been living with him. But when he got worse, his business went bad and all his money disappeared. I came here to sort of look after him, and a little later took this job with the Cables. I'd visit Uncle John every week or so, at first. But it became more and more trying."

There were tears on her cheeks and she wiped them away with the heel of her hand. It was, of course, a fairly touching story. And after listening to it, I couldn't see upsetting her further by asking about her conversation with McCrea on the night he'd been murdered. There was also the small matter of her uncle appearing at the dinner and posing as her employer. I wasn't really sure how to work that into the discussion. So I was relieved by what followed.

"I'd prefer Mr. Moran not know I'm here. So I'll prepare the dinner, but someone else will need to serve it, if that can be arranged."

"Hal and I will take care of that."

"Hal? Poor Hal."

"Why poor Hal?"

"He just deserves better. He'll figure it out."

Since she would be avoiding the dining room, I decided to keep her uncle's presence a secret. Margaret came back in and Lottie returned to the sink.

"I believe Elizabeth is done tormenting Gloria for the evening."

We went out to join them and soon after Gloria and I were on our way home.

"How'd it go this evening?"

"Oh, fine. We had dinner at the hotel again. This time it was all about what you do when you aren't actually eating. I'd hoped she'd tell me what I should talk about. But she mostly told me how to act when someone else is talking. Said I should look like I think it's all extremely interesting, even when I haven't any idea what it is they're talking about. It's much harder than you'd think. She said that's what being charming is all about. Especially where men are concerned."

"Yes, it's dull work, no doubt about it. Say, you remember that fellow Hal got into a fight with at the depot, McCrea, I think?"

"I know him," she said, somewhat defensively. "Like I know lots of people."

Given how freely she spread her attentions, I didn't know quite what to make of that.

"Has he been bothering you?"

"No more than he did the others."

"Like Jane Grundy, for instance?"

"Well, she might be leading him on some. It's hard to say with Jane. The whole thing... Oh, never mind."

"I don't suppose this has anything to do with the Neigh-itties?"

"Who told you about that? Hal? You haven't said anything to Aunt, have you? Or Cousin Emmie?"

"All I know is the word. If it is a word."

"Jane says it's a Greek word. Means nymphs. They're girls who like to frolic in the river."

"And you all frolic in the river?"

"Promise not to tell?"

"Absolutely."

"We'd go at night... in the altogether.... But just us girls."

"Well, I think the secret is out."

"That was Jane's doing, mostly. See, town girls get jealous of all the looks the college girls get. So Jane figured we needed to do... something. It started last September, when it was still hot. She let a few boys find out, but now hardly nobody doesn't know."

"Is that where you were going on Sunday night, when Emmie intercepted you?"

"Yes, but I was glad she caught me."

"A little chilly for an early morning swim, isn't it?"

"Don't I know it. I told Jane I wasn't keen on it anymore.... Least not 'til it's hotter."

"How many of you were there?"

"Never more than half a dozen, but now most of the others have stopped going too."

"So on Sunday, Jane might have been by herself?"

"She told me when no one else showed up, she went on home."

"Did she mention seeing anyone? Boys, I mean?"

"No. She said no one was out watchin' anyway, so it didn't matter."

And with that, whatever qualms I'd had about maneuvering Gloria into marriage with the valet of the esteemed author she thought she was marrying evaporated.

13

After breakfast the next morning, Emmie went out-side with her mother to help with the garden and I was left in the house alone. I'd been waiting all week for this opportunity. I knew Emmie had a stash of hard currency somewhere because she kept producing banknotes at regular intervals. Her little purse sat right atop the dresser, but contained a grand total of one dollar and seventy-eight cents in copper and silver. I took two quarters.

Next, I pawed through her wardrobe. Nothing. I flipped through the pages of her manuscript. Again, nothing. Then I flipped through the books she'd brought—the last being James's *Roderick Hudson*. Still nothing—until I saw a corner of something peeking out of the paper pocket used for the library card, forty-three dollars altogether. I took thirteen and returned the two quarters to her purse. I like feeling magnanimous.

I went outside and told her I wouldn't be home for lunch. She rose from her crouching position and locked me in a piercing stare.

"Oh?"

"Yes. It involves... It involves that matter you want nothing to do with. I don't suppose you've changed your mind?"

"No, I haven't."

"Well, I should be off or I'll miss my train."

"Harry..."

"Sorry, no time." I trotted off down the block.

Well, I knew then I'd put my foot in it. Mentioning the train was a dead giveaway. By the time I made it to the depot, she'd have discovered the theft and begun plotting her revenge. Emmie is no slouch when it comes to plots generally, but she saves her best stuff for those promising some form of merciless bloodletting. Luckily, I had a scapegoat already picked out.

I took a train north to Greenfield, then another west to North Adams, the mill town where Lottie and her uncle had lived before his commitment. It was right around noon when I arrived. At the depot, I found a city directory and copied out the addresses of several real-estate agents. Then I had a pleasant meal at one of the hotels. The food was no better than adequate, but I took comfort in being able to differentiate one dish from another.

On leaving the hotel, I went by the police station. It took some wheedling, but eventually I got in to see a detective who remembered Anthorn.

"Funny old guy. Off his nut. But never caused any trouble.... Until..."

"Until he heard the upstart McKinley would be coming?"

"Yeah. Really lost his head over it. We thought of just locking him up until the President left town, but he had a lawyer. So the mayor found a doctor willing to commit him."

"I'd heard he was actually fairly well off. Any truth to that?"

"Oh, he did OK. No idea how well. You might talk to his lawyer. Henning's his name. He could tell you more."

Henning had an office just a few blocks away, but a girl there told me he'd be out until late afternoon. I looked up the first of my real-estate agents, the one who had the largest ad in the directory. Parsons was the fellow's name. He told me Anthorn had been successful—very successful, timing the boom and bust of the nineties perfectly.

"Owned a slew of mill-worker houses, triple-deckers, mostly. Bought them for a song when the mills closed. Then when things turned for the better, he raked it in."

"What I'm curious about is what happened to his assets after he was committed?"

"Well, when things turned around, he sold off the houses, one by one. Where he put the money, I can't say. Didn't spend much of it. Never lived high."

"What sort of money do you think we're talking about?"

"Tens of thousands. Twenty, thirty maybe, from those houses. Plus he was making money right along. Seems odd, but the nuttiness never hurt his business. Crazy like a fox, I guess."

"Can you tell me anything about his niece?"

"His niece? No, I don't think I ever met her. We weren't chummy. Just knew him through business. He had a partner, fellow named Ransom. He wasn't in on the killing, but they shared an office later on. He's still around, I think. Retired."

It took some doing, but I tracked down Ransom's address. It was one of the big frame houses shared by several families of mill workers. But unlike most of the others, it was obvious it had previously been a home of some distinction, then later divided into apartments. It needed painting, badly, and there was a trench running through the yard, as if someone had started to lay plumbing of some kind and then abandoned the project. Ransom wasn't in, but from the looks of the place, it seemed plain he hadn't shared in Anthorn's savvy, or his fortune.

It was after four when I finally got in to see the lawyer, Wilbert Henning. I told him I was a distant relative of Anthorn's and was making inquiries on behalf of an aunt.

"I didn't know he had a sister."

"A cousin. Second cousin."

"Well, family or not, I don't know what I can tell you. Mr. Anthorn was my client, and that bond remains even after I've left his service."

"Of course. I just have some general questions. Did you fight his committal?"

"Yes, but unfortunately it was a lost cause. The eccentricities were one thing, but he'd made too many threats regarding the President's visit. That's all part of the public record."

"Have you made any effort to have him released?"

"I did consult with his doctors at the hospital, about three years ago now. They assured me he was better off there, and when I talked to him, he exhibited no enthusiasm for returning here. I suppose it's not a bad retirement. People see to his needs. And humor him."

"Yes, he seems comfortable enough. Did you handle the paperwork for his real-estate transactions?"

"I handled all his work."

"So you must have a good idea of how set he was."

"If you mean financially, of course."

"It sounds as if he sat on a good sum of money."

"He did very well for himself. But beyond that..."

"Well, without going into specifics, what happens to someone's assets when he's committed?"

"That depends on the actions of the other interested parties. If his family goes to court, it might make a case that the owner is no longer capable of managing his assets and thus gain control."

"Did that happen in this case?"

"No."

"Did his niece…"

"What niece?"

"I understood that his niece, Lottie, lived with him."

"Lottie isn't his niece. She's his wife."

"His wife?"

"You're shocked? Because of the age difference?"

"Yes, there's that."

"It was an arrangement born of greed."

"She was after his money?"

"No, not her. Her father, Ransom."

"Ransom? Anthorn's partner?"

"Ransom was never his partner. Not in any formal, business sense. They shared an office and a stenographer. But they operated separately. Ransom had been caught with his pants down when the crash came, in '92. He had bought big on borrowed money and never climbed out of that hole. I think it might have been partly out of guilt that Anthorn took him in."

"His fortune came at the cost of Ransom's?"

"Not directly, of course. Still, there had to be some feelings of resentment on Ransom's part. Not surprisingly, he envied Anthorn's success. So he used his daughter to get his hands on his cash."

"And she approved of the scheme?"

"No, I think she was just a dutiful girl who followed the wishes of her father. I would have stopped it if I could have. It was about the time of the marriage that Anthorn started exhibiting signs of his illness."

By the time I left Henning, it was after five—already too late to catch the last train back to Northampton. And now I was especially keen on seeing Ransom. I went by the depot and sent a wire to Emmie, telling her I wouldn't be returning until the following day. Then I revisited Ransom's house. He still hadn't returned, and none of the neighbors knew when he might be back.

After booking a room in the hotel I'd dined in earlier, I found the offices of the evening newspaper. Given that the last edition had been put to bed, I surmised its news staff could be found holed up in one of the nearby barrooms. And so it was—Kilkinney's Saloon. Mr. Kilkinney's establishment had just the right combination of moody atmosphere and inexpensive liquor which appeals to the sensitive nature of the newsman.

I knew from long experience I'd entered dangerous territory. There are, of course, any number of professions which exhibit a strong taste for drink. But none of the others are as agile at avoiding the check. I'd wager my last dollar that the words "This round's on me" have never passed the lips of a journalist over the age of seventeen.

I took a spot at the bar, within listening distance of the table where the ink slingers were holding conference. They were easy enough to spot by the stacks of empty shot glasses, and the pleasure they took in disparaging one another's parentage and diction.

Next, I struck up a conversation with the bartender. He stood several feet away, washing glasses, so I had an excuse to raise my voice. I asked if he remembered President McKinley's coming to town. He said he did. Then I mentioned I'd met Anthorn in Northampton. He didn't remember Anthorn, so I gave him an abridged version of the old man's biography.

"I hear he has some money socked away," I added.

"Who told you that?" One of the scribes had gone for the bait.

"Seems common knowledge up at the hospital."

"Anyone seen this money?"

"Can't say, myself. But someone's looking pretty hard for it, and I doubt it's on the old man's word."

"Looking where? Down there? In Northampton?"

"Seems so."

He came over and joined me at the bar. He was about my age, with sandy hair and that jaded mien which gives cops and newspapermen an aspect of impenetrability.

"These people think he has a pile of loot hidden somewhere?" he asked.

"That's the idea."

"You got any names?"

"Well, I might." I tapped my empty mug.

"Jack, bring the man a beer…. And put it on the paper's tab." Then he turned back to me. "So?"

"Bill McCrea," I said. "The name mean anything to you?"

"McCrea? No. Should it?"

"Well, I had a hunch he might be from up around here. Works at the State Hospital now."

He consulted his companions, but when none of them recognized the name, he asked the barman for a city directory.

Over the course of the afternoon, I'd reached several conclusions. First, and most obvious, Anthorn had a middling-sized fortune put away somewhere. Second, neither Lottie nor her father had gotten hold of it. As a rule, women with twenty thousand dollars in the bank show a disinclination for taking jobs as domestics. And rich old men only rarely live in run-down mill housing. Third, McCrea knew about both the money and Lottie's relationship to Anthorn. That would explain the conversation they had which Hal witnessed the night McCrea was murdered.

"How long's he been down there?"

"Can't say. But he left town last Sunday—I thought he might be here." If he weren't dead, of course.

The reporter had been scanning the directory as I spoke.

"No Williams, but maybe one of these is a relative he's staying with." He jotted down three addresses. Then he paused, staring at the list. "I suppose there might be a story in this. More likely, I'll just waste another Friday night.... Oh, well. You want to come along?"

"Sure."

"I'm Donaldson."

"Reese."

"This Thomas McCrea works in a mill. I suggest we start with him."

"Why's that?"

"If your father's a mill hand, landing a job at the State Hospital is a step up. If your father's Patrick McCrea, the railroad superintendent, it's a step down."

Thomas McCrea wasn't in, but his careworn wife was. They lived on the third floor of a large frame house which reeked of cabbage. There was a growler of beer sitting on the table she'd tried to cover with a towel. Mrs. McCrea confirmed she had a son named Bill and that he worked at the State Hospital. She spoke with a slur, and I realized she wasn't so much careworn as soused. The distinction can be a fine one.

"Is there some sort of trouble?"

"No, none at all," Donaldson assured her. "Just thought he might be in town. I'm doing a follow-up piece on old Mr. Anthorn. Remember him?"

"No, can't say I do."

"Well, he's at the hospital also. As a patient. Just thought your boy could tell me something about life there. So you aren't expecting him home anytime soon?"

"Said he'd try to get up for Memorial Day."

"I see. Well, sorry to trouble you."

As we were leaving the neighborhood, I realized we were just a block from Ransom's house. I kept that to myself for the time being.

"How about letting the paper buy you supper and you can tell me what you know?"

"Suits me. But isn't much to tell."

He asked me where I was staying and then suggested we dine there. But I saw through his ruse. Never enter an establishment in the company of a journalist which serves liquor and has a bill running in your name. He'd offered to buy dinner and he was going to have to make good.

We went on to a little café and ordered chops.

"I take it you're hoping to come into some of this fortune yourself," he said. "What's the angle?"

"What if I told you I was working as someone's agent?"

"Oh, I get it. The wife. What's her name?"

"Lottie."

"*Are* you telling me that?"

"Only as a possibility."

"Who else is there?"

"Well, there's her father."

"Who's he?"

"Ransom. The fellow who worked with Anthorn."

"His daughter is Anthorn's wife?"

"Didn't you know that?"

"Must not have come up at the time. Are you saying he hired you?"

"No, I just meant he might be another interested party."

"You mean, hoping to get Anthorn's dough through his daughter?"

"The idea's been suggested to me."

"By who?"

"Anthorn's lawyer."

"I guess he'd know. Maybe we should have suspected something. It was Ransom who got him put away. Well, I shouldn't say that. Anthorn had gotten angry with a couple people. Broke a mirror in a saloon when the bartender needled him about McKinley coming. But it was Ransom's word that sealed it. He told how Anthorn went nuts whenever the newspapers mentioned the President. There was no reason to think he was lying. But..."

"But perhaps Ransom also goaded him, and for a very good reason."

"Could be. Can't say I know him well enough to tell one way or the other. He seems to have fallen through the cracks, don't hear about him anymore."

"He lives not far from the McCreas'. I've stopped by twice today, but he's been out."

"What say you we make another visit?"

"All right."

When we reached the place, I let Donaldson knock on Ransom's door. When no one answered, he knocked harder. Then, within a few seconds, he had it unlocked. A neighbor poked her head out of a door at the end of the hall.

"He ain't in. Won't be back tonight," she said.

"That's OK," Donaldson told her. "We're friends. Asked us to check the place for him. Gave us the key."

She didn't look convinced, but nonetheless disappeared back into her own apartment.

"Better he's not here. Gives us a chance to look around." Inside, Donaldson lit a gas jet. "Man, what goes on here?"

We were in what looked to have been a parlor or study before the house was subdivided. The walls were peppered with holes, and there was a gap where some floor boards had been pried up and never put back.

"Creepy," he said.

"This house—was it Anthorn's?" I asked.

"Somewhere around here. Yeah, come to think of it. So Ransom moved in and now he's tearing up the place."

"And the yard."

"Looking for Anthorn's money?"

"Seems a safe bet. He must finish with a room and then rent it out."

"Let's see what else we can find out here. Maybe we can start with that desk."

It was a beat-up old rolltop, with papers crammed into all the little nooks, and drawers packed with files. We started flipping through it, not even sure what we were looking for. Not until we found it—a little notepad in the middle drawer. The first few pages listed a number of real-estate sales dating between 1894 and '98. It had the prices and addresses, but no names. They totaled over forty thousand dollars. This must have been Ransom's estimate of Anthorn's fortune. The following pages were more curious. The first was headed "Next of kin." Underneath was a short list of half a dozen names and addresses. Two had the surname Anthorn, and all had been crossed out. Next was a page headed "Bank account?" and below was a list of various banks, most of them local, judging from the names. One after another they'd been crossed out. The fourth page was titled "Real estate elsewhere." Then followed a list of county names and their seats. One was "Hampshire – Northampton." All of them were likewise crossed out.

"Seems clear enough," Donaldson said. "He's using the process of elimination to figure out where Anthorn put his fortune. First, he checked all Anthorn's relatives. Then the local banks, probably using the pretext of his daughter's marriage. Then he must have traveled to all the nearby county seats and checked the deeds. He really went to some effort."

The next page of the notebook, and the last one with writing, had a single word. It was written large, then underlined and circled: "Lottie."

Suddenly, we heard a voice from behind.

"OK, stick 'em up!"

14

Before I go any further, I'd like to point out how free the previous chapter was from the usual sort of absurdities which populate a book involving Emmie. What you had was a glimpse of my life when I'm not operating in her realm. I had certain facts to investigate and I did so in a logical, forthright manner. And the people I encountered were, for the most part, the typical sort of people one encounters in everyday life. Sadly, my sojourn in the land of the rational was destined to be a brief one.

We turned around to see a boy standing in the doorway aiming an index finger at us. A boy I knew all too well. Little Cousin Pluribus. *Emmie's* cousin.

"What the hell are you doing here?" I asked.

"Followed you up on the train."

"Where'd you get money for a ticket?"

He shrugged.

I went over and cuffed him. "Little thief. How'd you get in here?"

"I saw you go to the cops, then that other fellow's, an' then here. When you were banging on the door, I climbed in a window. Wanted to see what you were up to. Then I saw Lottie's picture."

"Where?"

"In the bedroom there, on the dresser. An' then I found a bottle."

"Bottle of what?"

"Said it was rye whiskey. Guess I had too much. Before I knew it, I was asleep."

"Friend of yours?" Donaldson asked.

"My wife's cousin. But we can turn him in to the cops if you want."

"Turn *me* in? What about you two?"

"Maybe we all three ought to get out of here. I think we found what we needed."

We followed Donaldson's suggestion and walked over to the hotel. There I deposited Pluribus in my room.

"I'm going out for a bit. You better lie low. I'll have a waiter bring you a sandwich."

"What fun's that?"

"Suit yourself. But don't expect me to post bail."

"Likewise."

I had planned to send a supplementary wire to Emmie, in case they were worried about the little truant's whereabouts. But after this last exchange I decided to hold off. With a little luck, I could lose the nuisance before reaching Northampton.

Donaldson took me to another barroom. As soon as we sat down, I told him I'd left my wallet back at the hotel.

"Say, you're good," he told me. "Ever work on a newspaper?"

"No, I couldn't drink at that pace."

"Takes learnin'. So you think Ransom has gone to Northampton, to bother his daughter?"

"Or found a minion to do it for him."

"McCrea?"

"Possibly—he was seen talking to her."

"Seen by you?"

"No, but a reliable source."

"Maybe I can head back with you and talk to her myself?"

"How about leaving that to me? I already know her."

165

"All right. City editor wouldn't be likely to go along with it anyway. Where do you think McCrea went when he left Northampton?"

"Not far, I'd guess. What do you say we each look into it and share what we find out? You see if you have any luck figuring out where the money went, and I'll find out what Lottie knows."

"You're sure she doesn't have it?"

"She's working as a cook for a family. I doubt she has forty dollars, let alone forty thousand."

"And what about McCrea?"

"Well, I'll keep an eye out for him, and you do the same with Ransom."

"OK. But I still don't see what angle you're working."

"Well, for one thing, my wife's cousin is hoping to marry Lottie."

"The squirt?"

"The squirt's older brother."

"But she hasn't divorced Anthorn, has she?"

"He has no idea she's married. *I* only found that out today. She told me she was Anthorn's niece."

"I'll see what I can learn. But it looks like Ransom covered the obvious."

"Then maybe the less than obvious? Maybe he bought shares in U.S. Steel. Or government bonds."

"Or maybe a coffee plantation in Brazil?"

"Sure, and don't forget rubber in Malaysia."

"Looks like I got my work cut out for me."

We finished our beer and I walked back to the hotel. I doubt it will surprise you to learn that when I arrived, the room was empty. Just in case he changed his mind, I latched the door. Then I crawled into bed—my first night in a real one since we'd left Brooklyn.

I slept like a log until sunrise. Then I noticed some-one beside me. He must have snuck in via the window. I left the bed silently, then carried my things out on the fire escape and dressed there. It meant leaving without taking the time to wash, but desperate times call for desperate measures.

Unfortunately, the beat cop who witnessed my de-scent interpreted the situation differently.

"In a hurry, huh?"

"Ah, it's not what you think, officer. I was about to go inside and settle."

"Sure you were."

It was a sticky situation, from which I saw no easy escape. Then it became palpably stickier.

"Where you going, Cousin Harry?"

Pluribus had come out on the fire escape, acting the forlorn child. No doubt he'd observed the cop, because now he whined an addendum, "Oh, please, Cousin Harry, don't leave me all alone again!"

The cop stared up at him, and then turned his head slowly back to me. His eyebrows were raised in a way I couldn't help but find worrying.

I sensed where his thoughts were running, and my supposition was confirmed a little later when he led me to the police station and booked me on suspicion of pederasty.

The desk sergeant was a friendly sort, as desk ser-geants go, even willing to listen to my explanation. And had I been able to think of a reasonable one, all might have gone well. But I was back in Emmie-land now. She herself may have been sixty miles away, but her psychic tentacles had me by the ankles and were drawing me into the abyss.

There was really only one choice: admit to skipping out on the hotel bill.

"Money's a little tight. See, the boy's an orphan. Had no one else to turn to. We're on our way to Northampton. The boy has an aunt there. I had thought he was right behind me, but seeing the officer must have frightened him."

If I were as good a liar as Emmie, that might have been the end of it. Unfortunately, I'm a very bad liar. The sergeant remained doubtful. Then came the unexpected. Pluribus put in with me.

"It's all my fault, officer," he sniveled. "Cousin Harry told me to follow him, but I went back for my slingshot. Please don't put him in prison! He's all I got now!"

He was Emmie's cousin, all right. The charges were dropped. And when they learned we barely had enough for train fare, they took up a collection to cover the three-dollar hotel bill. It was a touching scene, though not as touching for those of us who know the lowest patrolman takes in that much through graft in a bad week.

For the first leg of the journey back, we both dozed. But after we'd boarded the train in Greenfield, I quizzed him about his activities.

"What were you planning on doing? Just spy on me?"

"I figured it had something to do with the murder, so I wanted to be in on it. But now I know you're looking for someone's money. Who's Anthorn? And what's Lottie got to do with him?"

"Well, that's all pretty involved. The less you know, the better."

"Ain't better for me. Not if there's money at the end of it. If I were you, I'd be considering what story you're going to tell Cousin Emmie when we get home. Be tough for you if I tell her you took me along and kept me out of school yesterday."

"Are you trying to blackmail me, you little degenerate?"

"Why not? All I'm asking is you tell me what's what."

"All right. But you have to keep it under your hat."

"Sure."

"And this time, mean it. Not a word to Hal."

"Yeah, yeah. OK."

"Remember that old guy who was hanging around McCrea's corpse that first day?"

"The nut givin' out pardons?"

"Right. Well, he's Anthorn. He made some money back in North Adams. A lot of money. Then he decided he liked being President McKinley and got sent to the hospital."

"What's that got to do with Lottie?"

"Well, in between making the money and going nutty, he married Lottie."

"Oh. So that's why she won't marry Hal."

"Of course, even if she didn't have a husband, she just might not want to marry Hal."

"But why shouldn't we tell Hal?" he asked.

"Well, it would be better if she told him. Let me talk to her and see what she says. But whatever you do, don't mention it to Hal."

"I said I wouldn't, didn't I?"

"Yeah, that's what you said."

"Now we better come up with a story to tell Cousin Emmie, somethin' that gets us both off the hook."

"Sounds like a tall order," I told him. "What if she

found out the teacher's been lying about you?"

"She won't talk. She'd lose her job. I got her over a barrel now."

This kid was like one of those dark villains you meet in a Dickens novel. I had to remind myself he was twelve years old.

"Did you tell Cousin Emmie about us finding the grave?" he asked.

"I told her you *said* you had found it. But at the time, we were both sure you were lying."

"Well, that's what you get for not trustin' me. You didn't say anything else, after you saw it yourself?"

"No, but I did talk to Hal about it."

"Yeah, me too. But he won't mention it to Cousin Emmie. So we just change it around some."

"How?"

"We tell her that I was lying then. But later, after school yesterday, I really did find it. And you told me you were going to North Adams. So when I found the grave, I caught a train and went up there to tell you."

"Why?"

"Well, 'cause I wanted to be in on the investigation, naturally."

"Sounds pretty weak. Maybe I'd be safer just telling her the truth."

"Maybe. And maybe Cousin Emmie can tell me what pederasty means...."

By now the kid had made me nostalgic for Snide Sam and his crony with the cauliflower ear.

"I bet you torture small animals, don't you?"

"Why'd you say something like that? I'd never hurt any animal."

"You save it for humans."

"Only ones who don't play fair. How'd you get the money for the train?"

"What's that to you?"

"Nothing. But you were flat broke the day before."

"You search my things on a daily basis?"

"Not just yours. I borrowed my fare from Hal. He ain't as careful as Gloria."

"It's amazing you've made it this far with no one drowning you."

It was mid-afternoon by the time we arrived at the house. Emmie had gone out and her mother gave us a late lunch. By way of explanation for his absence the night before, Pluribus told her a story so ludicrous I myself couldn't follow it. It involved rescuing me from a couple of bomb-tossing anarchists who were bent on my destruction. I suppose it was having spent twenty years living with Emmie which allowed her to accept his story without question.

"Well, at least you're safely home now," was all she said, then went back out to her garden.

"What do we do next?" Pluribus asked.

"After I take a bath, I'm going over to the Cables' and see if I can talk to Lottie. Alone."

"What about me?"

"What do you usually do on a Saturday afternoon? Rob banks?"

"Thought about it. Never tried it. You?"

"Me? No, that's not my line. I'm more of a bounty hunter."

"Shoot anyone?"

"Not yet. But if I do, you'll be the first to know."

When I arrived at the Cables', I walked around the house to the kitchen. I hoped to see Lottie without encountering anyone else. Unfortunately, Elizabeth was reading in the garden and saw my approach.

"Harry, there's something I left unmentioned. It's a rather obvious point and I expect you thought of it yourself, viz., James's lecture this evening."

"His lecture? What about it?"

"Well, obviously it's imperative that we keep Emmie from attending. My stand-in for James should pass muster with someone who has only seen old photographs, but won't if she's seen him in person the evening before."

"Given the whole reason Emmie's come to town is to see James, that might prove difficult."

"I'm sure you can manage it if you put your mind to it. Also, I'd like to see her manuscript for myself. Do you think you could arrange that?"

"Doubtful. At least not without risking my life. But isn't the idea to get her to hand it over to your fake Henry James tomorrow?"

"Yes. But in case that doesn't come off, I'd like to at least have a chance to peruse it. Oh, and one more thing. You might have a talk with Gloria. She's become rather difficult."

"How so?"

"I took her to dinner again last night, at the hotel. The waiter had just served a confit of goose breast...."

"Wrong fork?"

"No, she has the mechanics of the table down admirably. But she greeted the waiter by his first name...."

"Well, she does work there herself."

"Yes, but that isn't the worst of it. She stopped him as he approached the door—'Say, Jim, why don't you show Mrs. Tibbitts your scar?' He demurred, but she insisted he pull up the leg of his trousers so I could see the salamander-shaped scar on his kneecap."

"And was it salamander-shaped?"

"Oh, yes, indeed. A very close resemblance. But that's not really the point. When I suggested having servants exhibit their scars during dinner might strike others as too familiar, she became contumacious."

"Contumacious?"

"Mutinous."

"Mutinous?"

"For God's sake, you went to college. Surely you know the word mutinous."

"Yes, just not in the context of the dinner table."

"Well, the point is, she now simply refuses to follow my directives."

"Ah. I'll have a word with her."

I realized then it had probably been a mistake to place a willful girl who grew up on a hill named for an insect under the tutelage of a condescending snob used to speaking in edicts. But one lives and learns.

I found Lottie in the kitchen and asked if I could speak with her. She put me to work peeling potatoes.

"I was up in North Adams yesterday, Lottie."

She'd been rolling out dough, and stopped midway through a pass. Then she spoke, quietly, and without turning toward me.

"Did you have business there?"

"Well, frankly, I was curious about some things. Do you know a fellow named McCrea? Works at the hospital?"

She turned toward me now. "What do you know?"

"That John Anthorn isn't your uncle, for one."

"I see."

"Also, that there are people looking to find out where his money went."

"There is no money!"

"Do you know what happened to it?"

"No. But I know John has no fortune stashed away somewhere."

"But McCrea thinks he does?"

"Yes. My... Well, someone told McCrea that."

"Your father?"

"Yes. My father. Did you talk to him?"

"No. He wasn't in town. Have you seen him recently?"

"No. Why?"

"Well, I suspect he may be planning to visit you."

"How would you know that?"

"That would be difficult to divulge. How is it you're using the name Flagg?"

"It's my mother's maiden name. I just didn't want to be found."

"Your father's obsessed with Anthorn's money, isn't he?"

"Yes. It's all he thinks about. He's the sick one. John would have been fine without him."

"Do you love your husband?"

"No.... He's a good man, but no, I never loved him."

"There are divorces."

"I couldn't do that to him."

"He seems content enough at the hospital," I pointed out.

"I'm glad. But you should go now and let me get dinner on."

"All right. I'll see you tomorrow."

"Tomorrow? ...Oh. Margaret's dinner. All right."

I left her and walked over to the Plymouth. I found Gloria folding linen in the basement.

"I take it things aren't going well with Elizabeth?"

"The woman's impossible. Treats me like a dog she's training."

"If it makes you feel any better, she treats everyone that way."

"No, it doesn't, really. I know enough now, Cousin Harry. You don't have to worry. I won't make a fool of myself."

"No, of course not. Still, it might be a good idea to at least drop by and thank her for her help."

"Why?"

"Well, Elizabeth isn't the sort of person you want to be on bad terms with."

"Are you saying she's dangerous?"

"Dangerous might be too strong a word. But she can be extremely unpleasant when she wants to be—and she often does."

"I'll send her a thank-you note. I suppose I do owe her that. She bought me a lovely dress yesterday. Will that be all right?"

"That would do nicely."

From there I started for the house. But up at the next intersection, I saw Emmie crossing the street toward me. I was all prepared with a story for her—based partly on the truth and partly on the construction of events Pluribus outlined on the train. But instead of grilling me, she just stared at me dejectedly.

"Hello, Harry."

"Hello, Emmie. Everything OK?"

"No. It's not. Is there somewhere we can go for a drink?"

"We can try Rahar's Hotel."

"Yes, of course. That will be fine."

I wasn't sure what to make of it. In nearly five years of marriage, I'd seen Emmie in this state only a handful of times. To call her indomitable would be an understatement. Particularly when it came to her literary ambitions. They'd been thwarted in every way imaginable, for years now, and yet she was always eager to try some new approach. I bring this up because I noticed then that she was pressing her manuscript up close to her chest with both hands.

We sat down and had the waiter bring us cocktails.

"Well, Harry, I imagine you'll be happy to learn that my writing career is over."

"Why? What happened?"

"I met with Mr. James this afternoon. He was sitting for some photographs in Miss McClellan's studio. She's a Smith alumna and I'd met her before. She allowed me to sit in. Then I managed to persuade Mr. James to look at the first few pages of my book. He groaned at the thought, but felt too constrained by circumstances to refuse. He read intently for a few minutes. Miss McClellan said he was at his most expressive while reading it. I thought that encouraging. But then, when he'd finished reading, he handed it back to me and asked, very pleasantly, if I'd tried my hand at dime novels. It was rather devastating, Harry."

"Well, the man's an ass, Emmie."

"It's kind of you to say so, but literary opinion is otherwise."

"Literary opinion be damned. Who cares about literary opinion?"

"Authors do."

Her point was difficult to contest, so I tried deflecting her attention.

"Cheer up, Emmie. Things are heating up in the murder investigation."

"Seriously? Have you really learned anything noteworthy?"

"I have indeed. I've lots of juicy intelligence."

She listened attentively as I briefed her on all that had happened. Starting with how Pluribus's story of finding the grave had turned out to be true. And how Hal feared he might have killed McCrea, and how he and Mr. Grundy transported the corpse.

"How perfectly gruesome," she said, her upper lip betraying a telltale smile.

I went on to recount the events in North Adams and what I'd learned about Anthorn's fortune, Lottie's evil father, and her marriage. Though nothing regarding my encounter with the police.

"Harry, this is turning into a proper case, isn't it?"

What she meant, ironically, was that it had all the elements of a dime novel. But given the recent remarks of the genius James, I kept that observation to myself.

"What do you plan to do next?" she asked.

"Talk to Mr. Grundy's daughter, Jane. I'm curious as to why her father convinced Hal to bury the body rather than contact the police. And I suspect it involves her. Do you know her?"

"Casually. Her older sister was a high-school classmate. That's how Hal got the job. Jane works at a café, just up the street. Maybe we could go there for dinner."

"Good idea. But there is one thing...."

"I have money, Harry. At least, what you left me."

15

I suppose I should have been thankful to Henry James for having accomplished what I couldn't. I only wished he had achieved it without so blunt an instrument. As trying as I sometimes found Emmie's haughty self-assurance, her moments spent in humble reflection were worse by far.

As we made our way to the café, she was again carrying the manuscript at her breast. Every few steps her eyes would drift down to it and I could almost feel her shudder. Poor Emmie. Humility didn't become her. A further diversion was in order.

I told her about the Neigh-itties, the river nymphs who swam naked for the amusement of Northampton's youth.

"Naiades?"

"Yes, I suppose that's what they're aiming for. It seems Jane is a sort of nymph-priestess. Gloria was headed to one of their gatherings that first night, when you caught her leaving the house. According to her, Jane went out alone. And there's a good chance she might have encountered McCrea that night."

"The night he was killed?"

"Yes. Hal told me that when he heard McCrea had been killed, he told Mr. Grundy and suggested they go to the police. But Mr. Grundy advised against it. He suggested they instead go out and bury the body."

"So you think Jane might have told him she had hit McCrea?"

"Something like that."

The café was busy, it being a Saturday night, but we did manage to be seated among Jane's tables. Once things slowed a bit, she sat with us. She and Emmie exchanged news. We heard all about her sister—the cramped home in Worcester and the various illnesses of the three children, plus an extended exploration of the husband's drinking habits and poor posture. Luckily for him, she was called back to work before she could delve into his bad points.

When she finished for the evening, we walked out with her.

"There is something else we wanted to talk to you about, Jane," Emmie told her. "Last Sunday night. Were you out at the river... swimming?"

"Has Gloria told you?"

"Only confirmed what I'd heard elsewhere," I said.

"We know about the Naiades. But that's not what we want to talk about. That night, Gloria had arranged to meet you, but I caught her leaving the house and she went back with me. Did you see anyone else that night?"

"No. No one else came at all."

"Where exactly is it you go?"

"Up above the pond."

"So not far from the Cables' home?"

"No, not far. Why?"

"Are you sure you didn't see that McCrea fellow?" I asked. "He was out along the river there."

"Yes, I'm sure. I went out and waited, then when no one else came, I went home. Why are you interested in Bill McCrea?"

"Well, it's tangential to another matter. Did you mention having gone out to your father?"

"My father? No, of course not."

"So he had no idea you were out that night?"

"Well, I think he suspected. While I was down along the river, I slipped on a rock. I didn't realize it at the time, but I must have cut my shin. I went home and got into bed without turning on a light. When I woke in the morning, I saw blood on the frock I'd been wearing. I rushed to the sink to wash it out. Father was just coming out of the bathroom."

"He saw the blood?"

"I don't know. But he was suspicious. He knows I go out at night sometimes."

"Did either of you mention McCrea's name?"

"No. Not then. Father had seen him talking to me a couple times and warned him off. But he treats every boy who comes near me that way."

"Except Hal," I noted.

"Yes, except Hal. Why are you asking about all of this?"

"Well, it's pretty complicated. But I think maybe you should tell your father just what happened that night."

"Not about the Naiades?"

"Just tell him you were planning to meet Gloria, but that I intercepted her," Emmie told her.

"And make sure you emphasize that you cut yourself."

"All right. He can see the scab if he likes."

She said good-bye and hurried off to meet her friends.

"Do you think she's telling the truth?" Emmie asked.

"Yes—I suspected something like that."

"Something like what?"

"Like her father seeing her washing blood from her

frock. He must have assumed she'd been out that night. So when he heard McCrea had been killed, he deduced she'd had an encounter with him."

"What makes you sure she didn't? What if McCrea, seeing her alone, and vulnerable, tried to force himself on her?"

"Not likely, and mostly for the same reason Hal couldn't have done it. They both were miles from where McCrea died. And his wound was on the back of the head. If she'd been resisting his advances, she might have managed to pick something up and give him a blow to the front of the skull, but not the back."

"Then who do you think killed McCrea?"

"That's the problem. Anthorn might have had the opportunity to kill him, but when the body was moved, he was locked up. The only suspect left is your dentist. I found the book he threw from the train not ten feet from the body."

She made a noise. "Why can't you just admit you threw the book, Harry? The spine is compromised, you know."

"I'm glad it isn't out in my name."

"Quit being silly. He wasn't killed by a book."

"Well, then I suppose we'll just have to think on it."

Unfortunately, leaving her to her thoughts was the worst possible course. I watched as her eyes drifted down to the manuscript once again at her breast. I had just one more arrow in my quiver.

"How about another cocktail before going home?"

"Why not?" she said without enthusiasm.

As we started back to Rahar's, I contemplated how best to introduce the subject of Elizabeth and her plot. Here, Emmie gave me some assistance.

"You know, I think all this worry about my writing is making me paranoid, Harry."

"How so?"

"This morning, I would have sworn I saw Elizabeth Strout. Or Tibbitts, I should say. Right here in Northampton. I even tried to follow her."

I responded with a noncommittal "hmm" and said no more until we had our drinks in front of us.

"Tell me, Emmie. Do you still plan to attend Mr. Cable's dinner tomorrow night?"

"Oh, that. I forgot all about it. No, I must send Margaret a note."

"Well, there's no need for that."

"Why not? It's a matter of simple courtesy."

"You see, that probably *was* Elizabeth you saw this morning."

"She's in town? To see Henry James?"

"Actually, I don't think she's interested in him, specifically. She's here to thwart your seeing him."

"I wish she had.... But how did she plan on doing that?"

"By having you attend an alternate dinner. One at which she supplies her own Henry James."

"Her own Henry James?"

"A friend of her father's. He apparently bears a striking resemblance to James. Or at least a passing one."

"How absurd. And where is this to take place?"

"At the Cables' home. The real dinner is being held at the Plymouth. Elizabeth is furnishing the phony James and I'm supplying the faux Cable."

"You? So you've been conspiring with Elizabeth?"

"I'm sorry, Emmie. I thought it was for your own good."

"You thought humiliating me in front of Elizabeth would do me good?"

"Frankly, Emmie, your literary pretensions were making you insufferable."

"I suppose I *had* let it turn into a bit of an obsession. Nevertheless, you conspiring with Elizabeth.... But I'll not be vindictive, Harry. There is some chance that someday, *someday,* I might find it in my heart to forgive you."

"Thanks. And besides, think what fun we can have. Now you can pretend to be taken in. Though it will require some serious pretending on your part. The cast is an eclectic one. First, there's Anthorn...."

"The man who thinks he's President McKinley and is really Lottie's husband, who may, or may not, have a fortune put away someplace?"

"Yes, that's him. He has agreed to set aside the duties of a dead President for the evening and will be playing Mr. Cable."

"Margaret agreed to that?"

"No, I led her to believe I was bringing in an actor from New York."

"But how will Lottie react when she sees her husband pretending to be her employer?"

"She already plans to avoid the company by staying in the kitchen. You see, the fellow playing Mortimer Vincent is a hospital attendant she's acquainted with and she wants to avoid him."

"So there will be three impostors at the table?"

"Yes, three. Unless you include Mr. and Mrs. Grundy."

"Hal's boss? The plumber?"

"Yes, he and Mrs. Grundy are playing a pair of

dramaturges masquerading as Shakespearean scholars. Apparently they stage a play at the Elks Club each year, so there is some justification for the first of their claims."

"And you thought I'd be fooled by these people?"

"Well, I admit at some point I lost sight of that goal and got carried away with the spirit of improvisation. But it should make for some interesting dinner conversation."

"Did you give yourself a role?"

"Hal and I will be waiting table. I thought you'd believe I was doing it for the money."

"What, work? That would be a change. And what is it Elizabeth expects to occur?"

"Of course, she didn't anticipate your meeting Henry James today, so she was operating on the assumption you would want to give him your manuscript at the dinner."

"And so she would have my manuscript. Well, now. We'll see about that."

We had another round, but by then Emmie was lost in thought. I could only hope that her morbid musings on her authorial career had been swept aside by healthier ones involving her former friend's ruination. She suggested a walk and I paid the check. When she left the table without her manuscript, I took it as a good sign. Though I dutifully went back for it.

We'd gone only a block or two when we encountered Gloria in the company of Mortimer Vincent—or his valet, if you're a stickler for detail. Not wanting to complicate things, I introduced him to Emmie as the real thing. She didn't seem pleased to see Gloria hanging on the man's arm, and that, in turn, led to some nervousness on his part.

"I asked Gloria to accompany me to Mr. James's lecture," he told us, hoping the serious nature of the outing would assuage Emmie.

"You went to Henry James's lecture on Honoré de Balzac?" she asked her cousin.

"Sure. It seemed like it would have been rude not to," the girl told her.

Emmie exchanged looks with me, then asked her what she thought of the talk.

"It was very illuminating, wasn't it, Mr. Vincent?"

"Oh, yes. Very illuminating. It's brought on a complete reassessment of my opinions in regards to the man."

"He's French, you know," Gloria added. "He and Mr. James must be very good friends."

"Yes, I believe they attended the same preparatory school," Emmie told her. "Now, if Mr. Vincent doesn't mind, perhaps you will join us for a walk, Gloria."

"Oh. Not at all. Until tomorrow evening, then. Good night."

We made little nods, and he went off.

"What's to happen tomorrow evening?" Emmie asked her cousin.

"Oh, well..." Gloria cast a desperate gaze my way.

"Ah. You see, Emmie, since we had this alternate dinner all planned for you, it just seemed like a waste to leave a seat empty at the real dinner."

"So?"

"So, I arranged for Gloria to go in your stead."

"On what pretext?"

"Well, on the pretext of being you."

"Mr. Vincent is going too, and it seemed like a perfect opportunity...." Gloria had gone too far. I signaled to her to cut it off. But not quite soon enough.

"A perfect opportunity for what?" Emmie asked.

"Well," I said, "for Gloria to gain some experience socializing."

She was dubious, but I could see the idea of subverting James's dinner appealed to her.

"I hope you aren't angry with me, Emmie. For taking your place. Cousin Harry thought it would be all right."

"Oh, it's quite all right. Though there is one small problem with the plan. Mr. James has now met me."

"Oh." Gloria made no effort to hide her disappointment. "I guess then..."

"Of course, I don't see why you can't go as yourself."

"But it's you who they invited."

"I'll give you a note, explaining that I was called away on another matter and didn't want to leave them short a guest at the table. Once you're there, propriety will dictate that they welcome you."

"Oh, that would be a relief. Having to pretend to be you on top of everything else..."

"And perhaps I can help you prepare?"

"Would you?"

"Elizabeth has been giving Gloria some pointers on how to conduct herself."

"Not anymore. That woman is such a shrew. I don't see how anyone can stand her. I'm sorry. I know she's your friend from school."

"Not friend, dear. What did she teach you?"

"Oh, just how to walk, and what fork to use for asparagus, and how to pose when someone else is talking. But nothing on speaking up myself!"

"Well, we'll take care of that."

This was Emmie in her element. She now had two adversaries and two dinners to undermine. And it being Emmie, you can be sure she'd take no prisoners. I had set the stage. But from then on, there'd be no controlling the script.

I was reminded of our own wedding, which included a denouement never to be forgotten—and I'm not referring to the ceremony itself, but to the episode at the reception in which Emmie had a friend of uncertain reputation pick the pocket of my then-employer, whereupon she mistakenly accused the man of murder. My employer, that is. This was just before we correctly fingered the father of Emmie's cousin Charlie's fiancée. It may sound like a recipe for disaster, but several in the party found it quite entertaining—though not said father, fiancée, or Charlie.

"I'm feeling a little sleepy," Gloria informed us. "If you don't mind, I think I'll just go home."

"All right," Emmie said. "But directly home. No visitations to the Plymouth... and no nymphing about in the river."

"You've heard about that, too?"

"Yes, I've heard about the Naiades. Fun's fun, of course, but there is taking a thing too far."

"I quite agree, Cousin Emmie. I'm too old now for such youthful indiscretions. It's time to think about settling down. Good night."

We bade her good night and she went off.

"'Such youthful indiscretions'? Where did she pick that up?" Emmie asked, I assumed rhetorically. "She didn't take that exactly as I meant it. Are you sure you've resolved matters with this Mortimer Vincent?"

"Oh, yes. No question. That's well in hand."

"What's well in hand?"

"Ah, well, the resolution."

"Do I have your word that Mortimer Vincent has no designs on Gloria?"

"Oh, certainly not. I mean, yes, you have my word. Mortimer Vincent is a confirmed bachelor...."

"And is that better? Or worse?"

"You saw the man she was with. I tell you he would never take advantage of the girl."

"Well, I suppose he didn't seem the type. But with a girl like Gloria, you can never be too careful."

"No, you're right about that. Which is why a fellow like Vincent might be just the thing for a girl like her."

"But you just said he's a confirmed bachelor."

"*He* is, of course. I just mean some fellow of that general type we met tonight."

"Meaning Vincent?"

"Who else?"

"Who else, indeed."

We walked in silence beside the pond they call Paradise. Still couldn't see it myself. But if we encountered any naked nymphs frolicking, I was willing to reexamine my position.

We went up a rise and sat down on a bench nestled among some shrubs overlooking the pond. We were both of us lost to our own thoughts. Where Emmie's thoughts were running, I can't say, but I was having a difficult time letting go of the frolicking nymphs.

Someone approached us, up the path from the opposite direction. From the sound of her footfalls, I surmised it was a woman out for a stroll. But before she reached us, she left the path, and then all was quiet. There was a gazebo not ten yards from us. As the moon was new, it lay in deep shadows. Nonetheless, it seemed reasonable to think she had stopped there.

Emmie held her finger to her lips. We were both anticipating a lovers' tryst. Perhaps not as diverting as frolicking nymphs, but still worth a listen.

About five minutes later, someone came from the other direction. Definitely male, but with an odd sort of gait. He'd walk for a bit, then trot, then walk.... It struck me as familiar, and apparently Emmie too. She turned to me with a sort of surprised look on her face.

The Lothario left the path for the gazebo, and our suspicions were soon confirmed.

16

"Pluribus?" the woman's voice inquired.

"Yeah."

"Do you have it?"

"No. She's out, an' musta taken it with her."

"Damn."

It was, of course, Elizabeth's voice we were hearing.

"Can you get it in the morning?"

"Sure. For a ten-spot."

"We agreed on five."

"Nix. You said five. I say ten. I'm the one takin' the risk. An' I want five in advance."

"You *are* Emmie's cousin, aren't you? All right, here. But if you don't come through..."

"What?"

"Don't you even think of crossing me."

"What makes you say that? No one's gonna cross anybody. Now, give me a kiss, so we know there's no hard feelings."

"Don't be ridiculous, you little vulgarian."

"A kiss or the deal's off."

"All right, dammit.... My God! ...Keep your hands to yourself! ...Now go before I call for help."

"OK, sweetie. If you want more in the morning, just give the word. I'll meet you back here at ten. She'll be at church with her mom."

"And not you?"

"Different church. They're Roman. Wanna try again?"

"Go!"

They went their separate ways and we sat in silence for a while. Then Emmie made the same observation I had earlier that day.

"He's only twelve years old.... I know they grow up faster in the country, but still...."

"He may have the body of a twelve-year-old, but he has the mind and proclivities of a fully formed social deviant. I don't want to tell you how to handle your family, Emmie. But if he were my cousin, I'd drown him before he got too big to handle."

"For God's sake, Harry."

"Suit yourself. But doesn't it bother you the little turncoat is plotting against you?"

"Of course it does. But I know how to handle him."

"Do you, Emmie? Like making sure he attends school?"

"Yes. Like making sure he attends school."

"He has you fooled there. He and the teacher are in cahoots."

"Don't be absurd."

"Imagine you were a schoolteacher and had him assigned to your class...."

"They're used to dealing with difficult children."

"Not on that scale. It was simply a matter of survival for her."

"What are you talking about?"

"They have a deal. He stays away, and she marks him present. Did you check on him yesterday?"

"When he didn't arrive home from school, I contacted his teacher, yes."

"And she said he had been in school all day?"

"Of course. You said he followed you to North Adams *after* school."

"In fact, he arrived on the same train I did. He just didn't show himself until later."

"But she'd be risking her job...."

"I'm sure she considers that a small price to pay to be rid of him. Face it, Emmie. We're not dealing with a mere delinquent, but a manifestation of pure evil."

"Oh, don't be hyperbolic. And I hope you realize you're only making the case that we need to take him in. It's all the more reason that someone needs to keep a closer eye on him."

"Over my dead body."

She made a noise—unfamiliar, and vaguely sinister.

While she dressed for church the next morning, Emmie called me into Gloria's bedroom. Her three cousins were off attending services at the Congregational church in which they, like most rural New Englanders, were brought up, and she wanted to take the opportunity to conspire. Emmie enjoys conspiring.

"Harry, I've decided I want Elizabeth to have the manuscript."

"What? You realize she'll probably just destroy it."

"She might. But curiosity will drive her to read it before she does, and that would give me great pleasure." She smiled to herself in the mirror, and looked thoroughly pleased with how pleased she was.

I could understand her thinking. Elizabeth did come off very badly in the book, particularly where she betrays her own father for a purse of gold.

"Besides, I have the previous draft at home, and I think that may be superior. I have to learn when to stop fussing with a book and move on to the next. I'm going to hide the manuscript in here. But not so well Pluribus can't find it. You mustn't interfere, but perhaps you can follow him and confirm he's taken it to Elizabeth."

"All right, if that's what you want."

Shortly after, she and her mother went off to Mass. I was reading the Sunday paper when her three cousins began trickling in. Gloria arrived first, and just behind her came Hal.

"For God's sake, Hal, take a bath!"

"I told you! I already did!"

While she went off to her room, Hal picked up a part of the paper and perused the headlines. A breeze wafting through a nearby window suddenly picked up and seconded Gloria's prescription. A rather sickening thought crossed my mind. I lowered the newspaper.

"Tell me you didn't go out and put back that body."

He seemed unsurprised at my introduction of the topic. "Mr. Grundy said we *had* to, otherwise we *would* be guilty of a crime."

"Too bad he didn't consider that four days ago. Wasn't it a little... liquidy?"

"It was awful, Cousin Harry. Putricafication, Mr. Grundy called it. See, he knew what to expect."

"Oh? From his days as a grave robber?"

"His readin'. I bet he's read more books than Cousin Emmie. He anticipatated it would be... well, sloppy. We brought some oilcloth we use in plumbing."

"So you dug it up and you put it back where you first found it?"

"More or less. It's further in the water, so it won't seem quite so obvious. Oh, and the head..."

"What about the head?"

"Well... it came off. I tried settin' it back on, but it rolled further into the water. But Mr. Grundy said that was all right, because it was naturalistical."

"Does he plan on contacting the police now?"

"No, he says he'll discover it in a nonchalantly manner. Out for a Sunday stroll with his missus."

"Does she know about all this?"

"No, not a thing."

"Isn't he afraid she might find the scene upsetting?"

"No, he says she's a trouper—n' besides, her screaming will add to the very simitune."

"Yes, no doubt."

He sniffed the air some, then went off for another bath. A minute or two later, Gloria emerged, now dressed more colorfully.

"I'm going out for a bit, Cousin Harry. But I'll be back by the time Emmie gets home. For my lesson."

She left, and just as I was returning to my newspaper, I heard someone in her room. I crept to the door and espied Pluribus through the keyhole pawing through Emmie's things. He must have snuck in through the window. He'd just found the manuscript when I swept open the door.

"I..."

"You what? You little Benedict Arnold! Selling out your own cousin!"

I took the manuscript and cuffed him hard. It was even more satisfying than before, having righteousness on my side, so I thought I might as well make the most of it and cuffed him again.

"Now give me that five dollars!"

"What five dollars?"

I cuffed him again, with even greater enthusiasm.

"Listen, you little thief, don't think you weren't followed last night. Now hand over that blood money before I do some real damage to your skull."

Happily it didn't come to that, as my cuffing hand was beginning to feel the effects. He pulled a small wad of cash from his pocket and I grabbed it.

"Hey! That's my every cent!"

"I'll return it to its rightful owners. Now, if I were you, I'd leave town. Emmie knows all about your deal with the teacher and she's already making arrangements to have you put in a home for delinquents. A big, ugly place in Boston, with big, ugly jailers who torture their charges on a nightly basis."

"An' I bet she also knows what pederasty is. I'll just ask her."

"Try it. Think she'll believe anything you have to say now? Get out while you still have a chance. If they take you to Boston, you'll find out what pederasty is, all right."

"Where am I supposed to go without money?"

"Don't tell me you haven't got some more stashed away. If I were you, I'd head to California."

"California?"

"Sure. It's the land of opportunity. You don't have to homestead, just pick someplace nice and safe, like San Francisco."

You might be thinking I anticipated the earthquake of the next year, but that was sheer coincidence. My only thought was to get him as far away from Brooklyn as possible.

"I'll think it over," he said.

"You do that. But you better think quick."

He walked out of the room and then the house. I didn't dare hope I was rid of him yet, but I *had* pierced his irritating insouciance.

It was almost ten by then, so I headed out to keep

his appointment with Elizabeth. I found her back in the gazebo overlooking the pond.

"Hello, Harry. What are you doing here?"

"Just passing. Thought I'd say hello."

"All right. You've said it. Now you may move along. I'm expecting someone."

"Not another young lover?"

"What are you talking about?"

"Your assignation last night was overheard."

"Are you spying on me?"

Elizabeth is one of those people who, though completely lacking in scruples themselves, are nevertheless quick to take exception when others follow their lead.

"Surely you must realize I can afford to trust no one in this," I told her. "If Emmie finds out the part I'm playing, it will be the end."

"Of your marriage? Then I would think I'm doing you a favor. What are you planning to do?"

"Sell you the manuscript for ten dollars."

I pulled it from behind my back and held it out to her. She seemed surprised. But when she reached for it, I pulled it away.

"I understand ten dollars is the going rate."

"I've already paid five."

"Not to me."

"Perhaps you and Emmie *are* meant for each other."

She pulled two five-dollar bills from a little purse she wore around her waist and handed them to me. I gave her the manuscript.

"I won't insist on the kiss," I told her.

"Don't remind me of it. What a vulgar child."

"You're too easy on him. Satanic would be nearer the mark."

"Do you think Emmie suspects? About the dinner?"

"No, not in the least."

"Good. I'll read this now. You can come back for it at noon. Do you think she'll look for it before then?"

"They're at Mass. We should be safe."

"Well, now that you have your money, Harry..."

This was her way of dismissing me.

I arrived back at the house just as Hal emerged from his bath. After he dressed, I suggested we practice his waiting at table. I sat down and had him pour me glasses of wine until I was sure he had it right.

"By the way, Hal. There's something you should know. The fellow playing Mr. Cable tonight isn't Mr. Cable, he's a patient over at the State Hospital. The real Cable has other plans for the evening."

"Do you think that's a good idea, Cousin Harry?"

"Well, I did when it first occurred to me. He's the spitting image of old Cable. But that was before I found out he's Lottie's uncle."

"Her uncle is in the State Hospital?"

"Yes, he's rather set on the idea that he's President McKinley."

"Dead?"

"No, not dead. Unlike the real McKinley, he had enough sense to avoid the crowds in Buffalo."

"Oh."

"Anyway, don't bring the matter up with Lottie. I'm just telling you so you understand why we want to avoid her going into the dining room, or the others going into the kitchen."

"Oh. All right."

"One more thing. There's also an attendant from the hospital coming, Pat Moran."

"Pat Moran?"

"Yes, do you know him?"

"Sure, I know who he is."

"Well, he's posing as a travel writer, Mortimer Vincent. And the guest of honor, Henry James, is being played by an acquaintance of Mrs. Tibbitts's, Margaret's friend."

"Will anyone be who I think they are?"

"You and I. And Margaret. And Emmie, of course. And Mr. and Mrs. Grundy are coming as Mr. and Mrs. Grundy—but playing professors of English drama, so you shouldn't act too familiar with them. Unless you'd like to be introduced as a student of theirs?"

"No, I don't think I'd like that."

"Suit yourself. But it would fit in nicely with the fictional theme."

It was going on twelve when I returned to the gazebo where Elizabeth had herself ensconced.

She was still reading when I arrived, and held up a finger to warn me off. I sat down against a tree and gazed over at the pond. I could just make out Gloria being ferried by Mortimer Vincent. Their boat glided across the water, then disappeared into a thicket of shrubs.

I didn't like the looks of it. Under normal circumstances, Vincent—or his valet, anyway—seemed a pretty decent fellow. But what would happen on a small boat in a secluded nook with a girl so comely, and so, let us say, accessible was another matter altogether. Still, I hesitated, and it was only when I heard her emit a little yelp that I charged down the bank and then around to the thicket in question.

But there my fears were put to rest. Whatever the fellow's intention, he had steered them into an ardor-arresting bramble of raspberry and wild rose. With no need to intervene, I climbed back up the bank. Gloria, meanwhile, continued to yelp, drawing the attention of the many passersby perambulating about the pond. When the boat finally emerged from behind the thicket, her dress was in a state best described as dishevelment, and the onrush of air brought on by the collective inhalation of the perambulators caused the willows lining the pond to shimmer.

"Harry, you seem to have brought me only part of the book," Elizabeth interrupted.

"Oh? Where's it leave off?"

"Not long after the introduction of Walt Whitman's pond-snipe."

"Ah. An arresting passage."

"Yes, quite," she agreed. "You know, Harry, I've been aware for some time that Emmie's been using my biography as fodder, but I had no idea of the fineness of detail she'd achieved. I don't know how to account for it. She actually quotes a passage from my diary. It's as if she had someone spying on me. How well does she know Mélisande?"

"As far as I know, they've never met."

"But Mélisande's met you."

"Just that one afternoon. And I had no idea she was the same Mélisande as the girl who accompanied you back from France."

"Emmie must have met her through Miriam Springer, a classmate of ours, in New York. Mélisande stayed with her for a while that summer."

"Could be. But did you read that preface of Emmie's?"

"The preface to the second part? Yes, I read it. Emmie really outdid herself there—an airship? Dropping a crate on Prospect Park? The problem with her is that she's incapable of checking her imagination. What lunacy."

"That was my interpretation, too. But that was how I first heard the name Mélisande. And Eugenia, for that matter."

"Are you saying this trove she speaks of exists?"

"It exists, all right. I had assumed Emmie had created it over time, and then simply presented it along with the myth of its arrival. But how was it she knew three months before your return that you'd be coming with a girl named Mélisande? Or that you would name your baby Eugenia?"

Elizabeth thought about this for a while, then smiled her own self-satisfied smile. Unlike Emmie, the gamut of Elizabeth's facial expressions runs only to three. There's threatening scorn, combining a slightly curved lip and a cold stare; amused scorn, illustrated with an embryonic smile and eyes that ridicule (oh, yes, they can); and then there's the smirk of self-satisfaction. It was an act of generosity on my part to call it a smile earlier in the paragraph.

"It's simple."

"What is?"

"The explanation. The child's name was a guess. Emmie simply conjectured my vanity would bring me to name a daughter Eugenia."

"Your vanity?"

"Oh, I admit it, Harry. I am vain."

"You'll get no argument from me, but how's that equate to naming your daughter Eugenia?"

"It's Greek, you dolt. It translates to well-born."

"Ah. And Mélisande?"

"This is the part that surprises me. You remember how I spent several months in France?"

"Yes. In Étaples, on the coast."

"That's right. Well, Mélisande showed up at the inn I was staying at sometime that fall. Then, over several months, she gradually wheedled her way into my confidence. She must have been an agent in Emmie's employ."

"An agent in Emmie's employ?"

"You're surprised at the lengths your wife would go to in order to get even with me?"

"Well, I don't question she'd be willing to go that far. But the logistics of it seem a little daunting. She didn't even know you'd been staying in Étaples until the next summer, after you'd left."

"She said that?"

"We learned it from a couple we met in Maine. Two women."

"Oh?"

"Yes. Mrs. Naggle..."

"Ah. Let me guess. Mrs. Naggle and her playful companion Miss Clack."

"That's right."

"But the inn where I was staying is owned by Mr. and Mrs. Chappelle, whom Emmie met when we were all in Washington, just a year before. She must have been in correspondence with them and had simply not confided that to you."

"That wouldn't surprise me. But how did she employ a spy on the north coast of France from our apartment in Prospect Heights?"

"There are ways...."

If you found this last part of the exchange confusing,

don't be alarmed. The characters mentioned have no importance to the present story. I merely wanted to convey the complexity of Elizabeth's reasoning. She's the type that would go to any length to settle a score, no matter how trivial. And arrogant enough to imagine everyone else behaved likewise.

I wasn't sure now which explanation was more absurd, Emmie's account of a visitation by a futuristic airship, or Elizabeth's saga of byzantine intrigue. Not that it made much difference. As usual, my only role was that of the bemused spectator.

She handed me back the manuscript. "Does she have the rest of it here in Northampton?"

"Probably."

"Well, either you provide me with it, or I shall insist on a refund."

"Partial refund."

With that, we parted company.

17

Back at the house, I found Emmie ministering to Gloria and her abraded face.

"Don't worry, dear. We can easily cover it with a little powder."

"Oh, I hope so. Otherwise I wouldn't dare go out."

"Care to tell me how you wound up in the bushes? I don't suppose you were alone."

"It was all perfectly innocent, Emmie. Mr. Vincent just had some trouble steering the boat."

"Yes, I'm sure... all perfectly innocent."

"I happened to witness it," I told her. "A simple error in navigation."

Vindicated, Gloria went into her room. Then Emmie took the manuscript I offered her.

"What did she say?"

"She's convinced Mélisande is a spy in your employ, and that's how you became privy to her secrets."

"Didn't she read my preface?"

"She did, but she remained skeptical."

"We'll see what she has to say after the next parts."

"Next parts?"

"Harry, what I've assembled so far is just the tip of the iceberg. The archive extends far into the future. Once my books begin to presage her life, Elizabeth will be forced to realize the power I have over her."

"Emmie, maybe you ought to lie down."

"Why?"

"I think that sacramental wine's gone to your head."

"Think what you like, Harry. You'll see. By the way, why is it you're bringing this back and not Pluribus?"

"He disappeared, so I took it upon myself to betray you. I hope you don't mind."

"No, but don't make it a habit, Harry." She now evinced the most disingenuous of all her expressions. It combines what a novice in Emmie-interpretation might consider an innocent, even endearing, smile, and a pleasantly suggestive movement of her eyelids. I imagine the female mantis offers her mate something similar—just before detaching his head. Emmie, mercifully, was satisfied with the unusually edible midday dinner her mother provided us.

The absence of Pluribus made it all the more pleasurable. Unfortunately, following as it did so closely on his disappearance two days before, Emmie and her mother were both displaying mawkish concern.

"Probably off swimming or something," Hal said.

"Swimming?" Emmie repeated, perhaps recalling my suggestion of the evening before. "Harry, are you sure you don't know where he is?"

"Me? What would I know?"

Her noise was skeptical. "Nevertheless, perhaps after eating, you and Hal might go out and look for him."

Not having much choice in the matter, we obeyed. Hal went off to search swimming holes and I headed off to the hideout the little truant had taken me to a few days earlier.

He wasn't there, and when I felt inside the knothole for his tobacco pouch, I found it gone. This elevated my mood, but now I worried that if there wasn't some definitive resolution, I'd be made to search for the brat until he was found.

I went back to the house and told them about the missing tobacco pouch. As I expected, they attached no importance to this clue. But I had a plan. I snuck into the boys' bedroom and fashioned a farewell message in something approximating the kid's scrawl. I took it into the kitchen, where Emmie and her mother were washing dishes.

"Well, I was wrong, Emmie. It seems he's run off to the circus...." I handed her the note and she read it aloud for her mother. "Probably the best outcome all around," I went on. "He'll be happy with them. Do him some good, too."

Emmie looked me over, assessing. I might have taken her in, if Hal hadn't shown up with the little delinquent in tow—soggy, and as unctuous as ever.

"You know I wouldn't leave you, Cousin Harry."

I cuffed him. "That's for worrying your poor aunt."

"Harry!" Emmie shouted. "I think you'd better step outside with me."

She led me into the yard and handed me back the farewell message.

"You wrote this, didn't you?"

"Well..."

"So I take it you *have* been encouraging him to run away again?"

"I may have mentioned the many attractions of life on the road. You have to admit, Emmie, civilization just doesn't suit him."

"This has got to stop, Harry. He's just a boy. Promise me you won't try anything like this again."

"All right—if you agree to forget about him coming to Brooklyn."

"Yes, all right."

She acceded too readily. Something was afoot.

We went back in the house, where I was forced to explain to Emmie's mother that I had forged the farewell note as a joke. I tried every tack imaginable, but she simply refused to see the humor in it. Finally, I gave up.

Pluribus, of course, found it very amusing. I followed him into his room and would have cuffed him again if the others hadn't been close enough to hear.

"You fool. How many chances do you think you'll get?"

He just looked back at me with his repellent smile. You may have noticed that unpleasant smiles provide a recurring motif for this tale. And yet none of the rest were half so unpleasant as those emanating from this scalawag.

"No go, Cousin Harry. You had me thinkin' for a while, but Aunt and Emmie both *love* me too much to send me to Boston."

"Well, I don't. I'll be visiting the head of the school department first thing in the morning."

"They wouldn't listen to you. Teacher says I was there."

"Yeah? We'll see what she says when they put her under the hot lights."

He wasn't smiling when I left the room.

Gloria reminded Emmie of her offer to provide lessons in conversation, and she in turn enlisted me to play the foil in bits of dialogue. We helped Gloria come up with responses to the usual sorts of questions—where she came from, etc. But the farm girl worried her biography would sound too prosaic when compared to those of the others.

"Would it be all right, do you think, if I maybe added little bits here and there?"

"Such as?"

"Well, instead of saying I grew up on a farm near here, maybe I could say it was a plantation."

"A plantation?"

"Yes, one of those grand places in Georgia, or South Carolina."

"I think that might be difficult to do," Emmie told her. "Mr. Cable is himself from the South. And there's the matter of your accent...."

"Oh..."

"But she could have been raised on a banana plantation in Central America. Most of those are owned by Yankees," I helpfully pointed out.

Emmie liked my idea, but felt it needed some elaboration.

"Yes, in the jungles of Dahomey..."

"I believe that's Africa. How about Honduras?"

"All right," she acquiesced. "At the headwaters of a long, sinuous river, in the jungles of Honduras... Your mother was an Italian opera singer, on a tour of Mediterranean ports...."

"Caribbean ports." Geography is not Emmie's strong suit.

"Quit carping, Harry. I'll lose my train of thought." Then, turning back to Gloria, "Your father was a fugitive from American justice, accused of murdering his partner in New York—falsely, of course."

Emmie had been reading quite a bit of O. Henry the year before.

"Oh, that's perfect, Emmie. What was my mother's name?"

I answered for her: "The Countess de la Salsiccia."

"A countess!"

"Why not?" Emmie agreed.

"But why am I here, and not with them, in Daho-mey?"

"Honduras," I corrected.

"Oh, all right, Honduras then."

"Why, you've come to clear the name of your father, of course."

"Yes! And do I, Emmie?"

"Not yet... you are still trying to locate one last piece of evidence...."

"What?"

"A note, written in an obscure cypher, which proves it wasn't your father who killed his partner, but his ne'er-do-well nephew...."

"Whose nephew? Wouldn't he be my cousin?"

"Not your father's nephew, the partner's."

"Oh. All right, I think I can remember that."

"Now, is there anything else we should cover?" Emmie asked herself.

"Well, shouldn't I be able to speak some about Mr. James's books?"

"Yes, of course. The safest thing is just to compliment his diction."

"Diction?"

"His use of language. The marvelous way he uses complexity of structure to make the simplest thought, or movement, seem fresh."

"For those, at least, who can stay awake until the end of the sentence."

"Don't listen to Harry, dear. He'll have you speaking like a philistine."

"What about his books themselves?" Gloria asked.

"I don't think there's time to cover all of that," Emmie told her.

"Particularly since you haven't read any yourself...."

"Shut up, Harry. There is one of his you might mention. It's called *Trilby*. I believe Mr. James himself considers it his favorite of all his works."

"What's it about?"

"Artists living in Paris."

"But what happens?"

"Well, a lot of love-making."

"Like Laura Jean Libbey?"

"Yes, dear, just like her. In fact, if you both compliment *Trilby* and tell Mr. James how like Miss Libbey's work you find his, I think you cannot fail to charm the man."

"That sounds easy enough.... There is one more thing. Suppose... well, it may be a long evening... and all that wine..."

"Ah," Emmie intoned. "How to excuse yourself, if you need to..."

"Yes."

"Well, that's simple—"

"Yes, very simple," I interrupted. "You stand up, and in your clearest voice say, 'Excuse me, ladies and gentlemen, but I'm afraid I must take a message to Señor Garcia!'"

She repeated it back to me, then asked its meaning.

"It's a witticism coined by your Cousin Emmie. It might be obscure to someone your age, but the others are sure to find it very amusing."

I thought it best not to confuse the girl with the intricacies of the story, but in case it's new to you, I'll explain. "Take a message to Garcia" is a catchphrase dating from the war with Spain, just a few years before. The first time Emmie used the line in its ironic sense was in a barroom full of newspapermen in Washington. I made mention of it in my account of that adventure, and rather than trouble myself with an original explanation, I'll simply quote from that:

You see, there was a fellow named Elbert Hubbard who peddled a sort of philosophical quackery from his citadel somewhere outside of Buffalo. Well, right about the time the country was feeling all noble about freeing the Cubans from the Spanish yoke—and before it started feeling sorry about having to put the Filipinos in ours— he wrote a little tract about an American officer who was ordered to take a message to Garcia, the leader of the Cuban rebels. In spite of innumerable trials, tribulations, etc., the American succeeded and lived to tell the tale on the lecture circuit.

Hubbard's hackneyed depiction of the event brought tears to the eyes of simpletons the length and breadth of the country, and it wasn't long before the phrase "take a message to Garcia" came to be a cliché. It was chiefly used to goad some poor fellow who had sense enough not to take on an unpleasant task with the promise he'd be ennobled if he did. Any profits from the endeavor, naturally, accruing to the man doing the goading.

"All right," she said. "That was the one thing I worried most about. That the others will be so sophisticated, and I'll look the hick."

"Not after that line, you won't," I assured her.

Gloria repeated it twice more, just to be sure she had it down.

"Oh. There is one thing I'm not clear on."

"What's that, dear?" Emmie asked.

"What's his name?"

"Who, dear? General Garcia?"

"No, the nephew."

"Oh. How about Septimus?"

This alone she wrote down, then went off for her bath.

"That was a very good idea, Harry. I would love to see James's face when Gloria stands and delivers. The only danger is he may have become so Europeanized, he won't know its meaning."

"Maybe, but the delivery alone should be worth something. And what's this about James having written *Trilby*?"

"Well, he didn't, of course. But I heard that he was rather jealous of its success."

"Ah. Well done, Emmie. And the comparison to Laura Jean."

"Yes. Touché, Mr. James. Well, Harry, I think we've saved what promised to be a very boring dinner at the Plymouth Inn. Let us hope ours is equally entertaining."

"Oh, I wouldn't worry on that score. By the way, the manuscript you provided Elizabeth was only the first half of the book."

"Yes—I haven't decided when I'll show her the rest. Did she seem anxious for it?"

"Oh, yes. She'd just reached Walt Whitman's pond-snipe."

"Good. Let's see now if we can get *her* to humiliate *herself*. This will be fun, won't it, Harry?"

Fun wasn't the exact word I was imagining. Risky came closer. Elizabeth annoyed was dangerous enough. The thought of Elizabeth humiliated, however satisfying, chilled me to my very marrow—and then some. I doubted she had ever been so treated before. And if she had, there were unlikely to be any survivors able to tell about it.

At six, Hal and I made our way over to the Cables' to help set things up. The guests weren't due until seven, so I was surprised to find Henry James sampling the sherry well before that hour. He introduced himself as the author-genius, but when Elizabeth passed through she informed him I was in on the conspiracy and he reintroduced himself as Archie Cobb. The name struck me as familiar, but from what context, I couldn't say.

"I wonder, Mr. Reese, if we might have a word...."

He led me out to a secluded part of the garden.

"Tell me, Mr. Reese, what do you know of this Henry James?"

"Not much."

"Oh. I was hoping..."

"Didn't Elizabeth prepare you?"

"Well, she handed me a stack of books as we were leaving Utica...."

"Utica?"

"Yes, where we're both living. Do you know it? Dreadful place..."

"I grew up there."

"Oh, I am sorry."

"Not half as sorry as I was. So Elizabeth set you up with some of James's novels?"

"Yes. Or tried to. I've been holed up at a local hotel with a pile of them, but I couldn't get past the third page of any."

"But I bet you've been sleeping well."

"Oh, yes. However, Mrs. Tibbitts told me to expect your missus to grill me rather closely. And I wouldn't want to disappoint Mrs. Tibbitts, dear woman."

"No, that would be unwise. But you're in luck—Emmie hasn't done any better tackling the great James than yourself."

"Oh, that *is* a relief."

"I can share one bit of information. Of all his books, I'm told James is most fond of *Trilby*."

"*Trilby?* I had no idea he'd written that. Svengali and friends. Takes place in Paris, doesn't it?"

"Yes. Have you read it?"

"No, but they made a play of it."

"How was it?"

"Never saw it myself. But I did see Nellie Farren's burlesque of the play at the Opera Comique."

"Ah. That's how I prefer to take in my literature as well. In New York they called it *Thrilby,* with Svengali rechristened Spaghetti."

"Quite admirable. Unfortunately, I don't remember much.... But no matter. If your wife hasn't read it..."

Holding up his empty sherry glass, he emitted a truncated "Well..." as if its vacancy completed his sentence. I followed him toward the house just as Margaret entered the garden from the kitchen. She looked troubled.

"Anything the matter?"

"Elizabeth is insisting on running the kitchen."

"She *is* an excellent cook."

"Perhaps. But that kitchen has been Lottie's domain for years now. Harry, if we can all make it through this dinner alive, I for one will be truly thankful."

"I believe Henry James is inside dispensing sherry. Perhaps he'd spare you a drop."

"I don't usually drink. But perhaps an exception is in order."

As she went into the house, she passed Elizabeth coming out. Margaret, thoroughly piqued, stared coldly ahead. Elizabeth looked back over her shoulder at her.

"I never realized how peevish Margaret could be."

"Any cause for it?"

"Certainly not. I merely suggested to her cook that if she laid a finger on my *bavarois aux avelines,* I'd take it off with a cleaver."

"In backwaters such as this, you'll frequently find servants treated like something almost resembling human beings."

"How quaint."

"Speaking of backwaters, how are you finding Utica?"

"Need you ask?"

"Let me rephrase the question. How are you tolerating Utica?"

"Not easily. But it has its compensations."

"Tibbitts?"

"I wasn't referring to him. But I do find it amusing to, let us say, influence his career. And with so little effort. People upstate are so agreeably pliable. And there's much more money about than I ever would have suspected. But enough of that. Do you have the rest of the manuscript?"

"In a word, no."

"But Emmie will be bringing it?"

"Yes, I'm sure of that."

"I sense something odd in your manner. You aren't thinking of double-crossing me, are you, Harry?"

"Whatever gave you that idea?"

"Your nonchalance about thwarting Emmie seems exaggerated."

"I've been drinking all afternoon."

"Well, I hope for your own sake it *is* just the bravado of a drunkard. I would hate to have to take measures...."

"What sort of measures?"

"Oh, whatever presents itself. I imagine you still have family in Utica?"

"No one I'm particularly fond of."

"A mere inconvenience. Surely you don't think you're safe in Brooklyn? I know quite a number of people in New York. And quite an interesting variety...."

"But you don't count Snide Sam among them? Because you'd be doing me a great favor if you could put in a word for me...."

"Harry, I don't know anyone named Snide Sam, and if I did, I certainly wouldn't put in a word for you. Don't you realize you're being threatened?"

"Sorry, but he was in line ahead of you. And he has that friend. A big, ugly fellow with a cauliflower ear."

"Perhaps you should go inside and prepare for the guests. And don't think I didn't mean what I said...."

18

The front parlor had been providently provisioned to receive the littérateurs, and as the soft sun of early evening streamed in via windows opened to admit the cooling breeze, it provoked a propitious radiance in the bountiful array of bottled goodwill.

After taking Hal into the kitchen to chop ice, I positioned myself beside the table where the pre-prandial refreshments were laid out. There was, for the nonce, little for me to do. Archie Cobb (in the role of Henry James, and standing stage left) insisted he took nothing stronger than sherry. Though I noticed he took it by the beaker. Margaret, wearing a flattering cornflower-blue dress, had stationed herself near the door, ready to welcome the guests. She was taking her sherry in the usual diminutive piece of glassware earmarked for the task. But consciously or not, she refused to allow the vessel's dainty capacity to impede her intake. Every minute or so, she would walk over to my post, look at me nervously, and say, "Oh, *Harry...*" while holding out her empty glass. I would smile encouragingly, refill the glass, and then watch as she paced back to the door, where she alternately fidgeted and drank. We soon fell into a fairly precise rhythm. It was only when Mr. James compared us to the movement of a mechanical clock that the spell was broken. Margaret looked down at her empty glass as if she were surprised to see it.

"Oh. How many?" she asked.

"Two—less than four, certainly," James lied.

"It's only, normally I don't drink—at all."

"Well, no matter," he assured her. "The more one drinks, the more one may."

"The more one may what?"

"Drink, I believe is the idea."

"Isn't that mere sophistry?"

"Sophistry?"

"A meaningless, circular argument."

"Might I suggest you have another drink and think on it again?"

She shook her head dismissively and set the glass on the table. Then the doorbell rang. She hurriedly picked up the glass, held it out for me to fill, downed it, and set it back on the table. Then, after calmly smoothing her dress, she went to the door.

She returned with the Professors Grundy. Mrs. Grundy, whom I now saw for the first time, appeared the typical burgher's wife, stout, middle-aged, but spry and in no way retiring. She was dressed more fashionably than I would have expected, as was her husband, who wore a suit I took to be tailor-made. Plumbing was indeed a good business, and it seemed only fitting that the Cable residence should be blessed with a display of what its largesse had afforded.

"Hello, Mr. Reese," he greeted me.

His wife set her foot on his. "Don't be familiar with the help, you'll only embarrass him." She spoke in the clear voice of a thespian, but an octave too high and altogether too loud for it to be called pleasing.

"What would you have, madam?" I asked in a tone I hoped reassuringly distant.

"Rum punch, dear. If you got it."

"Certainly. I'll just fetch the milk."

In the kitchen, I found Hal working the ice pick while watching Lottie stir a pot. Though she didn't seem to be stirring with much vigor, her body swayed perceptibly with each circumnavigation of the pot, while the bow of her apron suggestively flagged the movement from behind. It was this bow, I believe, which had arrested Hal's attention. The ice bucket was overflowing onto the floor.

I pried the pick from his hand and ushered him back to the reception room. Mrs. Grundy greeted him excitedly.

"There's our Hal!"

She held out her arms. Hal went to her and received a kiss on the forehead.

"Remember, Mouse," her husband chided, "not too familiar with the help."

"But Hal's family."

"Not today, *Madam Professor,*" he reminded.

The genius James had shyly retreated to a corner, careful to take the sherry decanter with him. Margaret flushed him out and introduced him to the Shakespeareans. With him distracted, I retrieved the decanter and refilled it, though not for the last time.

"I imagine you're a great reader of the Bard, Mr. James," Mr. Grundy said.

"No, but I do frequent the theatres."

"Covent Garden? And Drury Lane?" Margaret asked.

"Oh, yes. And the Garrick, St. James's, and so on."

"And what have you seen this past season?"

"Well, to be honest, I rarely go in. Mostly, I just like to mingle among the crowd."

"Oh, I see," Mr. Grundy said. "To listen to their conversations, to help you with characters and whatnot?"

"Yes. And whatnot."

"I imagine you can pick out a good many little gems...."

"Sometimes," James told him. "More often than not I must content myself with some more trifling treasure."

"Trifling treasure?" Margaret asked.

"Oh. A mere euphemism... for a thing..."

"Please, Mr. James!" Mrs. Grundy interrupted. "I'm sorry, but I will not abide euphemisms. And most particularly *things*. Isn't that right, Monk?"

"It's true. We subliminate the word from all our productions."

"What word exactly?" Margaret asked.

"Why, any *thing* we come upon, my dear."

"Anything?"

"Oh, no, of course not. Just some things are *things*. It's only those which we must strike. Though I leave the striking to Mr. Grundy—he's more fallacious with the pencil."

"Though it ain't easy, I can tell you. The Bard, God bless him, was rather fond of it. And without a *thing*, there ain't no *it*."

"But *what* it?" Margaret asked.

"Oh, how does your father do it? And by it, you can be sure I don't mean *it*. I mean how does he keep you so innocent? Our Jane..."

"*Our Jane...*" Mr. Grundy chimed, mournfully.

"What's the matter with Jane?" Hal asked.

"Not a thing you couldn't put down, dear boy," the lady told him. "But let there be an end to this obstrepteraneous talk. I'll have no more of it."

I mollified her with another rum punch just as the bell rang again. This seemed to catch Margaret off guard.

The academics' digression on things euphemistic, not to mention the pronoun suggestive, had knocked her off her pins. I refilled her glass and slid it toward her. She seemed not to notice. Then, all at once, her hand shot out and brought the elixir to her lips.

Once restored, she set down the glass and went to the door. She returned with Mr. Anthorn and Pat Moran, introducing them as her father and Mortimer Vincent, respectively.

Mr. Cable (Anthorn) saw me hand Mrs. Grundy her rum punch and smiled broadly. I sent Hal to the kitchen for more milk while I poured Vincent (Moran) the three fingers of rye he wasted no time in asking for. Having detected from his manner—and been assured by his breath—that he'd already imbibed, I sought to dilute it. But he pulled the tumbler away before the water got within a foot of it.

When Hal returned with the pitcher of milk, I suggested he go in and set the table. This may have been optimistic on my part, but I was loathe to leave the guests, as I found the conversation reminiscent of certain exchanges I'd had with Miss Clack up in Portland two summers before. She too was a scholar of the Elizabethan vernacular.

But the room had, for the moment, gone quiet. Margaret, ever the hostess, took it upon herself to rekindle the colloquy.

"As I'm sure you are all aware, Mr. Vincent is a travel writer of no small renown," she announced. "Perhaps you could tell us of your latest adventure, Mr. Vincent?"

Having directed attention away from herself, she tapped with a fingernail her abandoned sherry glass still sitting on the edge of the table. She didn't take her eyes off of Vincent while I filled it, and then only briefly to down it.

"Well, let's see. I took a steamer.... Yeah, took a steamer to the Emerald Isle, land of my forefathers."

"Is Vincent Irish?" she asked.

"Ah, no. The forefathers of my mother. Foremothers, I suppose you could call 'em. Come from a place called Katie's Bend, or Bent Katie. She goes both ways. Real jay town. Only stem can't run more than two blocks. An' still manages six barrooms and a pool hall. Take the bend, an' there's three more saloons and a burlesque house that puts on a respectable leg show—ladies free, Thursday matinee."

"How... charming. And did you make it to Europe proper?"

"Proper? Well, let's see. Think it was up the Low Countries next. That proper enough?"

"The *Netherlands?*" Mrs. Grundy asked, with more irritation than one might expect.

"I suppose you could call 'em that, yeah."

"Am I to understand you put in down Netherlands way *after* taking the ramp in Ireland? And you call that proper?"

"Should it be the other way around?"

"*Properly,* there's no getting around to *it* after a visit to the bogs," she told him decisively.

Mr. Grundy wiped his brow, the Messieurs Vincent and James stared vacantly, and Margaret tapped her glass. Only old Mr. Cable seemed unaffected by the lady's unbending posture: she would not have Ireland taken out of turn.

"I always wanted to visit the Low Countries," Cable whispered wistfully.

This time, Mrs. Grundy's mate anticipated her indignation and his anguished groan provided a synchronous complement to her affronted brow.

"Visit the Low Countries?" she asked. "You of four daughters and a son? One of whom stands in your presence? Please, sir, no more of this humor."

Now the entire company—save Mrs. Grundy—stared vacantly, each in a different direction, while the lady approached me and asked for another rum punch. A long silence followed, broken only intermittently by the lady's slurping of her drink.

"Lovely weather we're having," Margaret ventured intrepidly.

"Yes," Mr. Grundy agreed. "Very nice, indeed."

"I hope it keeps up for the length of your visit, Mr. James," Margaret added. "And yours, Mr. Vincent."

Mr. Grundy eyed his wife warily, but she was too occupied with her punch to offer a response.

"Perhaps later we can take a stroll by the river," Margaret went on.

"We took a stroll this afternoon, didn't we, Mouse?"

"Oh. So dreadful. I wouldn't bring that up, Monk."

"Suppose you're right. Sorry, Mouse."

"But it was truly horrible," Mrs. Grundy herself went on. "A body. Rotten. Oh, what a stench!"

"And headless!"

"Really, Monk. This is hardly the time." The lady looked for a moment as if she might faint. "But it's true, nonetheless. No head to be found at all!"

"I sent for the police and they came out with their hook. Couldn't find a trace of it."

"Good God," Mr. James said, seemingly involuntarily.

"Ah, where was this exactly?" Mr. Vincent inquired.

"Out along the tracks, past the hospital," Mr. Grundy told him.

"Any word whose body it was?"

"McCrea. Bill McCrea. Police found his wallet. Worked at the hospital."

Mr. Vincent licked his lips and then held out his glass to me.

"Treasury, wasn't he? Never liked him," Mr. Cable said to no one in particular.

Margaret looked at me, pleadingly.

"I expect Mr. Cable is confusing him with the current Secretary of the Treasury," I told them, "whose name, I believe, is likewise McCrea." Not surprisingly, no one in the party seemed to have any more idea who the current Secretary of the Treasury was than I did.

"How far from the hospital?" Mr. Vincent asked.

"Not far. Out by that stretch of the old canal. I often take Mrs. Grundy by the old canal when we go out on a stroll."

"Take me by the canal? When we're out on a stroll? What would you have these gentlemen, and this lady, think, Monk?"

"Oh, I only meant out that way."

"Then take me by the hand, and I will forgive you. But the *old* canal, I cannot. Perhaps you find it *too* old to navigate?"

"No, Mouse. I know its every nook and cranny...."

"Mr. Grundy!" Her shock this time was not so sharp, and ended in a not quite stifled titter. Her husband whispered something in her ear, which caused her to blush. She slapped him playfully.

Seeing now the path to conviviality, I refilled her punch.

The whole company relaxed with the Grundys' reconciliation and soon Mr. James was entertaining his fellow authors, Vincent and Cable, with a deck of cards. The bell rang again, and while Margaret went to the door, I slipped off to the kitchen to see how dinner was coming.

"Has everyone arrived?" Elizabeth asked.

"Yes. I believe Emmie is at the door now. Shall I take the guests into the dining room?"

"What were they doing when you left?"

"Mr. James was offering an exhibition of his talents with a cold deck. I believe he hoped to interest the other gentlemen in a game of three-card monte."

"Oh, damn him! Pull him aside, Harry, and remind him he's being paid handsomely."

"What's the going rate for impersonating a genius?"

"Go on! Is the table set?"

"Hal's attending to that now."

"Well, make sure he doesn't muck it up. I want this to come off right, Harry. You *do* want to bring Emmie to heel, don't you?"

"Bring her to heel?"

"Why not?"

"The way Tibbitts has with you?"

Lottie let loose a truncated snort and Elizabeth glared at the back of her head. The poor cook shuddered at the unseen assault.

"Never mind Tibbitts," Elizabeth said, turning back to me. "Do you want Emmie spending her time writing books without prospects, and mooning over any author who gives her the time of day?"

"No, I suppose not."

"Well, then, we must work our subterfuge and get that manuscript from her. Now go. The soup is ready."

I found Hal in the dining room, straightening the name cards. There being an odd number of guests, four men to three women, I had placed Mr. Cable at the head and the others three to a side. Hal had balanced the entrée plates atop the smaller dessert plates and the fish plates upon them in turn, with the soup bowls taking the top position. Though not perhaps altogether proper, I noted he had them ordered correctly, and admired the economy of effort it would afford us later. As to silver, he had the general idea. But rather than an even distribution of implements, he had allocated them by size according to sex: women given the petite dessert forks and teaspoons, while the men were provided the more virile dinner forks and soup spoons.

"Looks perfect," I told him.

"And which of the glasses are for water?"

"Let's use that dessert wine glass, the little ones there, for water and save the goblet for claret. Go ahead and fill them now. And keep them filled, whatever you do. Things could get ugly if this crowd starts to sober up."

Mr. James had by then drawn the Grundys into his felonious game, and it was now Mrs. Grundy trying to correctly pick which of the three cards on the table was that which she'd been shown a moment earlier—before it had found its way back into Mr. James's dexterous palm.

Emmie stood near Margaret, enjoying the sherry and observing from the far side of the room. On my approach, Margaret excused herself and went off to the kitchen.

"Do you know who that is, Harry?" Emmie whispered.

"That depends on which *who* you're speaking of and what you mean by *is*. But I believe I know the cast as well as anyone."

"Why are you speaking so pompously?"

"Sorry. It comes with the servitude."

"I'm speaking of the flimflam man calling himself Henry James. I believe that's Archie Cobb."

"I can confirm that it is. But why is the name familiar?"

"From my book, you gink. Cobb is the con artist who travels from Europe with Mrs. Biddle."

Just so you aren't left in the dark, in Emmie's book, the thinly veiled fictional portrayal of Elizabeth is dubbed Mrs. Biddle. The name chosen as an additional gibe at her friend's expense.

"Oh, yes. Lord Archibald."

"Lord Abernethy," she corrected.

He was not an actual lord, even in Emmie's fantastic book, but had been given the title by his employer for some reason which now escapes me. Much of the reasoning in Emmie's books is elusive, so this didn't concern me. What *did* concern me was that I had once again been introduced to one of her characters. Whatever basis in fact her book might have had, you can be sure Emmie adorned it heavily with her imaginings. Even her journalistic work, which purported to be entirely factual, had been, by her own admission, invented from whole cloth.

My previous such encounter was with a character from one of those invented stories. Oh, but he was real enough. And once I had him trussed... Well, that's another book. Suffice it to say, I wasn't the least bit pleased about encountering a second figment of her unbalanced imagination.

I'd had a good deal of wine that day already, what with rehearsing Hal, and then Gloria, but decided reinforcements were now in order, and sent a large draft of rum down after it.

"Is that proper, Harry?" Emmie asked.

"Not just proper, but essential. And if you take my advice, you'll work on catching up." I paused to refill her sherry. "Oh, and you might try to avoid the word proper. And *thing*. And *it* should only be used with the utmost caution."

"What are you talking about, Harry?"

"You'll find out soon enough. Cheers!"

19

I coaxed the guests into the dining room through a combination of suggestion and coercion.

"The soup will be served shortly," I announced, then, fearing that with so literate a crowd my lexical imprecision might invite misinterpretation, added, "I mean, the soup will be served in a short while... and certainly not with any lack of civility." No one moved. They just stood there looking at me dumbly. So I stowed the liquor away while casually mentioning the claret was on the table in the other room. This carrot-and-stick work had the desired effect. Though not commonly acknowledged, the similarities between hosting a dinner party for literary luminaries and one for hollow-legged jackasses run deep.

While Hal helped them to their seats, I went to the kitchen and fetched the tureen of cold leek and potato soup. We managed to dish out the course without spilling more than a modest *soupçon*... per guest... on average. Poor Emmie got the worst of it, but only due to her own carelessness in distracting Hal by removing his tie from the tureen just as he was ladling.

"Perhaps Lottie can sponge it off for you," Margaret suggested.

Upon mention of the name, Mr. Cable (played this evening, as you no doubt remember, by Mr. Anthorn, late of his role as President McKinley, and, not incidentally, Lottie's husband) looked up toward the ceiling. "Lottie!" he echoed.

I feared now that he would insist on seeing the girl, who I had earlier assured him would be at the dinner. (But only before I'd been made aware that *his* Lottie was *our* Lottie, you see, for I was, quite innocently, simply trying to mislead him.) Fortunately, he chose instead to pass out, falling gently face first into his soup. So gently, in fact, not a single drop splashed from the precariously positioned bowl. I went over and lifted back his head and mopped his face with a napkin. He revived in short order and returned to his soup as if nothing had happened.

By and large, the guests seemed to appreciate the uncertainty of their stacked china, Mr. Grundy having the sense to buttress his with three well-placed dinner rolls. But his wife, sitting catty-corner to him, found the wobbling inexplicable. She went so far as to push away her claret. From then on, she watched the bowl suspiciously as her soup rippled with each movement about the table, imagining, perhaps, that at any moment the lost head of Bill McCrea would come floating to the surface.

The second time Mr. Cable fell into his soup, I repeated my ministrations and he once again revived. The third time, however, annoyed me. I pretended not to notice. As did most of the others. But as at any table of jackasses, there's always one squeaky wheel.

"He ain't gonna drown, is he?" Mr. Vincent asked.

"I think it unlikely," I told him. "The gentleman had all but emptied the bowl."

"I'd just hate for anything to happen to him—if you know what I mean."

I suppose as Anthorn's keeper, Mr. Vincent, né Moran, had some basis for concern, but I still thought it forward of him. His ersatz daughter, Margaret, showed not the slightest interest in her faux father's predicament—

unless the speed with which she drained both her own and then Mrs. Grundy's claret was indicative of something other than mere thirst, or esteem for a fine vintage.

When Hal returned, we went about removing the soup bowls. It was Mr. Grundy who came upon the helpful scheme of using Mr. Cable's loosened tie to bind his upper torso to the chair back, thus enabling me to reach his bowl without waking him. He was still out cold, but his drooping head now safely above the table.

"Lottie get that stain for ya?" Mr. Vincent asked Hal.

"Yeah, she did," Hal said, displaying the wet silk.

As my eyes fell on Mr. Vincent, I noticed him smiling at me. It was a disagreeable smile. He had a disagreeable face, so there was no way of knowing if there was any meaning to the smile beyond general amusement. Still, since I'm remarking on it so long after the fact, you'd be wise to make note of it.

Hal took the bowls into the kitchen and returned with a platter of sole in a tasty cream sauce, which I was able to sample when I licked off the finger I'd needed to steady a portion while serving Margaret. Luckily, she was preoccupied with the Sauternes dispensed immediately before.

She'd been quiet up until then, the memory of her previous conversational forays still fresh. But fortified by food, and not a little wine, she charged once more into the breach.

"Tell us, Mr. James, which of your books do you find the most satisfying?"

"Oh, no contest there. The one that made the biggest pile, of course."

"And which would that be?" Emmie asked. "*Daisy Miller*?"

"*Daisy Miller*?" he asked. "Good lord, no. What an insipid name. Are you sure that's one of mine?"

"Oh, quite certain," Emmie told him.

Margaret held up her wine glass and I refilled it.

"Well, whatever I made from that was nothing compared to *Trilby*. I set the Thames on fire with that little flirt."

"And I was always under the impression George du Maurier wrote *Trilby*," Margaret said good-naturedly. "One learns so much at affairs such as this."

Emmie, however, was not so complacent in the face of his plagiaristic assertion, even if she herself had set it in motion during our preparation of Gloria.

"I feel quite certain it *was* Mr. du Maurier who wrote *Trilby*," she told James rather sharply.

James studied the wine glass he revolved in his hand, then glanced over at me, then back to the wine glass. The great man was thinking.

"It pains me to say it, but that was all a fraud."

"So you admit it?"

"Admit it? Why shouldn't I? That I allowed a lesser author's name to appear on my work, out of pity for the wretchedness his own failure had brought upon him? Why should I not admit it, Mrs. Reese?"

"I see. You sacrificed the acclaim the work garnered... but not the money?"

"Certainly not the money. There is a limit." He took a long sip of wine, then went on the attack. "But what of your own work, Mrs. Reese? Tell me, where might I have encountered it?"

"I'm afraid I've yet to find a publisher worthy of it."

"Ah, how disappointing. Then you must condescend to tell us about it."

"I'd be most happy to.... I think you especially will find it interesting. As it opens, it follows a young American woman, a newly minted mother, as she returns to her homeland after a long sojourn in France. She is a woman of the lowest order. A confidence trickster, a charlatan, a thief—a woman uninhibited by even the slightest scruple, a woman who knows not the meaning of shame."

When I brought a stack of fish plates into the kitchen, Elizabeth pulled me aside.

"Has she given Cobb the manuscript?"

"Not as yet. She's providing him an oral summary of the book. She was enumerating her heroine's myriad qualities as I absented myself from the room."

"Yes, I'll bet she is. Why are you talking like such an ass?"

"I thought it part of the job."

"Your job is to make sure I get that manuscript. Has she definitely got it with her?"

"She has her satchel, and I'm sure it must be in there."

"Where is that?"

"She's kept it with her, on the floor beside her chair."

"Well, let's not wait to see if she hands it over to him. You may take in the lamb now. While serving it, you must contrive a way to get the manuscript and bring it to me. I'll be in the garden."

"To hear is to obey, O Great Mistress."

"Shut up and do as you're told."

After filching a roasted fig in a tasty wine sauce, I took in the rack of lamb. Emmie had just reached the point where Elizabeth, as Mrs. Biddle, betrays her father.

"Her confederate in that affair was a man named

Cobb, Archie Cobb. Perhaps you are familiar with the name, Mr. James?" Emmie asked.

Cobb took a long draft of wine, then looked skyward for a moment.

"No, no, I don't believe I am, Mrs. Reese. But do go on...."

Emmie looked annoyed. Obviously, she had hoped to shock the old fellow with her knowledge of his and Elizabeth's underhanded dealings on the boat over.

Meanwhile, Hal held the platter and I served the lamb. Mr. Anthorn had awoken, so we untrussed him for the entrée. When we got to Emmie, I slid her satchel away from the chair with my foot. She gave no indication of having noticed, beyond a smile flashed at me briefly as she continued with her antagonizing of Henry James.

"This Cobb is himself a fraud of the first order."

"Of the first order? Why, good for him," James told her. "That which is well done, is twice done."

"You sound as if you know the double-dealing man. One affair I could relate would leave no doubt as to his duplicity. It isn't in this book, but I expect to make use of it later...."

"And what is this affair you find so shocking?"

"Cobb seduces the wife of his host, an eccentric entrepreneur named Dexter. And under the man's own roof!"

"Are you sure?" James was sincerely interested now.

"Oh, I'm quite sure. One evening, when her husband is away, and after much consumption of drink... Well..."

"And tell me, how does his hostess take to the idea?"

"Excuse me?" It was not the response Emmie had expected.

"I'm curious to know the attitude of the lady."

"Oh. Well, she has been long neglected by her husband... and is, after all, only human...."

"Ah, you need say no more." James appeared quite satisfied with the fictional lady's disposition, but Mrs. Grundy not so.

"*Only human?* Human as a common trull, perhaps. You must strike her from your book, Mrs. Reese! Make no accommodation for this Doll Tearsheet!"

"Madam," Mr. James interrupted, "I will not have you speak of an honorable lady in this way. One must never judge from appearances."

I suspect the others at the table found it incongruous that the two were disputing the virtue of a character plucked from Emmie's invented world. Mrs. Grundy's views on fictional propriety were by now well known, but what Mr. James's motivations were in taking the opposing view were difficult to imagine.

Mr. Grundy groaned, and continued to do so when his wife started up again. She was more excited than ever, and her pitch rose with her ardor. The combination of his unremitting drone and her ever-shriller modulations brought to mind a college roommate, a fellow named Prinski, who took up the bagpipes and was nearly drowned in a fountain the school maintained for that purpose. I used this cacophony as cover to sneak Emmie's manuscript from the satchel and then spirit it from the room.

In the garden I found Elizabeth, patiently awaiting my arrival.

"Hurry up, you slouch, give it to me!"

I complied, and she took up the sheaf of paper like a boy anxious for the next installment of his nickel-an-issue adventure.

"Go!"

"As you wish, Mistress of All She Surveys."

I reentered the house through the kitchen door, and there found Lottie nearly prone on the floor, probing under the stove with a broomstick.

"Lost something?" I asked.

"Oh!" She quickly raised herself up off the floor, then patted down her apron. "It's nothing. Are they ready for dessert?"

"Not yet. Everything all right?"

"Yes. The blancmange—or baverwah, or whatever she calls it—is in the icebox."

Just as I entered the dining room, Moran rose theatrically from his seat and held up his napkin.

"Excuse me, ladies and gents, but I must take this message to Señor Garcia!" Then he turned to Margaret, his voice reverting to the conversational. "Ah, where would I find it?"

"Find what?"

"The, ah, washroom."

"Oh. Upstairs, second door on the right." When he left, she looked about the table, perplexed. "What a strange man."

"All writers are a little nutty," Mr. Grundy opined.

I worried briefly that Mr. Anthorn might be offended by the comment, but he was safely lost in his lamb. When he finished, I brought him another helping. I was hoping to make use of Moran's absence, and of the fact that Mrs. Grundy had, for some reason unknown to me, taken the floor again to condemn riverine fishing generally and the peculiar pastime of trout groping most particularly.

"Tell me, Mr. President," I said, sotto voce. "Had

you some recent trouble with your Secretary of the Treasury?"

"Greedy little viper. Never a thought for anything but money. But we won't be bothered by him."

Some might think a concern for money in a Secretary of the Treasury not altogether a bad thing. But Mr. Anthorn was evidently not among them.

As I refilled Emmie's wine glass, she motioned for me to come closer.

"Did you take Elizabeth the manuscript?"

"Yes, wasn't that the idea?"

"Of course. I just didn't want it to be too obvious. By the way, did you prompt Mr. Vincent's use of my exit line?"

"No—I meant to tell you. It seems it's taken on a life of its own. I heard a fellow use it in Philadelphia a few months back."

"How extraordinary."

"Don't be so modest, Emmie. It's a first-class line, and people are always looking for a novel way of going to the toilet."

She smiled. She was pleased with herself, of course. Not as much as if her writing had gained the same universal appeal, but we must take our satisfaction where we can get it.

I, for one, wasn't the least bit surprised it had caught on. There are, and I imagine have always been, innumerable euphemisms for the function in question. But one gets tired of seeing a man about a dog, and even the hospitable Widow Jones loses her appeal on the one thousand-and-tenth visit. Emmie's literary efforts may well pass unnoticed by humanity, but I have no doubt her euphemism for visiting a toilet will outlive us both.

We cleared the dinner plates and then brought out the blancmange, a jiggly sort of chiffon concoction made out of one part of the egg or the other. We had just served the last of the guests when Mr. Anthorn made an unpleasant noise and fell face first into his dessert. Once again I pretended not to notice, and the others followed my cue.

In my defense, I would just point out that by this stage in the meal, napkins were in short supply—due in no small part to the gentleman's previous submersions in his soup. And the sticky pudding promised to be even more difficult to remove.

With the serving completed, I allowed Hal to go to the kitchen for his dinner, while I remained dutifully at my station and helped the guests finish off the wine. It was some minutes later that Mr. Moran returned from his trip to Cuba, looking more disagreeable than ever. Apparently the mission had not been as successful as he had hoped.

He immediately set upon his dessert, and it was some time before he noticed his charge facedown in his own.

"Hey, he ain't gonna drown, is he?"

"I think it quite impossible to drown in something so airy," Emmie assured him.

"Still," Margaret said, slurring the word only slightly, "I wonder if you wouldn't mind righting Father, Mr. Reese? He's been like that so long, it's a little disconcerting."

Well, even if she *was* tight as a tick, I could hardly refuse the woman. Though I wish I had. I picked up the old fellow's head and found it just as sticky as I had imagined. I was surprised, however, to find it cold to the touch.

20

For the most part, the company took the news that their supposed host had drowned in his blancmange with great equanimity. The two exceptions were Moran and Margaret. The hospital attendant pulled me into the front room for a private conference. He worried about how he would explain to his superiors the demise of a patient he had brought to the home of a venerable author to imper-sonate said author. He became excited, even irrational, going so far as to accuse me of having a hand in the affair. I reminded him that as a mere waiter, I could hardly be held responsible. Unfortunately, this did noth-ing toward calming him—so I broke out the rye and poured him another three fingers.

Margaret's response was by far the more remarka-ble. When we got back to the dining room, she was laughing uncontrollably. And it wasn't a pretty laugh. By then she'd put away the better part of two bottles of wine and a half-cask of sherry, all in the futile hope of getting the better of her ever-rising nervous tension. Now the dam broke and let loose a flood.

"Oh, dear," Mrs. Grundy said. "I wonder if we shouldn't take her up to her room?"

"Yes, I think that's an excellent idea," Emmie agreed. "We'll leave you to clean up your mess, Harry. Good luck."

She looked back at me over her shoulder as the two of them escorted Margaret upstairs, smiling.

"Who would have thought you could drown in a

pudding?" Mr. Grundy said, chuckling.

"Ain't nothing funny about it," Moran told him. "I don't suppose you'd like to explain it to the doctor?"

"There's no need for a doctor, is there?" James asked, as he ferried a bottle of Calvados from the sideboard to the table. "When the ewe is drowned, she's dead."

"Who's you?" Moran asked.

"*What* ewe. The ovine female."

"What the hell are you talking about? And where are you from, anyway?"

"Boston, I'm told. But frankly, I don't believe it."

Personally, my views ran closer to Moran's. I had more or less arranged for Anthorn's being there and I wasn't looking forward to explaining the situation to the real Mr. Cable, who would likely be returning from his own dinner in the not too distant future.

Surmising that Grundy was too cheap to spring for a cab, I asked if he had driven his van.

"I did, Mr. Reese. The missus hates to walk in her good shoes."

"Then perhaps you might consent to helping Mr. Moran here return Anthorn to his rooms?"

"You mean help Mr. Vincent?"

"Yes, of course, Mr. Vincent. You see, it was he who brought along his friend, Mr. Anthorn, who happens to be a guest at the State Hospital."

"I get it. And now you want to sneak him back in?" Grundy said to Moran.

"Yeah. Something like that."

"I don't know if I could be a party to that sort of malpedience of the law, Mr. Reese. Much as I'd like to help."

"I see. You find the moving of bodies objectionable, do you, Mr. Grundy?" I asked, pointedly. "I've heard rumors...."

He looked back at me, nonplussed. "What sort of rumors?"

"The sort that would lead one to believe you were more open-minded on the subject."

He rubbed his face as if thinking the matter over, but now he knew that I knew.

"All right, I'll do it. As a favor to a gentleman."

"Great," Moran told him. "Now let's get going before he gets stiff."

Given Mr. Grundy's bad back, it was left to me to assist Moran in carrying out the corpse. I thought about calling Hal out from the kitchen. But I was a veteran of enough conspiracies to know that the fewer people involved the better.

When we got to the front gate, I tried holding my end with one hand while I fiddled with the latch. Tactlessly, Mr. Anthorn chose that moment to release a blast of vapor from his lower depths. The noise startled Moran and he dropped his end. This, in turn, caused the corpse to spin upside down. I was now in danger of losing my grip, and so quickly swung my free hand up under him, catching him hard in the belly. The blow dislodged something. A small object shot out of his mouth and landed under a viburnum. Preoccupied with the precarious corpse, I left it lying there.

The van had been washed free of the mud which coated it after its outing to the canal, but the odor lingered. We put the new, relatively fresh, body into the back and Moran and Grundy hopped up at the front.

"Tell the missus she'll have to take a trolley home."

But before he could pull away, Mrs. Grundy came out of the house.

"*What,* leaving without me?"

"Well, I offered to give Mr. Vincent a ride back to his... ah... hotel."

"We can drop him on the way, can't we?"

"Sure. Only I ain't stayin' at a hotel exactly. I'm roomin' with a buddy what works out at the hospital."

"The State Hospital?"

"Yeah, it's cozier than you might think."

"Well, let's go then, or we'll be out all night."

Her husband helped her up and Moran looked back at me and shrugged. By the time they reached the end of the block, I'd retrieved the ejecta. As I rinsed it off in a horse trough, a carriage passed them from the other direction. In it were Mr. Cable and a young woman.

They alit at the front gate and their hired driver went off.

"Mr. Reese, isn't it?"

"Yes, that's right."

"This is my daughter Lucy."

"Pleased to meet you."

"And you, Mr. Reese. We passed the plumber's wagon as we came in. He wasn't here today, was he?"

"Plumber?"

"I'm sorry, never mind. I suppose you were attending Margaret's affair?"

"Yes, my wife and I and several others."

"How did it go? For some reason, Margaret was in a terrible fret about it."

"Oh, I think everything went as planned. A wonderful meal. By the end, however, Margaret felt a little under the weather. I believe she's upstairs, lying down."

"Poor thing. I'm feeling a bit exhausted myself. I think I'll join her. If you'll excuse me."

"Certainly, my dear."

She went into the house and her father and I followed. Emmie met her on the stairs and they exchanged greetings while Mr. Cable and I went into the dining room. I introduced Cobb as himself and he graciously offered to share the Calvados he'd been husbanding.

"None for me, thank you," Cable told him. Then he looked about the room, as if doing an inventory of the empty bottles.

"Thirsty group," I offered.

"Oh, I'm not shocked. I used to travel the lecture circuit with Mark Twain, you know."

We had just sat down when Emmie entered. Cable rose from his seat and made a little half bow. Emmie reminded him who she was and he politely pretended to remember her.

"I think I'll join Elizabeth in the garden, if that's all right."

"Why, of course, Mrs. Reese."

Cobb and I toasted Cable with our brandy and then I asked how the dinner with the real James had gone.

"Delightful. A very attractive man. Always feels more than he says."

"Quiet?" Cobb asked.

"Oddly shy. He has an amusing manner of speech, strongly indicative of the studious finish of his writing. Though the effect is not quite the same. He will say, 'Hm-m—I walked-eh-I walked to the—hm-m—the-eh—hm-m-m—the—what shall I say?—the corner! And took a—hm-m—a—I suppose I may call it—hm-m—a hansom cab!' Very amusing."

Cobb eyed me dubiously over his brandy.

"And how did you find Mr. Vincent?" I asked.

"Oh, most informative. Most informative. He's been all over the world, you know. And not nearly so, well, portentous as I'd been led to believe. Very down-to-earth."

"And my wife's cousin Gloria, how did she get on?"

"Oh, very well, I think. A most amusing way of excusing herself from the table, 'I must take this message to Señor Garcia!' she told us. Wonderful. Though we had some trouble explaining it to Mr. James. I'm afraid that sort of humor escapes him. Yes, very amusing girl. Though we couldn't dissuade her from thinking that Mr. James had written *Trilby*. She came back to the topic several times, much to the man's discomfort. With each repetition, he winced as if a whip had been cracked at him and in his worst stammer mildly repudiated the attribution. I think we all found his polite distress howling funny, though none dared laugh in his presence."

While he was talking, Cobb had taken out his cards and was shuffling them absentmindedly.

"What an admirable idea," Cable said. "Shall we play something? Three-handed? Or perhaps one of the ladies can be enticed to play."

"I think they may be occupied in conversation," I said. "And perhaps I should join them. It's been so long since we've seen Mrs. Tibbitts."

"By all means, Mr. Reese. Go and join the ladies. I'm sure Mr. Cobb and I can come up with a two-handed game."

"Oh, I can think of several."

I stopped in the kitchen, where the smell of food finally fired my appetite. Regrettably, Hal had devoured everything save a healthy helping of soup and a modest one of the pudding. While I served myself from the tureen, I suggested he go and clear the bottles. Then Lottie brought me some bread.

"Quite an evening," I said.

"Yes—I'll be glad when things are back to normal. And that Mrs. Tibbitts has gone back to wherever she comes from. What a shrew."

"I've heard her called that before."

I'd also heard Elizabeth called much worse, of course, but shrew was the hands-down favorite. I once lent her husband a copy of Shakespeare's treatise on the little insectivore. But it didn't seem to do him much good. That was right before she went off to France. She came back to him, all right, but it's doubtful the homecoming involved any acts of contrition. In Emmie's version, the reconciliation comes only after they've run out of ways of tormenting each other.

"Don't forget the dessert," Lottie said, setting the last of the blancmange, or baverwah, before me. "It *is* good, I'll admit that. She used filberts in it."

I ate a couple spoonfuls, then came upon something metallic.

"Looks like a wedding ring," I said, holding it up to the light.

"Oh." She instinctively put a hand to her chest. I handed her the ring.

"You wear it on a string around your neck."

"How would you know that?"

"My wife did the same thing when she wanted to hide the fact she was married."

"Oh. You were estranged?"

"Off and on. And only for a few days at a time. I suppose that's what you were looking for under the stove?"

"The string broke. Must've been when I was putting that in the icebox. Only, I didn't notice 'til later. Thank goodness no one choked on it. Who'd expect to find something like that in a pudding?"

"Well, personally, I've been suspicious of soft-seeming desserts ever since an occasion in Washington when a German count choked to death on his Charlotte Russe."

"His Charlotte Russe? But how?"

"Seems a chicken bone found its way into his portion."

"But how could a chicken bone get into a Charlotte Russe?"

"If you'd met his wife, you wouldn't need to ask that."

"Oh. What a world we live in, where a woman could do that to her own husband."

Not knowing where I'd found the ring—under a viburnum by the front gate—there was no way she could appreciate the irony of her commentary.

"Well, Mr. Reese, if there's nothing else you need, I think I'll go on upstairs. Please say good night to Hal for me."

"All right. Though there is something else I ought to mention. Do you remember I told you Pat Moran would be here?"

"Yes, I remember."

"Well I suspect he may have searched your room."

"Searched my room?"

"For the money your husband's hidden away."

"For God's sake! There is no money!"

"I should have said the money he believes your husband has hidden away."

"What fools. Well, he would have found nothing there of value. Good night, Mr. Reese."

"I'd better make it good-bye, Lottie. We'll be leaving soon, and I doubt I'll be back here. Good luck."

"Thank you."

Outside in the garden, I found Emmie and her college chum renewing their acquaintance.

"...and what of you, *Dame Perfidia?*" Elizabeth asked, and not without feeling.

"How dare you call me that!"

"After all I've done for you."

"What did *you* ever do for *me?*"

This seemed a not unfair question. Elizabeth had never been what one might call altruistic, and after thinking about it for a minute or so, even she gave up.

"I won't be interrogated in this way, Emmie. It's *you* who need to explain yourself. You even quote my diary verbatim!"

"You should feel flattered."

"Flattered? You didn't even notice that it was a parody of *Bleak House*. And a damn good one."

"Oh, I noticed your plagiarism. I simply didn't want to draw attention to it."

"*Plagiarism.* What nonsense. And coming from you, who suffer from a terminal case of alliteration."

"Are you mocking my writing?"

"And why not? You've gone to great lengths to make *me* a source of amusement."

"Great lengths? That would hardly be necessary. And you've no one to blame but yourself. If you weren't such an unbearably haughty virago, people wouldn't so easily find you comical."

"Comical? What a cruel thing to say, Emmie."

I suppose it was in a way. If you were to call Elizabeth a calculating hellcat, or a self-serving viper, she would take it as a compliment. But the thought of people laughing at her was more than she could bear.

"Oh, I didn't mean comical, Elizabeth. Only, you must see how your always needing to come out on top feeds a certain resentment in others."

"Well, I can certainly see that. But what am I to do about it? Fail deliberately?"

"No, certainly not. You must, I'm sure, remain just the way you are."

It was not the ending I'd expected. Emmie had her on the ropes—and then at the sight of blood, she settled for a draw.

"Thank you for that concession," Elizabeth told her. "I'm willing to forgive you, but I must insist you allow me to finish reading the manuscript."

"That will be fine, dear." Emmie gave her a peck on the cheek. "We'll see you tomorrow."

"Yes, all right. Oh, and what was Cobb up to, Harry?"

"I believe he was trying to interest Mr. Cable in a game of chance."

"Is your actor still here? Or do you mean the real Mr. Cable?"

"The genuine article."

"Good lord. Coax him away, will you?"

"We'll take care of it," Emmie told her.

We left her reading by the light of a lantern. Then, as we neared the kitchen door, Emmie stopped me.

"What happened with the corpse, Harry?"

"The Grundys offered *it,* and Mr. Moran, a ride back to the hospital."

"Shouldn't a doctor have been called?"

"It was thought that might prove an embarrassment."

"But you're sure he wasn't murdered?"

"Quite sure."

"Oh."

"Don't be disappointed, Emmie. McCrea was certainly murdered."

"Yes, I suppose," she agreed. "Did you tell Lottie about her husband?"

"No, I thought it better to let her find out later. I expect Moran will announce he found him dead at the hospital."

"So who knows what actually happened?"

"Hal was in the kitchen the whole time, so just those of us at the table—the Grundys, Cobb, Moran, and Margaret. Do you think she'll mention it to her father?"

"The only way we could calm her was to convince her the man had merely fallen asleep again. She was quite content to believe what we told her."

"Good. And the others all have reasons of their own for keeping quiet."

We found Hal in the kitchen, stowing the empty bottles.

"Come along, it's time to go home," Emmie told him.

In the dining room, Mr. Cable was just excusing himself. We all said good night, and then escorted Cobb out of the house.

"That man wouldn't wager a nickel," he complained.

"Do you gamble, Mr. Cobb?" Emmie asked.

"So you know?"

"Yes. I know a great deal."

"And that about, eh, Mrs. Dexter?"

"You'll find out in time."

"Yes, I'm sure I will. But back to your question—I do gamble, on occasion. And yourself, Mrs. Reese, do you enjoy a game of cards?"

"On occasion. Provided the stakes are sufficient."

"My feelings precisely. It's early yet. Perhaps you'd like to come back to the hotel...."

"Oh, I hardly think that would be appropriate."

"No, I suppose not."

"But we're staying at the home of my mother, if you'd like to come along?"

"I'd be delighted, Mrs. Reese. Delighted."

"I think I'll go for a walk, if it's all the same to you, Emmie."

"Of course, Harry."

"I'll go with you," Hal said.

"By the way, Emmie. You'll find a deck of cards in my bag."

"Oh, I have one right here," Cobb offered.

"Yes, I'm sure you do," she told him. "But the house should always provide the deck. As a matter of courtesy. Thank you for thinking of it, Harry."

"You're welcome, Emmie. Good luck."

Hal and I wandered off toward the Edenic millpond.

"How are things going with Lottie?" I asked.

"Oh, I tried again, but still got the same answer. I wish she'd just tell me what she finds wrong with me."

"Well, give her another try in a week or so. Things might change."

"What could change in the next week?"

"You'd be surprised."

We walked in silence for a while. Then as we got closer to the pond, I espied Mortimer Vincent's valet staring off into the distance. I hailed him and introduced Hal.

"How was your dinner?" I asked. "I hear Gloria made quite an impression."

"Oh, yes. I'm afraid she did."

"It didn't go well?"

"It was bad enough when she kept insisting Mr. James wrote *Trilby,* in spite of his protestations to the contrary. But when she proclaimed his writing 'almost as good as Laura Jean Libbey's,' I thought the poor man would expire. I can't imagine what Mr. Vincent would have said in that situation."

"No sense of humor?"

"None whatsoever."

"Well, she's trainable, I'm sure."

"Perhaps, but I'm not certain that's a risk I can afford to take. You see, I've worked hard for my position. No, much as I like the girl... Well, good night. And goodbye. I'll be leaving town tomorrow afternoon."

This attitude of his annoyed me. Perhaps I should have appreciated that prompting Gloria to goad the genius James was at cross purposes with having her impress Vincent's valet with her deportment. But if the scheming fake thought he could renege on the family that easily, he had another thing coming.

21

Back at the house, I found Emmie with Cobb in the kitchen. She'd made a large pot of coffee and set out a plate of cheese. While Cobb shuffled, she sat back and watched. I cut myself a slice of cheese, then said good night. Neither saw or heard me. There was nothing left for me to do but hope that Emmie would prevail—and by a margin large enough to satisfy Snide Sam and his pugilistic friend.

Hours later, I woke to the smell of bacon. I joined the others—sans Emmie—at the breakfast table.

"Any signs of life from your cousin?" I asked Gloria.

"Dead to the world. Didn't get to bed 'til an hour ago."

"How's she look?"

"Look?"

"I mean, is she smiling?"

"Couldn't say, really. Her mouth was hanging open."

"Well, did she still have the gold inlay?"

"Gold inlay? Oh, yes. Back there." She stuck a finger in her own mouth to illustrate.

"Well, things can't have gone too badly then."

After she and Hal went off to work, and their aunt to the kitchen, Pluribus came out of his room carrying a little grip.

"Well, guess I better be off before Cousin Emmie wakes up."

"Decided to take my advice?"

"Yeah. How long's it take to get to California, you think?"

"Oh, just a few days."

"I only got fifty-two bucks. Think that's enough?"

"That's plenty. Any more and you'd have to worry about it." More crucially, it was enough to get him out there, but less than he'd need to get back should he change his mind. "Well, good luck. I'm sure you'll make a big splash in San Francisco."

I took it as a given that if he made it that far, he'd wind up drowned in the bay. Frankly, I saw it as even odds some Samaritan would dispatch the little barbarian before he reached Cleveland. But I shook his hand, and as I watched him go out the door even felt a glimmer of apprehension—until I'd made sure my watch lay safely in my vest pocket.

After giving him a five-minute lead, I followed him to the depot. Then kept an eye on him as he boarded a train to Springfield, where the Chicago-bound trains stopped. One down, two to go.

I hadn't yet figured out how I would maneuver Mortimer Vincent's valet to the altar. The best I could think of was to tell him that Emmie and I had set Gloria up, and that left to herself, she knew nothing about Garcia, or *Trilby*. But that was hardly a ringing endorsement of her literary acumen, even if she *was* a devotee of Laura Jean Libbey.

What I needed was some sort of leverage. More precisely, something I could blackmail the man with.

That something dropped into my lap a few minutes later, when I encountered a weeping Gloria two blocks from home.

"They let me go, Cousin Harry."

"Who let you go?"

"The hotel. Some busybody saw me out on the pond

252

with Mr. Vincent yesterday. They say he accosted me. How ridiculous!"

"Ridiculous, perhaps. But timely."

"How do you mean?"

"What are your feelings toward Mr. Vincent, Gloria? I mean, if he were to offer you his hand, would you accept?"

"Well, first I'd need to demur, of course. But yes, most definitely."

"Good. But you may need to keep the demurring to yourself. He's set to leave town this afternoon, so we'll need to work fast."

"An elopement! Oh, how romantic!"

"Terribly. But let's make sure the knot's tied before boarding the train, just to be safe."

"All right. Has he said that he plans to ask me?"

"He doesn't know it yet. But there is another small detail I should tell you about."

"What's that? Oh, don't tell me he has a wife already! Who was lost at sea, and presumed dead... but is certain to show up just as I'm expecting our first child?"

"Ah, no. Nothing as complicating as that. It's just that the man we know as Mortimer Vincent is not actually Mortimer Vincent."

"I don't understand. Then who will I be marrying?"

"Mortimer Vincent's valet. Name's Joe Griep, I believe he said. You'd still be traveling, and living well. It's just the social standing would be of a lower order. And there may be some domestic duties...."

"Oh, that's impossible," she interrupted. "Totally impossible."

"I suppose it *is* a big step down...."

"I don't mean that. Honestly, I'd be relieved not to

have to put on airs all the time with the snobs. But just imagine, Cousin Harry. My name would be Gloria Griep. It sounds like a vaudeville farce."

She was right, of course.

"What's Floyd's last name?"

"Floyd?"

"Your fiancé we met at the depot. The day we arrived."

"Oh. I'm not sure...."

Not sure? Someone needed to get this girl out of circulation but quick. "Well, it might have been even worse."

"Yes, I suppose. Oh, all right. I *am* looking forward to seeing all these exotic places—China, and Egypt, and Paris, and Saskatoon.... What do I need to do?"

"Go home and dress for the occasion. And pack a bag. I'll be by with Vincent within the hour. Or Griep, I should say."

"Let's keep it Vincent as long as we can," she suggested.

"Good idea. Best not to let on to Emmie or your aunt about the valet part of it until absolutely necessary. You'll have enough trouble selling them on the idea of marrying Vincent."

"Yes, how shall I manage that?"

"There is one sure way...."

"What? Oh... you mean tell them that what didn't happen yesterday *did* happen."

"Yes. Might risk some fireworks, but should bring them around."

"Yes, all right."

I found Vincent's valet in his room, packing.

"Hello, Mr. Reese. I didn't expect to see you again."

"No, I'm sure you didn't."

Blackmail nearly always involves some unpleasant-ness, and I'm not the sort who enjoys putting the screws on some other poor slob. But there was a job to do, so I rolled up my sleeves and waded into the mud.

I told him that he was responsible for Gloria losing her position and, almost certainly, her reputation (what there was of it). I even hinted at the confessional she was performing at that moment with her cousin and aunt.

"I can't imagine what Mr. Vincent would think of all this," I said.

"I should think he'd believe his loyal retainer, a man who's served him honorably for seven years."

"Would he? Even after he's informed that his loyal retainer has been impersonating him? Going so far as to attend a dinner with the noted authors George Washing-ton Cable and Henry James? Quite a fellow, your Mr. Vincent. I'm thinking I might mail him an item from the newspaper detailing the event."

He mulled the matter for a moment, but I'd turned his flank and now threatened his baggage train.

"All right, Mr. Reese. You win."

"Cheer up. She is a very attractive girl. And keen."

"But will she be when I have to tell her I'm merely Mr. Vincent's valet?"

"Already knows. Doesn't mind a bit. Despite the un-fortunate name."

"Unfortunate name?"

"Ah, never mind that. What do you say we go over to the house and get the preliminaries out of the way? Then it's just a matter of obtaining the license and finding a justice of the peace. An informal wedding luncheon, and off you go to Argentina."

"New Orleans first. I'm to meet Mr. Vincent there."

"Wedding night on a sleeper? Well, that ought to provide some entertainment for the rest of the car."

My observation in no way increased his enthusiasm for the business. Nonetheless, he went with me back to the house and there things were settled to everyone's satisfaction—or at least mine and Gloria's.

She was looking particularly fetching that morning, save some recalcitrant welts from the run-in with the bramble, and by the third glass of brandy, Joe Griep was gazing upon her with a genuine fondness. Lust, a more scrupulous writer might call it, but occasions such as this beg for some delicacy.

I took them around to city hall, where they acquired a license. Then we scheduled a noon session with a justice of the peace. While Gloria went home to help her aunt and Emmie prepare for the ceremony, I took Griep to Mr. Grundy's shop so I could introduce him to his future brother-in-law.

Hal seemed not the least bit surprised. Nor did he voice any objection to his sister marrying a valet. Mr. Grundy, however, was another matter. When he was told that Griep was Mortimer Vincent's valet, he inquired after the man he had dined with the evening before. When Griep told him Vincent was in New Orleans, Mr. Grundy accused him of being a fraud.

I pulled the pipe-fitting thespian aside and tried explaining the facts of the matter. But that got me nowhere. He was firmly convinced he had met the real Mortimer Vincent, and the real Henry James, for that matter. Short of taking the convincin' wrench to his head, I saw no hope of dissuading him. So I told him Griep was merely covering up for his boss, who was wary of being implicated in the disposal of the faux Cable's body. This explanation he found acceptable.

I then suggested that Hal and I treat his future brother-in-law to a few rounds at a local barroom. When informed he would need to foot the bill, Hal became uncharacteristically terse—as if he had some grounds for irritation. He took us to a low saloon, as a comeuppance, I imagine. It didn't work, however, as I've no pride in such matters. Like anyone with sense, I prefer sponging drinks in some posh hotel bar. But I'll settle for a basement dive if it's that or nothing.

Griep seemed to be of the same mind that morning, and he was thoroughly lubricated by the time we left— just the condition needed for what lay before him. I had Hal take him to the justice of the peace while I went back to pick up the ladies.

It was nearly noon by the time I got to the house. They were ready, but troubled that Pluribus would miss the wedding of his sister.

"Leave him a note he'll see when he comes home for lunch," I artfully suggested. "By the way, there is something I should tell you so you aren't surprised by it later."

"What should you tell us?" Emmie asked warily.

"Just that Mortimer Vincent is a pen name. He's Joe Griep in his off hours."

Gloria's cousin's reaction to the infelicitous name was not unlike her own. But there could be no turning back now. Not with the girl's ticket to the pudding club having been putatively punched.

The ceremony lasted about ten minutes. Emmie's mother again voiced some regret about Pluribus's absence, but once we sat down to the celebratory luncheon, he was all but forgotten.

Afterward, we escorted the newlyweds to the depot. The requisite minimum of tears were shed, but the speed and seemingly sordid nature of the betrothal did a fine job of inhibiting any crass displays of sentimentality. Not unlike our own departure from Buffalo five years before.

When we arrived back at the house, Pat Moran was waiting on the front porch. I introduced him to Emmie's mother. Then after the two women went inside, he and I took a stroll.

"How'd things work out?"

"That's what I come to tell you. It went without a hitch, so the less said the better. A buddy helped me sneak him on the grounds. Then a little later, I just happen to find Anthorn and call the doc. He says he choked to death on something, but couldn't tell what. Didn't seem to care, either. So ain't no one suspicious. They didn't even notice he was gone. So as long as we're sure no one else will talk, everything's jake."

"Then I think we're safe. My wife convinced Margaret the old man was fine. And she never knew his name. But I suppose someone should tell Lottie."

"You mean she don't know he was there yesterday?"

"No, she was keeping out of sight, to avoid you."

"Well, if they got her name there as next of kin, one of the docs will go by."

"You find anything searching her room?"

"What's that?"

"Your trip to Cuba."

"Oh. No, nothing. I suppose that's what you're after too, the money?"

"Five will get you ten, there is no money."

"I'm beginning to think that too."

"Who told you there was—McCrea?"

"Yeah, he was sure of it. See, he comes from the same burg. Or came from."

"Was it Anthorn who killed him?"

"That's my guess. I was out of town that night, but I knew McCrea was up to something. When I get back the next morning, they tell me Anthorn's on the loose and I should go find him, on account of me being his Secretary of State. I found him, not long after you told me about seeing him. He said something nutty about the Secretary of the Treasury getting what he had coming to him. I get him back and then, taking off his jacket, I see some blood on his shirt sleeve. I ask him where the Secretary of the Treasury is and he tells me, 'lying out in the old canal.' Then he hands me McCrea's wallet. I went back out there, and there was McCrea, dead."

"And then you sunk the body?"

"I figured no one else had seen it. 'Cause if you did, why wouldn't you mention it?"

"Go on."

"Well, like you say, I filled his pockets with stones and sank him."

"Because you didn't want Anthorn to be accused of the murder?"

"Yeah. I figured now was my chance to find out where this money is hid. So I get even chummier with Anthorn."

"What did you do with the wallet?"

"Put it back on McCrea, before I sank him."

"Then you saw my ad in the newspaper?"

"That's right. So I go out there at midnight. I see a lantern on the far side, and start to make my way toward it. Then I see you sneaking up on me, only, I didn't notice it was you then. Just someone trying to get the jump on me."

"So you sapped me?"

"Sure. Only 'cause I figured you were there to do the same to me. No hard feelings?"

"Well, I wouldn't make a habit of it. What next?"

"When there's nothing in the paper about a body, I figure whoever was out there didn't want McCrea found either. Then when you show up, pretending to be Anthorn's nephew, I figure it was you out there, and it's a sure thing there's money."

"So you did recognize me?"

"Sure. But why let you in on it?"

"But you didn't know Lottie worked at the Cables' until last evening?"

"No. All I knew was her name, and that she was his niece, from when she come by to visit him a while back."

"Actually, Lottie was his wife."

"His wife?"

"Yes. But she's at the Cables' under the name Flagg. It might be they don't have that in their records, so maybe you could make sure they know."

"All right. What's *she* say about the money?"

"She insists there isn't any."

"McCrea was sure there was."

"Well, at some point Anthorn did have a pile stashed away. What exactly happened to it, no one seems to know."

"So you giving up on it?"

"Me? I was never really looking for it. Just trying to figure out what happened to McCrea."

"Why?"

"No good reason, really. It's just something I have to do to keep the franchise."

"*What* do you have to do?"

"Investigate murders."

"Any money in it?"

"Not much. At least, not that I've seen."

"Huh. Well, I kinda like the stuff, so maybe I better get back to the hospital. See you around, maybe."

"Yeah. Maybe."

With the matter of Anthorn's demise having been satisfactorily resolved, I went back to the depot and sent a wire to Donaldson, the newspaperman in North Adams. I told him about Anthorn's death and suggested he come to town. An hour later, a messenger came by the house with an answer. He'd be arriving on the southbound 7:48.

Emmie's mother was out in the garden, and I took the opportunity to ask Emmie about her game with Cobb.

"Oh, I came out well enough. I can advance you twenty dollars, if you'd like."

"I would, yes."

"And I'll take care of this month's rent. And the grocer, the butcher, and the telephone company."

"There is one other small expense that will be awaiting us."

"What? And how small?"

"Niggling, really. It's just that there's this fellow who is under the impression I owe him some money."

"Does this have something to do with your outing with Mélisande?"

"Indirectly, though it's not her. A fellow named Sam. Nice fellow."

"Good, then he won't mind waiting for his money until you can afford to pay him. I assume you aren't so dimwitted as to expect me to cover the cost of your tryst."

"I would hardly call it a tryst. The idea's laughable."

"From her telling, I believe Mélisande would agree with you."

Given her attitude, I decided to hold off mentioning the magnitude of the debt, or the fellow with the cauliflower ear.

22

Later, when Pluribus didn't show up for his supper, Hal and I were dispatched to look for him. Knowing the futility of it, I went by a saloon and killed time until Donaldson's arrival.

After we'd exchanged greetings, I told him about Anthorn's accidental death at the hospital. Then I handed him the evening newspaper. The front page held a detailed account of the discovery of McCrea's headless body. (Just for closure, I'll mention that the head did turn up that evening. Apparently a farm dog had thought it worthy of investigation and carried it off. His astonished owner found the gnarled remains in his woodshed.)

When Donaldson handed me back the newspaper, we were seated in the barroom of Rahar's Hotel.

"So no one has any idea who killed McCrea?"

"No. But there's reason to think it was Anthorn. McCrea had been hounding him about the money. Then he started hounding Lottie, too, and may have made the mistake of telling Anthorn about it."

"And the body's just sitting out there, rotting, for most of a week before anyone notices?"

"Guess no one goes by there much. Have you learned anything?"

"Yeah, plenty. A couple days after you left, I found out where Ransom went off to."

"Not here? To see Lottie?"

"No. I tracked down everyone who had any connection with Anthorn. Finally, I came to this carpenter who had apprenticed with the guy who did repairs on those houses Anthorn had bought in the '90s. First thing he tells me is that Ransom had come by a few days earlier. Probably that day you and I were searching his house."

"Let me guess. He'd made a secret room in the house where Anthorn stashed the money."

"Yep. This fellow I'm talking to wasn't in on the building of it, just his boss. A guy by the name of Stebbins. He was the only one besides Anthorn who knew where it was."

"And so when Anthorn gets sent off to the hospital, Stebbins helps himself to the money...."

"Actually, it was *before* they sent Anthorn off. Stebbins disappears, leaving a wife and four kiddies. Ransom must have known about that, and suspected something like a secret room. But here's my theory: he figured Anthorn had killed Stebbins, so he could never tell about the room."

"Sounds out of character for someone like Anthorn, doesn't it?"

"Sure. But not out of character for Ransom, and people like him get to thinking everyone else thinks the same way. Anyway, as soon as he gets in the house, he starts looking for the secret room. Eventually he finds it. But not the money. So *now* he realizes Stebbins must have made off with it, and goes and talks to his old apprentice."

"It'd be next to impossible to track this Stebbins down. With thirty, forty grand and eight years, he could be anywhere. Probably has another wife and family."

"Yeah, that's how I figure it. But there was one clue this fellow, the apprentice, had. He has a brother who'd moved out to Denver. That brother sent him a letter a few years ago saying he thought he saw Stebbins on a train headed to Salt Lake City."

"So maybe two or three wives. Did he tell Ransom about Salt Lake City?"

"At first he plays dumb, then Ransom offers him twenty bucks. That does the trick. An hour later, Ransom leaves town. It only cost me ten to get that out of him."

"Bit of a long shot."

"Yeah, but I guess it's all he lives for now. Think I should tell his daughter?"

"Why not? She'll probably be relieved to know he's gone. She's working as a cook, under the name of Flagg. For George Washington Cable—I can give you the address. She's never told them about her marriage, or any of the rest, so maybe you can keep her out of the paper, and not let on to the Cables?"

"All right. I can say I came by to interview old Mr. Cable. But even if I don't identify her, Ransom will appear big in the story, and that his daughter Lottie married Anthorn."

"Well, if you don't mention the name Flagg, I don't see how anyone will make the connection."

"All right. Well, here's to lost fortunes."

I helped him work through his travel money for the next hour or two, wanting to defer my return to the house as long as possible.

When I did arrive back, the three of them were in conference around the kitchen table. Hal had found a note from his brother outlining his plans for a trip to California. It was in a drawer of his dresser and apparently he'd been meant to find it the next morning. Emmie was looking at me accusingly, but her mother, though teary-eyed, didn't seem overly upset.

"I better pack a bag and go after him," Hal said.

"You can't be sure what route he took," Emmie said. "There's no use going into a panic. Tomorrow I'll send some wires. But we mustn't worry." She patted her mother's shoulder. "He is a very resourceful boy. And when he runs out of money, I'm sure we'll hear from him."

"Oh, you can be sure of that," I added.

Now I had three sets of eyes looking at me accusingly. Mere amateurs, Hal and his aunt soon tired of the effort and went off to bed, leaving Emmie to finish the job.

"Well, I hope you're happy, Harry. You realize if anything happens to him, it will be on your account."

"Anyone acquainted with the brat would chalk it up as a credit."

"How can you be so heartless?"

"Emmie, there's no use trying to blame me for that little plague's behavior. His character had been set in stone long before I met him. You all act as if this is some childhood phase he's going through. Well, it's not. He'll be a liar, a cheat, and a thief all his life."

"Not like you. Tell me, Harry, when did *you* last pilfer? I seem to remember, just a few days ago, finding thirteen dollars missing. Immediately after you hurried off from the house. And as to lying—well, has a single hour gone by in the past week in which you weren't involved in some dissimulation?"

She'd gone too far, I thought. But in the name of magnanimity, I let it pass. Plus, I wasn't altogether sure which of my dissimulations had been exposed and which hadn't. There was still the matter of Joe Griep's real occupation, for one.

"I'd like to catch a morning train, Harry. If that suits you."

"Suits me fine. To anywhere in particular?"

She smiled. "So, you really are in deep with this Sam?"

"Deep enough. And Sam's the doggedly persistent type. In lieu of an intriguing mauve envelope, he sends his duns via a giant plug-ugly with a cauliflower ear."

"A cauliflower ear?"

"That's right. And a permanently split lip. The sort of fellow you're introduced to when, after a few rounds in a Bowery concert saloon, you notice you left your wallet at home."

"Good night, Harry," she said, then started toward the bedroom.

"I thought maybe we could bunk together tonight. Seeing how Gloria's side of the bed is empty."

"Did you?"

She went in and closed the door behind her. But a half hour later, when she turned out the light, I snuck in beside her.

"Elizabeth came by today," she whispered. "When you were out."

"Did she give you back the manuscript?"

"She wanted to keep it, and I told her she could. I think she may have some plan herself to get it published."

"*She* wants to get it published?"

"What you must remember about Elizabeth is that she is, above all else, supremely vain. She was even complimentary, to a point. She said she admired the humor of it."

"I suppose any praise from Elizabeth is high praise."

"Yes, she is nothing if not discriminating. That's what makes her superior attitude so difficult to stand. If she were less deserving of it, it wouldn't be nearly so galling."

"Well, then you must be happy she was so flattering."

"As I said, she was, but only to a point. She told me she thought my work would stand in the first rank—of folk literature."

"A bit of a comedown."

"I certainly took it that way. But she insisted she meant nothing pejorative."

"Then she must not have. Otherwise she wouldn't have passed up the opportunity."

"Yes, I suppose. Still... folk literature?"

I did what I could to distract her.

The next morning, after a late breakfast, we said good-bye to her mother and then visited Hal at the shop. I reminded him about trying again with Lottie in a week or so. Then we bade him farewell and went off to the depot.

A block before reaching it, I noticed Emmie's dentist walking toward us.

"You must be relieved that cad James has left town," I said by way of greeting.

He looked at me askance.

"Little Emmie Reese," I said, pointing to her. "McGinnis then." Still askance. "Remember, just a week ago. You threw her book out of the train."

"Young man, I have no idea what you're talking about."

"Open your mouth, Emmie. Show him the inlay."

"Harry! Please excuse my husband.... He's only now been released... from the hospital."

"Ah. Say no more," he told her good-naturedly. "But are you certain it's time?"

"Oh, I've been assured I can always send him back."

"Well, good luck to you, madam. And you, sir!" He smiled at me, as you would to a driveling dotard, then hurried off.

"What was that all about, Harry?"

"Your dentist. I told you, he was the one who threw your book out of the train."

"Dr. Wilkinson? That wasn't Dr. Wilkinson."

"Oh. Well, he looks just like him."

"I suppose there is a resemblance. But perhaps you should refrain from making your accusations public before substantiating them. And please remember, I'm not in the habit of displaying my dental work for the amusement of passersby."

I could have set her straight on that score, but this was hardly the right moment.

During the first leg of the trip, I told her about my conversations with Pat Moran and the journalist Donaldson the day before.

"I was right, Harry. About it not mattering. Suppose we had never come to town. McCrea's murder would have been left unsolved. And now? It's still been left unsolved! At least as far as the world at large is concerned."

"There is the personal satisfaction from having figured things out."

"For you, I suppose."

"Well, next time we encounter a corpse, you need to make more of an effort to involve yourself."

"Do you think there will be a next time, Harry?"

"Need you ask?"

"No, I guess not. It is amazing how circumscribed our lives are, isn't it?"

"It could be worse. How'd you like to find yourself in a Hardy novel?"

"I guess you're right. I should just embrace it. And I've decided to embrace Elizabeth's verdict as well."

"What do you mean?"

"What's wrong with folk literature? It would be nice to simply set aside all the posing and pretense, and just accept my writing for what it is."

"And maybe not be so obsessive about it?"

"Yes, and not be so obsessive about it. There is more to life."

"Sure there is. Cards, for instance."

"Are you encouraging me to gamble, Harry?"

"Well, the train from Springfield includes a parlor car. What harm's there in it, really?"

"Apparently you don't remember the time I was forced to hide in the baggage car. *Or* the time we were kicked off the Empire State Express."

"Distant memories."

"Whereas Sam and his plug-ugly are vivid ones? All right, Harry. But if I get you out of this, you're going to need to be more accommodating."

Thinking she was speaking in vague generalities, I agreed. But when we got back to the apartment, I learned she had something specific in mind. There he was: my nemesis. She'd actually given him a key to our apart-ment. I suppose I should have wondered why she was willing to let me off the hook back at her mother's.

Pluribus ended up spending the better part of the summer with us. But it wasn't quite as bad as I had feared. For one thing, I didn't need to do any minding of him. He took seriously my threats of violence and did what he could to avoid my company.

But what was worse, for him, Emmie made a project of his education. I suspect he did more reading and recitation in those three months than in the previous three years. By August, he had thoroughly tired of the regimen and actually begged to be allowed to return to Northampton. He even attended school most days that next year. And, in time, he and I reached an understanding. We ignored each other totally.

Much to Hal's relief, Lottie, freed from her ill-starred marriage, began entertaining thoughts of a new match. Unfortunately, not with him. It seems there was an electrician who also milked the Cable cow, ten years Hal's senior and owner of his own business....

But Hal recovered. And, to no one's surprise but their own, the next spring he and Jane were married. They professed to be genuinely in love, but it's always difficult to know where warm-hearted affection leaves off and hard-nosed practicality takes up. Especially since by then, Hal had become involved in not only the family business, but its theatrical affairs as well. His debut came in an original production of the Grundys', *The Knight of the Burning Plume.* By all reports, it was a blazing success.

Emmie continued with her writing, but, just as she had promised, not so obsessively, or so pretentiously. And happily, it was some time before I was again entangled with her fictional world. There's something unnerving about coming face to face with characters you've met on the page, even under the best of circumstances. But when prophecies of these encounters arrive via a time-traveling airship, well, a fellow begins to wonder what's real and what's not. And who knows where that might lead?

With Emmie's winnings, we were able to settle our debts. And our financial dry spell soon gave way to a period of comparative prosperity. Life became pleasantly predictable—until, quite unexpectedly, we happened upon a body....

A Grundy Glossary

Mr. and Mrs. Grundy are very loosely based on George and Nell, or the Citizen and his Wife, characters in Francis Beaumont's delightful *The Knight of the Burning Pestle*. This play was published in 1613, and was the most thoroughly modern (in the literary sense) dramatic work of the next three hundred years. But the commentary of George and Nell is never quite as learned as that of Mr. and Mrs. Grundy....

bogs : 17th-century slang for a latrine

canal : Mrs. Grundy's own, rather obvious, euphemism for a woman's secret

Doll Tearsheet : a prostitute and associate of Falstaff in *Henry IV, Part 1*

Ireland : the buttocks; from *The Comedy of Errors*, III.i.110

it : 17th-century slang for the act of love

Low Countries : 17th-century slang for a woman's genital region

Monk : short for Monkey; Shakespearean slang for a lecher, used here by Mrs. Grundy as a term of endearment

Mouse : a 17th-century pet name for a woman; used by George in *The Knight of the Burning Pestle*

Netherlands : a woman's secret, a reference to the Low Countries (see above); from *The Comedy of Errors*, III.i.110

put down : Shakespearean slang for a man's taking of a woman

ramp : 17th-century slang for a wanton woman

thing : 17th-century slang for a woman's secret

trout groping : from Shakespeare's "groping for trout in a peculiar river," a euphemism for "it," with the watercourse standing in for "thing"; from *Measure for Measure*, I.ii.83